By J. Kenner

THE STARK TRILOGY
Release Me
Claim Me
Complete Me

STARK EVER AFTER NOVELLAS
Take Me
Have Me
Play My Game
Seduce Me
Unwrap Me
Deepest Kiss

STARK INTERNATIONAL NOVELS

THE JACKSON STEEL TRILOGY
Say My Name
On My Knees
Under My Skin

THE DIRTIEST TRILOGY
Dirtiest Secret
Hottest Mess

MOST WANTED SERIES
Wanted
Heated
Ignited

hottest mess

hottest

mess

A STARK INTERNATIONAL NOVEL

J. KENNER

 Bantam Books New York

Hottest Mess is a work of fiction. Names, characters, places, and incidents either are the product of the author's imagination or are used fictitiously. Any resemblance to actual persons, living or dead, events, or locales is entirely coincidental.

A Bantam Books Trade Paperback Original

Published in the United States by Bantam Books, an imprint of Random House, a division of Penguin Random House LLC, New York.

BANTAM BOOKS and the HOUSE colophon are registered trademarks of Penguin Random House LLC.

This book contains an excerpt from the forthcoming book *Sweetest Taboo* by J. Kenner. This excerpt has been set for this edition only and may not reflect the final content of the forthcoming edition.

Library of Congress Cataloging-in-Publication Data
Names: Kenner, Julie, author.
Title: Hottest mess / J. Kenner.
Description: New York : Bantam, [2016] | Series: Stark international ; 5
Identifiers: LCCN 2016006717 | ISBN 9781101967478 (paperback : alk. paper) | ISBN 9781101967485 (ebook)
Subjects: LCSH: Man-woman relationships—Fiction. | Billionaires—Fiction. | BISAC: FICTION / Romance / Contemporary. | FICTION / Contemporary Women. | FICTION / Romance / Suspense. | GSAFD: Erotic fiction.
Classification: LCC PS3611.E665 H68 2016 | DDC 813/.6—dc23
LC record available at http://lccn.loc.gov/2016006717

Printed in the United States of America on acid-free paper

randomhousebooks.com

9 8 7 6 5 4 3 2 1

For the Kenner Krew—you guys rock!

hottest mess

My earliest memories are of Dallas. Being with him. Laughing with him.

Loving him.

I don't remember when I realized that it was wrong, when I truly understood that we had to keep our growing desire secret. I only know that it glowed inside us, a spark just waiting to burn. And that when the worst happened—when we were captive together in the dark—we no longer cared about rules and expectations, taboos or punishments.

All we wanted then was to survive. All we cared about was finding comfort in each other's arms, the world outside be damned.

In some ways, those long, dark weeks were the best of my life. Terrifying and horrible, yes, but we belonged to each other. Fully. Completely.

After, in the real world, we were torn apart, everything we'd been to each other pushed aside. Buried.

A precious memory. A traumatic interlude.

A mistake.

Because we are brother and sister—bound as tightly by adoption as if we were tied by blood—and yet equally bound by need. By desire. By love.

For seventeen years, we fought a battle against our desire, but that is over now. Neither of us can fight any longer, and we have succumbed to heaven in each other's arms.

It's a forbidden love, a hidden passion.

It's a secret, and it has to stay that way.

But secrets scare me, because things hidden in the dark have power.

Dallas and I know that better than anyone.

So even though I am happier now than I have ever been, I am also more frightened than I can ever remember. Because I fully understand the stakes now.

I know the power of secrets.

And I'm terribly afraid that our secret is going to destroy us.

Pretty Little Liars

The universe is completely unfair.

For four long, luxurious days this Southampton mansion had been my personal paradise. Here, my body had been adored. My skin stroked. My blood had burned with a passion that had been building over seventeen long years. I'd been touched and kissed and worshipped by the man I've loved my entire life, and I'd relished the freedom to explore every inch of him in return. My lips on his strong jaw, his tight abs. My tongue tasting the sweetness of his skin and the saltiness of his cock.

We made love tenderly, then violently, then tenderly once more. We curled together in each other's arms. We watched late night television with our legs twined, until the sensation of skin against skin overwhelmed us and we muted the drone of talk show hosts, and explored each other again in the flickering light of the television.

We swam naked in the pool during the day, then walked along the beach in the moonlight.

Those days had been a gift. A reward.

A decadent, sensual heaven.

But all that changed this morning, and now this mansion that I love has transformed into hell. A luxurious hell with cool ocean breezes, a wet bar, liveried waiters offering sushi and canapés, and the man I love fondling the ass of a pert blonde with tits that are going to pop right out of that barely there dress if she so much as sneezes.

Bitch.

And I'm not the only one mentally plotting Blondie Bitch's demise. On the contrary, I'm certain that every female in the vicinity would take her down in a heartbeat in order to take the twit's place at his side. *Dallas Sykes.* The infamous billionaire bad boy. The man known publicly as one of the two heirs to the Sykes family fortune, and who women all over the country reverently refer to as the King of Fuck.

The man I love.

The man I can have in private, but never in public.

The man who is my brother.

Well, fuck.

The bitch leans closer to him, and as her teeth tug at his earlobe, I turn away—there's only so much torment I can take—and make a beeline for the bar.

"Woodford Reserve," I say to the bartender. "Two ice cubes." I recall the way his hand cupped her rear. "Actually, let's make that a double."

"Sure thing, miss."

Beside me, a runway-thin model-type with at least four inches on me takes a sip of red wine. "The hard stuff, huh? Guess you're singing the same song I am."

I glance at her, confused. "I'm sorry?"

Her mouth curves up in a way that makes her cheekbones even more prominent. She looks like a fairy with her pale skin and short dark hair. A devious fairy, I amend, seeing the glint in her pale blue eyes. "The Ode to Dallas," she clarifies. "The siren's song to make him ditch the bimbo and come straight to you. Or, in my case, me."

"*Oh*. Oh, no." My cheeks burn, and right then I'd totally welcome a natural disaster. A sinkhole, perhaps. Or a tsunami blowing in off Shinnecock Bay. "Me? With Dallas? That's not even—"

I clamp my mouth shut before I get in a serious *the lady doth protest too much* situation. How the hell could I have been so obvious? Could she really see the lust in my eyes? Surely not? Surely I was more careful. Because I *have* to be careful. I've been careful my whole damn life.

Yes, but before you two weren't together. Now you are. At least when you're alone. But not here. Not in the world. Not where it matters.

Her smile is knowing. "Oh, come on. Don't tell me that you don't—*wait*." She tilts her head, studying me, and as I watch, her eyes go wide, and she presses four long fingers over her blood-red lips. "Oh, shit. I'm sorry. I didn't—"

"Didn't what?"

"Didn't recognize you. You're Jane, right? You're his sister. God, that was totally lame of me." She drags her perfectly manicured fingers through her pixie-style hair. "I just saw you looking at him, and I assumed that you—anyway, never mind." She draws a deep breath and extends her hand. "I'm Fiona. Did I mention I'm an idiot?"

I can't help but laugh. "Honest mistake. Really. I was looking at him. But that was irritation you were seeing. Not lust." That, at least, is half true, and I allow myself one deep breath in relief. Crisis averted. Bullet dodged.

But I'd be lying if I didn't admit that some tiny, screwed up part of me wishes that she'd called my bluff. That she'd felt the heat that burns in my veins for him—and that she'd figured it out.

Because as much as I love Dallas, I hate that we have to hide. And some rebellious, hidden, bold, *stupid* part of me wishes that we could be open and out there and real.

We can't, though. I know we can't. The law and our parents and the threat of public humiliation keep us trapped firmly in the shadows. And, honestly, I've never been too fond of the spotlight, so the idea of having tabloid attention focused on me because I'm sleeping with my brother really doesn't sit well.

But it's not just family and privacy and social mores that are keeping us apart. There's Deliverance, too. Because as long as Dallas is Top Secret Vigilante Guy, everything in his life is going to remain hidden, including the man he truly is. A man so very different from the one he shows the public. A man that even I don't fully know or understand, because we haven't yet talked about how Deliverance operates or about its core mission to track—and presumably kill—the miserable excuses for human beings who kidnapped us both seventeen years ago. We need to, of course, but neither of us wanted that conversation to intrude on our four days of bliss. We only wanted each other.

"Hey," Fiona says, her forehead creasing as she peers at me. "You okay?"

"Fine." I force a smile, even though I feel like crying. Because for the first time it's fully hit me. *He's mine.* Dallas Sykes is absolutely, one hundred percent, totally mine.

And yet I can never truly have him.

Not in the way that counts. Not in the way that matters.

We're living a lie that is shiny and perfect and wonderful in the shadows, but that shrivels and dies in the harsh light of day.

I love him. I do.

And even though we promised each other that we would make this work, I can't help but fear that's a promise we never should have made. Because it's a promise that is impossible to keep.

2

Rear Window

An hour later I'm finally alone and on my third bourbon. Fiona has overcompensated for her faux pas by prattling on about nothing and everything, which was good in that her constant attention kept my eyes from drifting to Dallas.

And bad, in that her constant attention kept my eyes from drifting to Dallas.

Even knowing I shouldn't, all I want to do is watch him. And imagine him touching me. And seethe about the fact that he is spending the party touching everyone but me.

Apparently, he's even touched Fiona.

"We went out a couple of times," she told me, eyes sparkling. "Everyone knows he hardly ever sees the same woman twice, but, well, he saw me three times." Her lips curved wickedly. "He saw all of me."

My stomach twisted as I smiled politely and said something about my brother's reputation and how I really needed to go take care of something with the staff. I escaped inside, hid out for half an hour, and when I returned, I didn't see her at all.

Dallas, however, caught my attention right away.

Now, I'm leaning against the corner post of one of the pool cabanas trying not to watch him. Or, at least, trying not to be obvious about the fact that I'm watching him.

He's moved on from the blonde. Now he stands next to a brunette with streaks of neon blue. Her long hair falls in loose curls over her back, bare in the designer halter she wears. She sports a tattoo on her shoulder—not a feminine one, but a skull against a blood-red background.

She wears a black leather miniskirt and five-inch heels, and I have no doubt that this is a woman who takes what she wants. I can tell simply from looking at her. I can also tell from the way she keeps leaning toward Dallas and running her tongue over the edge of his ear.

I've never met the woman, but I'm going out on a limb and saying that I don't like her. Not at all. Not even one little bit.

I realize I'm staring again, and so I pull out my phone and make an effort to go through my emails. The attempt is futile—I see words, but they make no sense to me at the moment.

At least not until a text message flashes across my screen.

Watch.

It's from Dallas, of course, and my body tightens merely from seeing his name. I react on instinct—my head lifting, my eyes going straight to where he stands with Skull Girl. He's not looking in my direction, but I know that he is aware of me. He always is. Just as I'm always aware of him.

I stand, my feet like weights holding me in place as I watch the scene unfolding in front of me. Dallas and the woman standing near the pool, chatting casually with a few of the guests. Dallas's hand, brushing lightly against her bare back. His fingers trailing down her spine, then over the halter's tie at her waist.

I expect his hand to stroke the soft leather and cup her ass, but that isn't what happens. Instead, his nimble fingers unfasten the button of her waistband, loosening it just enough so that he can slip his hand inside her skirt and slide it down over her ass. For just a fraction of an instant, he looks up, his eyes finding mine. Heat pours through me, turning me liquid, making me wet.

I know what he is doing—we've done this before. Him touching another woman. Me watching. And both of us pretending that he is touching me.

The first time, it was hotter than sin. I'd been alone in a bathroom, watching the scenario play out on video. We weren't together yet—in fact we were doing everything to stay apart—and that moment had been a turning point for both of us. A bold—albeit completely fucked up—statement of just how badly we wanted each other. Of what we were willing to do.

Of how far we were willing to go.

I bite my lower lip and swallow, wanting to take what I know he is giving, but also wanting to run far and fast. My reaction surprises me—but at the same time it doesn't. I don't want this. Yes, it's hot. Yes, it's exciting.

But I really, really don't want it.

Before, it had been my only option. Vicarious lust. Fantasy fucking. I'd allowed myself to get lost in a sensual haze while I watched him with another woman. I'd touched myself and come violently, over and over again, pretending that it was Dallas stroking me. Knowing it was me that he wanted, and that the woman with her mouth on his cock was nothing more than a poor substitute.

But back then, I wasn't his. Not yet. Not really.

Now I am.

Now he can have me whenever and however he wants.

Except that's not really true. Because he can't have me now. He can't touch me here in his own backyard. Not with all these people around.

He and I have to stay in the shadows. But he can fondle Skull Girl whenever the hell he wants to.

God. Fucking. Dammit.

I turn away, my skin still tingling. My breasts still tight. I want to watch—so help me, I do.

But I really, really don't want to want to.

The door to the cabana is now right in front of me—*our* cabana. Where it all began between us, and where we finally, fully committed to each other, promising that we would some-how, someway, make this impossible situation work.

Memories flood over me as I move toward the door. I want to lose myself in them even if I can't lose myself in the man.

I push the curtain aside, then stop dead. I don't know the people on the daybed, but I know only too well what they're doing. I watch, transfixed, as a fully clothed man with his fly down thrusts his cock into a very naked, very willing woman.

I make a small noise, my hand going immediately over my mouth to stifle it, but I make no move to leave. I'm hidden from their view, I think. From where I stand, I am mostly behind the man, at an angle to the daybed. There is the curtain behind me that leads to the pool deck, and also a solid sliding pocket door that I'm surprised they didn't close and lock. Maybe they didn't know it was there.

In front of me are two more layers of gauzy curtains, de-signed both for privacy and to repel bugs in the evening. The lighting is dim, and although I'm sure they would realize I was there if they looked closely, I know from experience that they would see only shadows. And that so long as I don't move, they probably won't even notice me.

I don't move a muscle.

Instead, I stand perfectly still, lost in the hot, decadent scene that is playing out in front of me. I don't care about these peo-ple, and I don't want to. Instead, I'm imagining that it's me on the bed, my body stripped bare. That it's Dallas behind me, still dressed for the party, his fly down, his cock hard and thick and thrusting inside me.

He bends over, his hands cupping my hips, then my waist, then sliding up to grab my tits. He squeezes hard, the pain shooting all the way down to my cunt, making me even wetter, making my muscles clench ever tighter around him as he pounds inside me.

His cock fills me, his balls slapping hard against my ass as he fucks me from behind, harder and harder, riding me until I want to scream from pain and pleasure and the wild, frantic need for release.

I taste blood and realize that I'm biting my lower lip in an effort to stay quiet. I haven't made a sound, but I have moved. My hand has slid down, brushing the thin cotton of my floral print skirt, easing it up slowly until I have to clutch tight to the material in defense against the overpowering urge to ease the garment all the way up.

I'm breathing hard, lost in my fantasies. I'm so wet now, and all I can think about is sliding my fingers under my panties and fingering myself.

I want to imagine it's Dallas touching me. Dallas wanting me.

Me, goddammit. Not some tattooed bitch he grabbed as a prop and who now thinks she's got a claim on him.

A warm hand falls on my shoulder and I jump, my cry stifled by the hand that is suddenly pressed over my mouth.

"Don't startle them." It's Dallas, of course. His voice low, his lips so close to my ear that his breath makes me shiver. "They haven't seen you. We wouldn't want to interrupt the moment."

I swallow, understanding that he doesn't mean their moment, but ours.

His hand slides over my rear, cupping my ass through my thin skirt. Slowly, he starts to inch the material up, mimicking what I'd been on the verge of doing only moments before.

"Dallas," I murmur, my voice whisper-soft. "The door—"

"Is closed." He fists his hand around the thin strap of my thong panties, then yanks them off, forcing me to swallow a gasp in order to keep our secret. "Do you think I want anyone else to see this?" He lifts the back of my skirt up all the way and tucks it into the waistband, completely exposing my ass. "Do you think I want to share such an incredible view?"

I close my eyes, overwhelmed by the rough passion in his voice. In front of us, the couple has shifted. Now she is on her back and he is on his knees beside the bed. He's removed his shirt, and her legs are over his shoulders. Her thighs are pressed to either side of his head, and her hips are writhing as he eats her out. No way can this guy hear a thing that we do. And the woman is too lost in the sound of her own moans to notice us at all.

"Does it turn you on to watch?" Dallas slides one hand between my legs as he asks the question. "I guess it does," he continues, slipping a finger inside me. "Fuck, you're wet."

"That's not from them," I protest. "It's from you."

He bites the edge of my ear. "Bullshit," he says, adding another finger and thrusting hard. "It's all of it. Watching them. Me touching you. Knowing that at any moment we might be discovered. I closed the door, Jane. But did I lock it?"

"Dallas . . ." His name is a moan, because he's right. I'm completely and totally turned on by everything. Excitement. Fear. Danger. And, yes, I know that he locked the door—I trust him too much to believe otherwise—but that doesn't mean that the fantasy of getting caught doesn't excite me more than it should.

"Tell me," he demands. "Tell me how fucked up this is."

"You know it is."

"Tell me you like it."

My body shudders as he teases my clit. "You know I do." And so help me, it's true. Being like this with him sets me on fire. I don't know why—as a rule, I'm all about control, and right now I'm most definitely not in control of anything, myself included.

Maybe that should bother me, but it doesn't. Right now my mind is too sex-blurred to even try to think analytically. I only know need. I only understand want.

I only crave him.

"Dallas," I murmur, grateful that I have at least enough self-awareness left to keep my voice down. "Please."

"Jane." His voice beside my ear is an incantation, taking all of my senses to the next level. "Do you have any idea how much I've craved you tonight? How much I've wanted you?"

"Have you?" I retort, and though I'd meant for the words to be soft—a tease—I know that he has heard the hint of genuine uncertainty in my voice. I can feel the way his body tightens, and he hesitates, the gap in motion almost imperceptible. But not to me; I know him too well.

"Oh, baby. Don't you know that I have?"

"Dallas, I—"

"Shhh. Let me show you. Let me prove it to you. Let me make you explode." He slides his fingers back, stroking my perineum until he reaches my ass. His hand is slick with me, and I gasp as he slides his thumb deep inside me, then eases his fingers forward again until he slips his forefinger in my vagina, effectively finger-fucking me both ways.

I close my eyes, lost in pleasure, then reach out with my left hand and grab the wall to support myself as I push back against his hand, forcing him in harder. Deeper. Wanting everything he is willing to give, and then more.

"That's it, baby. God, that's so fucking hot."

In front of us, the couple has shifted again. He's fully naked on the bed now, and she's riding him. His cock is deep inside her, and as she grinds against him, I mimic her motions. My hips gyrating. My stomach tight. My back arched.

"All of it," Dallas whispers. He obviously understands exactly what I'm doing—including the fact that I'm imagining that his fingers are his cock. Something I want so desperately, but know that I can't have. Not now. Maybe not ever. I feel my cheeks heat, because that's not something I wanted to reveal, but he is unperturbed. "Touch yourself," he whispers as he closes his free hand over my breast, pinching my nipple so that threads of pleasure zing from my breast to my core. "Stroke your clit and ride me."

I don't hesitate. How can I when I belong so fully to him? When I will do whatever he demands because it is Dallas asking, and because I don't want this feeling to end.

My clit is hard and swollen and incredibly sensitive. But I'm so wet and slippery I can barely get enough friction. Even so the sensation is incredible, and as he thrusts his fingers deep inside me, I feel my body shudder. My muscles tighten to draw him in further, and my fingers play wildly over my clit, bringing me closer and closer.

He tweaks my nipple hard, then releases my breast and slides his hand down to press over mine. Now he is both guiding and following my actions, teasing my clit with me as his other hand fucks me so very, very thoroughly. He's hard, pressed close so that I can feel his erection against my hip.

I draw in a breath and pull my hand off my clit so that I can twine my fingers with his. Then I move his hand to his cock. "With me," I say, the words little more than a groan.

He understands, then strokes his cock with one hand while he fucks me with the other, and I take care of my clit myself.

It's wild and wicked and crazy and it feels so right and perfect to be in his arms. Even like this. Even hidden. Even watching other people fuck from this place in the shadows and—

"Come for me, baby," he says, thrusting hard and deep inside me. "Christ, sweetheart, come with me now." He is pressed up against me, and I feel his body tremble as he explodes, and that sensation pushes me over the cliff as well.

"Oh, god." The cry is ripped from me as I shatter, riding his fingers hard as my body buckles and breaks.

"Is someone there?" The girl lifts her head from where she'd been sucking her partner's cock, our roommates having shifted into a sixty-nine.

"Just a noise," the guy says, his back to us. "Forget about it."

But she's staring right at us. I know she can't possibly recognize us from the shadows, but I duck my head anyway and start to smooth my skirt, tugging it down from where it's hiked up in my waistband. I'm not about to say anything of course. On the contrary. I'm going to get my clothes straight and follow Dallas through the door before either of them decides to investigate.

"Who is that?" she asks. "Who's there?"

I motion to Dallas that we should go.

Dallas, however, has a different idea. "It's just me," he says, and I immediately want to sink into the floor. First in embarrassment, then in horror. What if this girl asks who he's with? What if she gets a good look at me?

I glare at him, but he just shakes it off, as if I'm the one being insane and unreasonable.

"Dallas?"

"Sorry to intrude, Christine. My friend's a little shy, but she likes to watch."

"Oh, really?" I can hear the lilt of excitement rising in her voice. "Billy likes to watch, too. Don't you, sugar?"

"Absolutely." Billy lifts his head long enough to bite Christine's hip, then dives back down to her pussy.

I just stand there, not sure if I'm turned on or scared or confused or what.

"Well, since they both like to watch," Christine purrs, "why don't you come join me?" She pats the daybed mattress.

"Tempting," Dallas says, and my gut twists a little because I honestly can't tell if he means it. "But maybe some other time."

"Suit yourself. Stay and watch some more if you want." She strokes Billy's hip as she aims a smile toward us. "I promise it'll be quite the show."

"We'll catch the rest of the act some other time. But stay in here as long as you like. I'll have someone bring you champagne."

"Thanks, man," Billy says, his voice muffled.

Dallas starts to turn, and I feel his hand at my back, ready to guide me out.

I'm breathing hard, shaking a little. And I don't wait for him to take the lead. Instead, I walk past him, slide open the door, and escape into the night.

3

The Man with the Golden Cock

The party is still going strong as I scurry from the cabana, my mind in a jumble. I know I should stop and talk to Dallas—but the truth is that I don't know what to say. What just happened in there was, well, absolutely fucking incredible. I can't deny that I liked it. Hell, I loved it.

Or at least I did until the fantasy ended and Dallas talked to Christine. *Christine.* He knew her name. Why? Because he'd slept with her, of course.

Well, fuck.

This is hardly a revelation, and yet I can't deny that it bothered me the same way that watching him touch the blond bitch or the tattooed brunette bothered me. Even though there's something so incredibly hot about that game of ours—even though I know he was thinking about me and only me—the whole thing just felt wrong tonight. And now that wrongness is sitting in my gut. Raw and sour and festering.

And I can't talk to Dallas about it, because the most wrong

thing of all is that it didn't bother him. To Dallas, it was play-time as usual.

To Dallas, nothing has changed over these last four days. But to me, the entire world is different.

Ergo, the running.

I keep my head down as I slide through the crowd, skirting the cabana and heading to the lush, manicured lawn. This section of the property isn't well-lit in order to keep most of the guests on the pool deck, in the house, or on the temporary dance floor that's been set up on the lawn closer to the residence.

Despite the dim lighting—or perhaps because of it—there are still a few people mingling about, but I soon leave them behind. By the time I reach the hedge maze that blocks this area from the more private family garden, I'm the only one around.

When Dallas and Liam and I were children, this maze was exceptionally easy to navigate, primarily because the hedge was only a foot high. Now, more than twenty years later, it's eight feet tall, but I still remember my way through, and I'm clear in under five minutes and heading toward the garden shed.

As soon as I reach it, I collapse onto the small wooden bench that sits flush against the stone wall. I breathe deeply, grateful to be hidden from view. Away from the party. From Dallas. From everything.

Except I'm not. He's followed me, of course.

I hear him first—the sound of his footsteps. Firm. Determined. Steady.

He's not running, but walking quickly. Then he is standing in front of me. My head is down, so I see only the soft leather of his Brioni loafers and the cuff of his Dior Homme jeans. Casual clothes for a casual party. But there's nothing casual about his manner. His stance alone radiates power, and though he says nothing, I know that he is worried about me.

Hell, I'm a little worried about me.

Slowly, I tilt my head up to look at him. I've stared at him for hours tonight, but despite my roiling emotions, I can't help but be riveted by him now. Or maybe it's because of those emotions. Because Dallas Sykes is beautiful. A living sculpture. A model of male perfection.

His legs are clad in the faded denim, tight enough to accent his muscular thighs, not to mention his semi-erect cock. He wears a plain white T-shirt under the thin gray cashmere sweater that I bought him for his birthday almost four months ago. He looks sexy as hell—like he just walked off the runway of a men's fashion show. And it's all I can do to still my fingers that want nothing more than to grab a fistful of cashmere and pull him violently toward me.

I don't. Instead I continue my inspection, tilting my head back further to see his face. I expect the hard line of his jaw to be tight with frustration and his emerald green eyes to burn with irritation. I expect those lips to scold me—to ask what the fuck is wrong with me.

Instead, he says, "I'm sorry."

I blink, the words as unexpected as a slap.

"I thought you'd like it," he says. "Something hot. Something for us."

"Something hidden. Something secret." As soon as I say the words I regret them. "I'm sorry," I say. "It was hot—incredibly hot. And I did like it. You know I did. It's just . . ."

"We can't be open," he says, then sighs. "I know."

He drags his fingers through his caramel-colored hair, and I watch as his expression hardens.

"It's not just us, you know," he says, moving to sit beside me. "Everything about these parties is secret. I'm playing a role. I know we haven't talked much yet about Deliverance, but you understand that, right? I'm—"

"The man with the golden cock," I say. "Yeah, I get that."

He winces. "We both know that's not true."

"Dallas." *Shit. Fuck.* "I didn't mean—"

"I know you didn't, and it's fine." He looks at me gently, his voice turning softer as he says, "I told you that I'm glad I've never actually fucked any of them. I only want you."

His words warm me, but they don't fully soothe. "I believe you," I say, matching his soft tone. "But being glad that you haven't fucked them is completely different from being glad that you can't."

He closes his eyes for a moment and nods, acknowledging the truth of my words.

I'd been shocked to learn that I was the only woman Dallas has ever penetrated—and that was seventeen years ago when we'd been captive and terrified. Before he'd been tortured.

Before he'd been broken.

Now he plays a game of smoke and mirrors, satisfying hordes of women, but never literally fucking any of them. And since no woman who's romped in his bed wants to admit that he didn't actually lay her out and fuck her hard, his reputation just keeps growing. And frankly, considering his skill in bed, I bet most women didn't even realize he was never inside them; they were too busy wallowing in the aftershocks of multiple orgasms.

Honestly, it's one hell of a marketing scam. All of it is, really. The playboy persona. The King of Fuck reputation. He flirts with, touches, and beds a procession of women because that feeds an illusion and serves his purpose—*Deliverance*. An elite vigilante organization dedicated to rescuing kidnap victims and punishing their tormentors.

Until I learned that Deliverance was essentially Dallas's brainchild, I'd been firmly of the opinion that it was a dangerous group that needed to be stopped. I'd done enough research and written enough articles and books on kidnappings and vigilante justice to know that mercenaries often do more harm than good. But I know Dallas; I understand his motives. And, honestly, I'm not sure what to think now, at least not about Deliverance. And so I'm officially withholding judgment until I learn more.

That in-depth educational experience hasn't happened yet. But I know enough to understand what he's doing. Creating camouflage. Hiding in plain sight behind the facade of a man who is too much of a player to be a threat.

"I've been living a life built on secrets for years, Jane." His voice is soft, pulling me back from my thoughts. "Secrets are familiar territory."

"We said we weren't going to have any more secrets."

"Between you and me. Not between us and the world." He draws a breath, looking away from me as if to gather himself before turning back to meet my eyes. "I'll tell you whatever you want about how Deliverance works. You know that."

"I do."

"So, do you want me to tell you now?"

"No. Maybe. I don't know." I sigh, then run my fingers through my hair. "That's not what's bothering me."

He nods. "Yeah. I know." He stands again and starts to pace, obviously frustrated. "Tonight—this party—maybe I should have sent you back to New York. Maybe you should be at your own house tonight."

I shudder, feeling suddenly cold. "You don't want me here?"

"Oh, baby, no." He stops in front of me and reaches down, taking my hands to pull me to my feet. "I want you with me more than anything. But I planned this party for one purpose only—I need to talk with Henry Darcy. I need to find out if he has any idea who's behind Deliverance. And I need a woman on my arm when I talk to him."

"Why?"

"Because I have to make sure he sees the playboy, not the man who might have set him up with Deliverance. I need him to talk to me, but I want his attention split. And a beautiful woman is an excellent distraction. This has been my camouflage for years, baby, and if I step out of character, I risk everything."

"Which means the woman on your arm can't be me." The statement is rhetorical; obviously I can't be the woman at his side. Even so, he opens his mouth to answer. I lift my hand to cut him off. "No. I get it. I do."

About a year ago, Henry Darcy hired Deliverance to rescue his kidnapped daughters. He'd jumped through all of the hoops to contact the group, and as far as Dallas and his team knew, Darcy was ignorant of the identity of the individual players in the vigilante group. For that matter, he didn't even know the name "Deliverance." Or, at least, the team had assumed he didn't. It was, Dallas explained to me, an internal code name only.

That's the way all Deliverance operations work. Contact is made through a very complex system that Dallas hasn't yet described to me. But the bottom line is total anonymity.

So when Henry Darcy revealed publicly that the vigilante group that had rescued his girls was called Deliverance, Dallas and the team were more than a little concerned. What else did he know? Was he a threat?

Apparently, Dallas decided that the best way to find out was to host a party, invite Darcy, and chat the man up. He wanted a sexy woman beside him as a visual diversion, so that whatever questions he asked or conversations he started would come off as simple chatter, not the interrogation of a man who masterminds an elite international vigilante group.

I draw in a breath. "I understand why you need a woman by your side," I repeat. "But understanding it and liking it are two different things."

"I know, baby. I do." I can see the pain on his face as he looks at me. "But I'm not willing to give it up. I *can't* give it up. Not

Deliverance as a whole, and not the women I use as camouflage."

His words are blunt and brutally honest, and I want to cry out, *Not even for me?* But I can't manage to force the words out. How can I ask him to be someone other than who he is? The leader of Deliverance. A man with a mission.

Maybe I don't entirely understand or agree with what he does, but it's part of who he is. It's there at his core.

And, dammit, I want the man. The full man, with all of his hopes and dreams and flaws. Not half the man. Not a man who compromised for anyone. Not even for me.

With a sigh, I shake my head. "I'm not asking you to. Really. I didn't even mean to open the Deliverance door. It's just that I—well, I didn't like you touching them. The blonde. The chick with the tattoos. And I didn't like that you've fucked Christine."

"I haven't fu—"

"You know what I mean."

"Yeah. I do."

He tilts his head, studying me. "Not that long ago, you liked it a lot. So did I. You watched another woman take my cock in her mouth and it got you off."

I nod, because he's right. Hell, just the memory of the game we played that night—the pictures he sent me, the things he demanded of me—make my body thrum. I lower my eyes to the ground, and softly admit, "I think I came harder than I had in a very long time."

He sits beside me once more, then puts his hand lightly on my thigh. He moves his thumb lightly back and forth, stroking me. "But?"

"But that was then. That was before we were together." I look up and meet his eyes. "That was when I had even less claim on you than they did."

"That was never the case."

I shrug. "Maybe not, but it felt like it." I press my hand on top of his. "It doesn't feel that way anymore. You're mine, Dallas, but you can't touch me like that. I love you, and we're not victims anymore, but we're still trapped. We're still held captive by this huge secret that we have to keep. And sometimes I think we're never really going to be free. We're always going to be trapped together in the dark. Maybe it's not a cement cell, but it's still a prison."

I squeeze his hand as I look imploringly at his face. "We deserve better," I say. "And I want better."

"So do I." He brushes a strand of hair off my forehead. "Oh, baby, so do I."

For a moment he says nothing else. Then he tilts his head slightly to the side. "Do you want to go public? Just be us, together, out there in the open?"

Yes. Oh, god, yes.

The words are wild and dangerous in my head. But they're not true. There are too many obstacles. Too many horrors. Our parents' reaction and the tabloid attention leap to mind. Just thinking of the way the cameras would inevitably focus on us makes me want to shrink into a ball and cry.

And oh, god, what would Grams or Poppy say? At eighty and one hundred, respectively, the revelation about me and Dallas would probably put our grandmother and great-grandfather in their graves.

I shake my head. "No. No, the idea terrifies me. I want it—I want so badly to be with you one hundred percent—but going public scares the crap out of me even more than I hate all the secrets."

He nods, and I think it's relief I see in his eyes. "I know," he says. "Eventually we'll figure out a way, but until then, going public stays tabled. Just as well. Better to deal with one obstacle to happily ever after at a time."

I frown, wondering what other obstacles he's worried about. "You mean the women on your arm?"

For a moment he looks confused, and he doesn't quite look at me when he nods and says, "Of course."

"Dallas?"

He looks straight at me, and I see no shadows on his face. No deception. Mentally, I roll my eyes at myself. I'm on edge—looking for secrets and obfuscation where none exists.

"Jane? Are we okay?"

I manage to conjure a smile. "I just don't like sharing you."

"You're not. Whatever I do—whoever they are—those women don't have a claim on me."

I nod, then close my eyes for a moment to gather my strength. "I get that you need them for appearances. That you need to touch them and put on a show. But I don't want—"

"To play our game anymore. I understand." He shifts so that he is facing me more directly, then strokes my cheek as he slides his hand back to cup my head. He pulls me toward him, then captures my mouth in a kiss. It's hot and deep and I feel my body start to melt.

"No more games," he says when we come up for air. "I only want you."

"Are you okay with that? You don't need to touch them while you think about me? You don't want to?" Just saying the words is making me wet, and I squirm a little as I wonder what kind of a hypocrite I am that I'm putting the brakes on something we both found so deliciously erotic.

I bite my lower lip thoughtfully before continuing. "It's just that I know you like sex dirty. That you need it—"

"Fucked up?" he interrupts. "I do." His eyes drop to my breasts, where my obviously hard nipples are apparent through the lace of my bra and the thin material of my simple pink T-shirt. "I think you like it, too."

I don't deny it. "So?"

His mouth curves up. "I told you before. That's just playing. I don't need it. Not with you."

"Oh. Well, then that's my—what do they call it?—my hard limit. No playing those kind of games unless—"

I cut myself off. I hadn't intended to go there.

"Unless?" His eyes sparkle with amusement, and I'm absolutely certain he knows what I'm going to say.

I glance down at his hand on my thigh. "Unless I start it." I don't look up, but I bite my lip as the hand that has been resting gently on my thigh starts to slide up, pushing my skirt as he goes.

"So, you're saying you like it? That watching me cup another woman's ass turns you on? That seeing her suck my cock makes you wet?" His words are raw. Almost vulgar. And yet I can hear the humor beneath them.

"It's not funny." Damn the man, he knows me so well. Lover. Brother. Friend. And he gets me better than anyone. Maybe even better than I understand myself.

"I'm not laughing." He's not. In fact, the humor in his voice has been replaced by a low, burning heat. His hand is midway up my thigh now, so close to my core that I'm practically shaking with anticipation. "Someone doesn't want to cut off her options," he says as he gently tugs on my thigh, urging me to spread my legs. "Tell me why."

Considering I'm losing the ability to form words, I find his demand entirely unreasonable. My skirt is up over my knees now, and I'm not wearing panties—those are probably still on the floor of the cabana. That means that with my legs spread, I'm completely open—and the cool night breeze against my hot, wet pussy feels beyond incredible.

"Jane." His fingertip traces along the soft skin between my pubis and my thigh. "Tell me why you want to keep the option open. Why you might want to slide your hand between your legs and stroke yourself while you watch me bite some other woman's nipple." As if in illustration, he strokes his finger over me from clit to core and I whimper from the incredible pleasure of it.

"Tell me," he demands again.

"Because I do like it." My voice is a whisper at first. "Even tonight, it was hot. I hated that I liked it, but I did. I just . . ."

"You didn't want to share."

"Now that you're mine—"

"I am yours," he says, pushing his fingers deep into me.

"I know." I move my hips, my body on a mission to draw him in further. Harder. "And I don't want to share." I tilt my head so that I can meet his eyes. "Not yet, anyway. But later. When I feel more certain, I—" I drop my eyes again. Another thing I hadn't intended to admit.

"Are you not certain about how I feel?"

"No." I blurt the word out. There is no doubt in my mind that Dallas loves me. Fully. Completely. Even painfully. "Never."

"Then you mean the future."

I nod.

"We'll make this work."

I want to ask how, but I don't. I just nod. "You're everything I want," I say. "You know that, right?"

"I know it, because I feel the same way."

"And I don't share my toys easily." I shift, sliding off his fingers as I rise up so that I can move to straddle his lap. "I'm pretty much a greedy little bitch."

"Oh, really? How greedy?"

"Very." I slide my hand down his chest and press my palm against his very stiff cock. "Very greedy."

His hand moves to my waist. "Come with me into the shed."

"No. Here."

His brow lifts. "Someone might see."

I take the hem of my blouse and tug it over my head, leaving me in only my sandals, skirt, and a very skimpy bra. "Only if they get through the hedge."

"Interesting," he murmurs as his hands move to my breasts, tugging the lace down so that I am fully exposed.

"What?" I reach behind and draw down the zipper on my skirt. I don't want to get off his lap even for a second, and so I lift the skirt over my head as well, then toss it onto the side of the bench with my shirt.

"This." He looks me up and down, his expression as hot and hard as his cock. "There's a bit of an exhibitionist in you." He leans forward and runs his tongue over my nipple. "I like it."

I shiver, as much from his touch as from his words. The truth is that I like it, too. And not just because the cool breeze on my hot skin feels delicious. I like the fantasy of discovery. Of having someone see us and realize what they're seeing. *Who* they are seeing.

I like the fantasy that our secret has been revealed and that, for better or for worse, we're no longer living in shadows and we just have to move forward and deal, all the hiding over. All the secrets finished.

I like the fantasy, yes. But the reality scares me to death.

Right now, I'm not scared. I meant it about the hedge. No one is going to come back here. Hell, none of the guests know this secluded section of the yard even exists.

We're safe to do what we want. And what I want is Dallas.

I lean forward to kiss him, then straighten before arching my back and cupping my own breasts. I watch his face, the expression of intense longing as I tease my nipples. Then I keep my eyes firmly on his as I lower one hand from my breasts and start to finger my clit as little frissons of pleasure shoot through me.

"That's it, baby," he murmurs as I succumb to pleasure and close my eyes, letting the sensations grow. "Get yourself off. Take what you want. Do it while you can."

It takes a moment for his words to sink in, and when they do, I open my eyes and peer at him. "While I can?"

"Do you think you're running this show, baby? You're getting off because I say you can get off. You're mine, remember? Every touch. Every orgasm. Your pleasure is my prerogative, and there will come a day when I'll take it away and make you beg for it."

"The hell you will," I retort, but it's a bullshit response. Maybe if I wasn't naked, I could pull it off. But it's only too easy for him to see how his words have made my nipples tighten. And it's too damn obvious that I'm soaked now, his jeans probably ruined from how incredibly wet his words have made me.

"I own you," he says, reaching out and capturing my clit between his thumb and forefinger. The wild, unexpected pressure makes me gasp, and when I jerk back a little, his hold tightens and I cry out from the sweet pleasure of an unexpected jolt of pain. "I've always owned you. Say it, Jane. Lift your hands up above your head and tell me that you're mine."

"You know I am." My voice is breathy. I'm so fucking turned on I can barely get the words out.

"Say it," he growls, pinching my clit again. "Say it and lift your hands."

"I'm yours," I say as I thrust my hands toward the stars. "I've always been yours."

I see the impact of my words on his face, the harshness melting into passion. I expect a kiss, but one doesn't come. Instead, he unfastens my bra.

"Arms behind your back," he says. "Wrists crossed."

I start to ask what he's doing, but I hold my tongue. I've told him repeatedly I'll go as far as he needs me to. And I want to see where tonight is leading.

Where it leads is to my hands bound behind my back with my very own bra. I'm still straddling his legs, my knees on the bench and my pussy over his crotch. My crossed wrists are against my tailbone, and my hands are pretty much useless for keeping my balance.

He's only bound me in that one place, but even so I'm antsy. This is Dallas, of course, and I trust him. For that matter, I've offered to let him tie me up before. We never got there, but he knows I was willing. More than that, he understands what a big step that offer was for me. I'd been bound and left alone during our kidnapping, and as a result, bondage isn't exactly my kink of choice.

Dallas knows that—and yet he's tied my wrists anyway. He did it boldly. Taking what he wanted. Taking charge. And not asking for permission at all.

I'm surprised to realize that the thought of being bound doesn't scare me. On the contrary, it makes me more excited. My body burning with desire. My sex clenching with need. He may not have asked, but that's because he *knows*. He knows my limits. More than that, he knows I trust him.

He meets my eyes, and for a moment his are soft with understanding. He waits, and I tilt my head in the tiniest of nods. He says nothing to acknowledge my assent, but I know that he has seen it when the corner of his mouth lifts. "Is this what you want?" he asks as he slowly strokes my sex, sliding his index finger in and out of me, and brushing over my clit with each and every stroke.

"Yes." My voice is barely a breath, and I arch back, supported by his other hand held firm against my spine. "Oh, god, yes."

"Then take it." He gently pulls his finger away, and I open my eyes, surprised at the sudden cessation of his incredible touch.

"I—what?"

"You want to come." His grin is hot. Wicked. "Do it."

I start to protest, but realize at once that it would do no

good. He knows perfectly well that I can't possibly touch myself with my hands tied behind my back. He probably expects me to protest—to beg.

No way.

I have a much better plan.

I lean back so that am using his hand at my back for support and balance, gaining leverage as if I had the use of my hands. It's dicey, of course—if he moves his hand, I'll tumble backward. But I trust him not to let that happen. Because the truth is, he wants the same thing I do.

I want to get off.

And he really, really wants to watch.

Right then, I'm ready to satisfy us both.

Slowly, I move my hips, grinding against the bulge of his cock, the friction of the rough denim against my sensitive clit all but driving me insane.

"Oh, baby." His voice is low, like rolling thunder, and I feel him grow harder. I'm wet and slippery and I'm sliding over him, harder. Hotter.

He reaches out with his free hand and holds me steady by the throat. I'm trapped like that—his hand behind me keeping me safe. His hand on my throat keeping me right there. Steady. Under his control.

He holds me in place even as I buck and slide and grind against him, and when he bends forward and tugs on my nipple with his teeth, I cry out, "Yes, oh, god, Dallas, yes," so loudly that I'm surprised the partygoers don't hear me all the way back at the pool.

He releases my breast and leans back with a self-satisfied expression, then he slides the hand on my spine down, lower and lower until it's not holding me in place anymore. I'm held steady only by his hand around my throat—tight and tense and dangerous enough to make me wet.

The finger that was splayed across my back is now inside

me, teasing and exploring even as I rock shamelessly against the bulge in his jeans. He brings his sex-slick finger around to my mouth and orders me to suck. I do, moaning as I taste my own desire. As I draw him in and tease him with my tongue. As I imagine it's his cock and I'm sucking him off.

He shudders violently, then groans with pleasure, the sound so intense it sends shivers through me. I meet his eyes, and I see a heated passion that matches my own, and when he tugs his finger free, I almost cry out in protest.

Then I see that he's using that hand to fumble at the button of his jeans. He manages it, then frees his cock. "Ride me. No, not like that," he says before I can protest that I don't want him trying to enter me and going soft. "Stroke me."

But even that I'm not sure of. "Can you—"

"Please, baby. I need to feel your cunt on my cock."

I don't hesitate. I want to feel him, too. Like velvet steel between my legs, and I rub myself shamelessly over the length of him, afraid at first that this is too close and he'll lose his erection. And then, when it's clear that he won't—when I realize that the moans of pleasure are full and rich and real—I buck harder and faster. I'm so caught up in the moment that I only notice that he's slipped his hand back around to my ass when I feel the finger that I'd just been sucking teasing the rim of my anus.

He thrusts his finger inside me, and even though the digit is thoroughly lubed, the sensual assault is both rough and without warning, and I bite my lower lip against a sharp, short burst of pain. But the truth is, I love this. I love that he is using me the way that I told him he could. More than that, I love the way this feels. Us together. Wild. Almost feral. It's dirty and fast and hot and edgy. And I absolutely fucking love it.

He is so incredibly hard, and I angle my body back, so that I can rock my hips so that my cunt strokes his cock, and also so that I can grind hard against the finger inside me. It's an exceptional sensation, and I close my eyes, wishing I could touch myself to take me this last little bit, but satisfied with exploring every touch and sensation. His hand at my throat, keeping me vulnerable. His finger in my ass—which is an entirely different kind of vulnerability. His hard, thick cock between my legs. And my own clit, swollen and stimulated and taking me right to the edge.

Not to mention the erotic sensation of the night air against my bare body.

It's all exceptional.

It's all pushing me closer to the edge, and any moment I will go careening over.

I'm not expecting it when he releases my throat to cup the back of my head. He twines his fingers in my hair, then pulls me roughly toward him. He captures me in a kiss so wild and hot that I swear I'm going to burst into flames, and I grind against him harder, wanting more. Everything. *Him.*

When he finally breaks the kiss, his expression is as raw as his voice. "You're at my mercy, baby."

"Yes." I can barely force the word out. "God, yes."

"Come for me, Jane. I want you to explode for me, now."

It is as if the primal command in his voice is the final piece of a puzzle I've been assembling, and I do as he commands, screaming his name as my body rips apart in one wild, sensational orgasm. I tremble all over with such violent rapture that I don't notice at first that his finger is no longer inside me. Now he's using that hand to stroke his cock, and the moment his eyes meet mine, we are locked together.

His breath is ragged, and I realize that mine is, too. We are perfectly attuned, and waves of pleasure crash through me as he explodes. He comes over my legs and belly, marking me. *Claiming me.* And I absolutely love it.

I keep my eyes on his, then slide my finger over my legs and stomach before lifting my hand to my mouth. I suck, relishing the salty taste of him almost as much as the look on his face. Lust. Desire. Appreciation. And, yes, love.

For a moment, we just look at each other, both our chests rising and falling as we breathe. Then he hooks one arm around my waist and another under one of my legs. He shifts me so that I am sideways in his lap, and I can cradle my head against his shoulder.

"You do know how to show a girl a good time, Mr. Sykes," I say.

I feel his chuckle rumble through my chest. "I try."

I smile, but the laughter never quite reaches my lips. I'm too overwhelmed by the moment. By what I feel. By the presence of this man I love. With a sigh, I tuck my head under his chin, snuggling close. "This whole thing is a hot mess, you know. How are we ever going to make this work?"

The silence between us is long, but then finally he answers. "I don't know," he admits. "But we will. Don't ever doubt it. Don't ever doubt us."

The passion in his voice calms me, and I close my eyes as he holds me tight. I cling to him, relishing his certainty. His strength.

And desperately wishing that he was strong enough to truly crush all of my fears and worries.

4

Sins of the Father

What the fuck was he doing?

He leaned forward, his hands clutching the marble counter-top. He was in his bathroom, naked from the waist down. He'd tossed his jeans—stained from her juices and his come—on the floor behind him. He should have tossed them in the laundry, but damned if he didn't want to wear them tomorrow. He'd be wearing them still if he didn't need to go back out to the party and find Henry Darcy.

He knew he should shower, but he wanted to hold on to the scent of her for as long as possible. The feel of her. The memory of how wild she'd been in his arms. How hard she'd rubbed herself against his jeans, then worked her slick, swollen pussy against his bare cock.

He groaned softly, closing his eyes as he let his mind drift back to the way she'd looked, her back arched as she ground herself against him like a wild thing, each gyration forcing his finger deeper into her ass even as the friction against her sensitive clit brought her that much closer to screaming his name.

He'd always wanted her—hell, some of his earliest memories were of wanting her. But now that they were together, that desire had changed. It was hard and raw. It was possessive and wild and desperate. He wanted to take her to dark places with him. He wanted her to understand what he needed now—and what he hated himself for needing.

He'd changed in captivity. *She'd* changed him. The Woman. One of their two kidnappers. The bitch who'd tortured him. Teased him. Tormented him in ways he hadn't understood at fifteen, but that had become a part of his sexual appetites. And Jane—oh, god, Jane—she'd sworn she wanted to go there with him.

Some part of him hadn't really believed her, and he'd intended to start slow. Asking. Explaining. But he'd lost his fucking mind tonight. He'd wanted—and he'd taken.

And fuck if she hadn't matched him. In power. In desire. In need.

Granted, tonight was a relatively tame appetizer—a first step on a wild and wicked journey—but she had been right there with him. More than that, she had loved it. He'd never seen her wetter. Wilder. He'd taken her to a desperate, primal place, and she'd been completely at his mercy.

And oh, the way she'd trusted him . . .

He'd bound her wrists. He'd gripped her throat. He'd given her reason to hesitate, to fear. And yet when he looked into her eyes, the trust and love he'd seen there had both melted him and left no doubt that she was his.

Trust.

He winced, looking down so that he didn't have to meet his own eyes in the mirror. *She trusted him.* And not just in bed, but in everything.

Most of all, she trusted him to keep his promise.

"No more secrets," she'd begged four days ago, when they had

finally stopped dancing around their desire and committed to being together for real. *"Not between us. Not again. Not ever."*

"No more secrets," he'd promised, and at the time, he'd meant it.

Then Liam had called, and Dallas had found himself holding on to the biggest secret of all. *Colin.* Jane's birth father. A man that Dallas considered a friend and had once thought of as an uncle.

A man who right now was topping Deliverance's list of suspects as the brains behind Dallas and Jane's kidnapping.

Fuck.

For years, Dallas and Deliverance had been on the trail of the six hired men who had physically pulled off the kidnapping. Five had slipped through their fingers—two had died before the team located them, one had killed himself rather than submit to the team's interrogation, and two simply didn't know a goddamn thing. And then a miracle had happened—they'd identified the sixth kidnapper. *Silas Ortega.*

Capture Ortega and Deliverance could extract the identity of the two people who'd masterminded the kidnapping—the Jailer and the Woman. It had been the first solid lead in years, and Deliverance had gone full force after the man, but they'd been too late—the authorities picked him up first. But before Interpol could get any solid intel, Ortega had killed himself in custody. Or so the story went.

In truth, the masterminds behind Dallas and Jane's kidnapping had arranged a fake suicide—a bold maneuver and one meant to prevent Ortega from offering any evidence about the Sykes kidnapping to the authorities. Dallas didn't have proof of that theory, of course. But that didn't change the fact that he was absolutely certain.

With Ortega dead, Deliverance was left to learn what they could of the man's involvement in the kidnapping by analyzing his property, including a netbook they'd found in his home in Argentina.

And that's when things became truly disturbing. Because even though the hard drive was encrypted, Noah—Deliverance's tech guru—managed to pull out a few bits and pieces. And what he found was Colin's name all over those goddamn files.

Maybe Colin and Ortega had legitimate business. *Maybe*. And even now the team was looking for more evidence to either inculpate or exonerate Colin. They were all hoping to hell the man was clean. But Dallas couldn't deny the tightness in his gut. A tightness that evidenced his belief that his friend—Jane's birth father—was guilty as shit. That he'd arranged their kidnapping. That he'd held them in a dank, dark basement. That he'd tortured Jane and Dallas for weeks.

To what end? To what goddamn end?

And now Dallas was carrying this secret despite promising Jane there would be no secrets between them. But how could he tell her? How could he dump such a horrible possibility on her unless he was absolutely certain?

He gripped the counter tighter in an effort to stifle the urge to throw something hard and shatter the goddamn mirror. *Colin*. This likelihood that Colin was involved had been fucking with his head ever since he'd learned about the contents of the netbook's hard drive. He was never far from his memories of the kidnapping, but over the last few days, his dreams had been more feverish, and he'd wake up sweating, his pulse racing. He'd sit up, gasping, as memories of what that fucking bitch had done to him clung to him like grime he couldn't scrub away.

Had Colin known what was happening? Had he simply looked the other way?

Or worse, had Colin been behind the torment? Had he urged the Woman on? Had he watched? Had he gotten off on the vile games that bitch had played?

The questions tore through him, seeping into his dreams, shifting into nightmares. Fucking with his head.

And, inevitably, yanking him from sleep.

Thankfully his violent awakenings hadn't disturbed Jane. He half-smiled, remembering how deeply she'd slept—how exhausted their lovemaking had made her. He'd sit frozen in bed, waiting until his heart rate slowed, and then he'd lay back down and hold her close, her warmth soothing him. And when she inevitably turned in his arms and burrowed against him, his chest would tighten with love and longing, and her warmth would banish the few dark remnants of the dream.

He took a deep breath, then another, reminding himself that they didn't really know anything yet.

Maybe Colin was entirely innocent. Maybe he'd been mixed up in something else altogether.

Or maybe Colin had gone completely off the rails after his parental rights to Jane had been terminated, and he'd used his underworld contacts to strike back at Lisa, Jane's mother and Colin's ex-wife. Except that theory was flawed because the kidnapping had been aimed at Dallas. Jane had been in the wrong place at the wrong time, and she'd been snatched with him.

Then again, Lisa and Eli were Dallas's parents, too. And Eli had been the moving force behind ousting Colin from Jane's life.

So maybe Colin set up the kidnapping to punish Eli, the man who at one time had been his best friend? Had Colin been determined to take away Eli's family the way that Eli had taken Colin's by having an affair with Lisa, then marrying her and adopting Jane? Could it be that screwed up?

It was possible, Dallas knew. Fucked up and depressing as shit, especially considering he actually liked the man. But possible nonetheless.

But no way was he telling Jane. Not until he was sure.

Telling her now would only taint her relationship with

Colin if he turned out to be innocent. And if he turned out to be guilty, it would destroy her. Colin had been the one she'd relied on after the kidnapping, going so far as to beg to attend a boarding school near her birth father because she needed to get away from Dallas. From everything that reminded her of the kidnapping. And from the reality that the love and comfort that they'd found in each other's arms while captive was forbidden out in the real world.

So yeah, he was holding on to one hell of a secret.

He only hoped that when the truth came to light, she'd understand that he'd broken his promise in order to protect her. Because he would always watch her back, even if doing so meant sacrificing himself.

Right now, however, he needed to let all of that go. This wasn't the time to get lost in the memory of the way she'd looked and felt. And it sure as hell wasn't the time to worry about how he would tell her the truth if the investigation proved that Colin was guilty.

Instead, right now he needed to focus on the reason he'd thrown this party in the first place—Henry Darcy.

He checked his watch and saw that it was almost ten. The party had been in full swing for two hours. He hadn't seen Darcy among the guests, but the man had assured Dallas that he was coming, and since Darcy had a reputation of showing up late to pretty much everything, Dallas wasn't yet worried about missing him.

What gave him more pause was seeing Jane downstairs.

They'd parted ways at the garden shed, deciding that it was safer to return to the party separately. He'd left first, circling the house and entering through the service entrance to avoid being noticed. He'd used the back stairs to head to the third floor and the master bedroom. Jane, he knew, had most likely used the same route to get to the second floor and her childhood bedroom.

She was just one floor below him, and it was so damn tempting to go down to her. To lock the door and strip her bare. To lay her out on the bed, spread her wide, and lose himself in the scent and feel of her.

Instead, he had to go back to the pool deck and pluck an anonymous woman from the crowd. Someone to look good beside him. Someone he could tease and tempt and put on a show with.

Someone who would expect him to take her to his bedroom and fuck her hard once they'd made the party circuit.

The thought made him cringe. Jane was the only woman he welcomed into his bed now. But that left him faced with the rather daunting problem of how to manage expectations, not to mention his own carefully-honed reputation as one of the biggest manwhores in the country.

Considering the scope of the investigations he ran for Deliverance, the dangerous calls that he made, and the sensitive data he handled on a daily basis, the fact that his biggest problem at the moment was how to deal with the rumors surrounding his cock seemed more than a little ridiculous.

Ridiculous, maybe. But still legitimate.

Then again, his cock wasn't actually his biggest problem. That honor belonged to Colin—who was currently in a holding pattern—and Darcy, who wasn't. And Dallas needed to get downstairs and talk to the man. Determine what exactly he knew about Deliverance. Did he know anything at all about the organization behind the code name? And if he did, Dallas would have to assess whether or not Darcy himself was a threat.

If so, he'd pull together the team and they'd come up with a plan.

If not, he'd breathe a sigh of relief and move on.

First, though, he had to find a girl he didn't want, but who would serve his purpose.

Suck it up, Sykes. You chose this life. You built Deliverance.

You know what it takes to make it work. Don't start acting like a pussy now.

Right. Good advice.

With his pep talk running a loop in his head, he pulled on a fresh pair of jeans. He continued to wear the cashmere sweater that Jane had given him. It was still clean, but it carried her scent, and he wanted as much of Jane with him as he could have.

Presentable again, he started toward his bedroom door, then caught sight of the blue envelope sitting on the small table that sat flush against that wall. Well, hell. One more thing to add to his list of shit that just kept piling up.

According to Archie, the letter had arrived last Monday, tucked inside the plastic bag in which the morning paper had been delivered. But Archie had told him that news at the same time that he'd told Dallas that Jane was waiting for him on the pool deck. Dallas had asked Archie to leave the letter in his bedroom to read later, and Dallas had hurried to Jane, the letter forgotten.

Now, he frowned at it, another one in a string that had started arriving about a year ago. He was tempted to just shred the thing, but reason told him not to. He didn't know who was sending them, and so far they'd been nothing more than a nuisance, but he also knew that could change.

He opened this one, then felt his gut twist as he read the words printed there:

My mouth, my pussy, my ass, my heart. You know you have all of me, so why aren't you mine?

The words made him cringe, all the more so because coming from Jane, they would make him hard.

"Bitch," he spat, cursing the unknown woman as he carefully folded the letter and replaced it in the envelope. He'd deal with it later. Right now, he had more important things to worry about than a woman who imagined herself scorned.

Forcing the letter from his mind, he hurried down the hall and through the double doors that separated the private rooms from the public area. He moved slowly down the stairs, using the vantage point to scope out possible companions mingling in the great room below. He didn't see Jane, and her absence both disappointed him—when didn't he want to see her?—and pleased him. Because right then, seeing her would only drive home the fact that she was the one woman at the party that he could absolutely not pursue.

He'd reached the second-floor landing when he saw Liam. His childhood friend turned business partner stood ramrod straight in the middle of the room, his perceptive gaze taking in every face. He was looking for Dallas, of course, but his military training was so ingrained that the man never entered a room without assessing the occupants and the space. Liam had been captured once, too, and held in Afghanistan. And Dallas knew damn well that his friend also fought his own personal demons.

Now, he tilted his shaved head back, his eyes going immediately to Dallas as if he'd known that Dallas was watching. Hell, he probably had. He grinned, his white teeth bright against his dark skin. Without hesitation, he pushed through the crowd, then paused at the base of the stairs like a wall of pure muscle and waited for Dallas to join him.

"I came here planning to put Archie on a couple of hours' worth of data analysis," Liam said, skipping over the prelims and getting right to business.

"He left Monday," Dallas said, referring to his butler and Deliverance's go-to guy, all rolled into one. "Had some personal things to take care of."

Dallas leaned against the balustrade, remembering how pleased he'd been to get the note from Archie saying that something had come up and he needed to take time off. Dallas hadn't relished the thought of explaining to the man who had helped raise both him and Jane why the two of them were sharing a bedroom.

Liam, however, knew the situation, and now Dallas flashed a quick grin at his friend. "A convenient trip, actually."

"I know." Liam smiled. "I heard you sent my mom away," he added, referring to Helen Foster, who had worked at the Southampton mansion as a housekeeper since before both men were born. "She appreciates the spa week. Said it was quite the surprise the way you hustled her into the limo and sent her off to the Ritz Carlton."

"Your mom works hard," Dallas said dryly. And it was true. She and Archie were the only two permanent staff he retained, not only because he valued his privacy, but he didn't want anyone who was unaware of Deliverance having unfettered access to the property. "I figured she deserved to be pampered."

"You just wanted to frolic naked with Jane."

"That, too."

"When's Archie back?"

"Tomorrow. You want to stay the night and catch him in the morning?"

Liam shook his head. "I've got plans in the city tomorrow morning before I head back to London. I'll leave instructions in the op-center," he added, referring to the mansion's converted basement that Deliverance used as one of its operational bases.

Liam started toward the bar that had been set up on the far side of the room, and Dallas fell in step beside him. "So you look all rested and refreshed," Liam said. "Not too tired out." His mouth quirked. "Must be doing something wrong."

"Fuck you."

Liam laughed, then ordered a tequila for himself and a whiskey for Dallas. "Seriously, you two okay?"

"If you're talking about her wanting to rip my balls off after she found out about Deliverance, then I have to say we've come through that just fine."

It had been hell for a while after she'd unexpectedly learned that truth, and Dallas had just about died thinking that he'd lost her. But they'd gotten past it, thank god, and Dallas knew that Liam had helped. "Thanks, by the way. I know you talked with her."

Liam shrugged. "You two are my best friends. That entitles me to butt in."

Dallas grinned. "Yes it does."

The bartender passed them their drinks, and they stepped away. When they were out of earshot, Liam spoke softly, "And Colin? You still haven't said anything to her?"

It was a fair question. Liam had been the one to call with the news about Colin's possible involvement in the kidnapping, and both he and Dallas had agreed that Jane shouldn't know. But that was four days ago. Four days of sex and intimacy, and Dallas could understand why his friend might think he'd changed his mind.

"I haven't said a word," Dallas admitted. "Honestly, though, I'm afraid that decision is going to come back and bite me in the ass." He looked hard at Liam. "This can't drag out forever. We need answers. Tell me you've decrypted the netbook."

Liam's expression darkened. "Not yet."

"Fuck."

Liam shook his head. "We will. But in the meantime . . ." He took a breath, then rubbed his temple with two fingers, a sure sign that he was troubled.

"Tell me."

Liam steered them toward a secluded corner and lowered his voice even more. "We found a lock box with old hard drives hidden under some floorboards in Ortega's house."

Dallas cocked his head. That really was interesting. "Noah's been working on them, I assume? You've found more intel on Colin?"

"Some of the data's corrupt, and some we haven't broken

encryption on. It's a lot to work through, but, yeah. From what we've seen, we know that there was email correspondence between Ortega and Colin about pulling a new job."

"When?"

"That's the kicker. About a month before you were taken."

"You think they were planning the kidnapping."

"It's possible," Liam agreed. "Or they could have been talking about smuggling drugs, arms, counterfeit bills. We don't know."

"But you don't think it's any of those things."

Liam met his eyes. "Neither do you."

Dallas dragged his fingers through his hair, trying not to let his anger and frustration show on his face, just in case anyone was paying attention. "I know this man," he said roughly. "I grew up around him. He fucked up, sure—he's done jail time, he's made some stupid decisions, and he put Jane in danger, especially that time when she was eleven. But I never believed he meant to hurt her back then."

"And when she was fifteen? When you were taken? Do you believe he could have done it then? To Jane? To you?"

"No," Dallas said, then dragged his fingers through his hair. "Yes. Fuck, I don't know."

Liam hesitated, then said, "You haven't really talked to me about what went down inside those walls, but I know you well enough to know—"

"That it fucked me up. Yeah," Dallas said, his body as tense and tight as his voice. "What's your point?"

"That it was personal, man." Liam met his eyes without flinching. "Seriously personal. And so you want to rule Colin out because you know him. You like him. Hell, he's even family. Maybe not legally—not anymore—but by blood he's tied to Jane more firmly than you are. But from where I'm standing, that's not a reason to rule him out. That's a reason to drag him straight up to the top of the list."

Dallas sighed, but nodded. "I know. I've thought of that my-self."

"I know you have, because you're smart and you know how this works. But I also know that you don't want to think about it because you're human and you care about him and you know it would kill Jane. So I'm playing the role of asshole here and telling you that you have to think it. You have to look at it. And if it turns out that he's our bad guy, you have to be ready to do whatever's necessary."

Liam's tone was firm, no nonsense. And when Dallas looked at his friend's face, he saw concern. He saw friendship. Most of all he saw respect.

"Thanks," he said, referring to Liam's support as much as his words. "I will."

"I've got your back no matter what. I've got Jane's, too."

"I know you do."

"And," Liam said, his voice taking on a lighter tone, "after giving you my *keep focused* speech, I'm gonna tell you to wash the man from your mind. Right now, you need to shift that focus from Colin—"

"—to Darcy. Believe me, I'm well aware. This isn't my first rodeo."

"He's out on the pool deck. I saw him right before I came in." Liam took a quick look around the room. "Found your distraction yet?"

"Not yet." Dallas, too, glanced around, looking for either of the two women who'd been at his side at various times throughout the evening. "I'm sure I'll find—"

He paused as a woman he knew caught his eye then started walking toward him. *Fiona.*

"Actually, looks like someone's volunteering."

Liam took a quick look at the girl, tipped his head to Dallas, then walked off toward the buffet.

As expected, Fiona took that as her cue to approach. "Hey, stranger."

He flashed what the tabloids always called his devilish smile. "Fiona, you look stunning." It wasn't a lie. She was an attractive woman. A little too thin for his taste, without Jane's alluring curves, but pretty in a waif-like way.

"I was going to get a fresh drink and head out to the pool deck," he said. "Come with me."

He didn't wait for her to agree, and wasn't surprised when she fell in obediently beside him as he approached the bar, then signaled the bartender. To be honest, he would have preferred someone else. His general rule was one woman, one time. There were a few he'd bedded more than once, though, either because he'd enjoyed their company or because circumstances just worked out that way.

Fiona was a combination of both. She was smart and funny and they'd gotten along. He liked her well enough, and she'd been more than willing to do some pretty kinky shit one night after a party. He hadn't intended to see her again, but when Archie had reminded him that he was obligated to attend a charity event the next night and that his intended date had come down with the flu, he'd invited Fiona simply for the sake of convenience.

Now she was convenient again.

"You know," she said as she took the martini he offered and hooked her free arm through his, "I was just telling your sister that this is exactly where I wanted to be."

"At my party?"

There was no mistaking the heat in her eyes when she looked at him. "With you."

"What a coincidence," he said, intentionally matching her heat. "That's where I want you, too."

"And in your bed?" Her voice was little more than breath and invitation, and it was all he could do to stay in character. To remind himself that this was a role. A job. That all he had to do was get through this and then he could get back to Jane.

"Do we even need a bed?" He didn't notice her reaction. His attention had been diverted as he was speaking by the woman standing a few yards behind Fiona, now facing him with a harsh, hurt look on her beautiful face.

Jane.

He felt his body lean forward as he instinctively started to move toward her, and he had to force himself to stop. When he did, he noticed the pressure of Fiona's hand on his crotch, and he dragged his attention from Jane to Fiona as a string of curses ran through his head. "You know," she whispered huskily, "I've seen your pool deck. Why don't we just head upstairs?"

Her hand moved, stroking and massaging, and like the well-trained asshole he was, he felt his cock grow hard.

Fuck him. And fuck this facade. And fuck the fact that he couldn't have the woman he wanted at his side.

Slowly, he stepped backward, lessening the pressure of her touch. For an instant, her brow furrowed in confusion. Then he caught her hand and traced his fingertip slowly along her palm. "Soon enough," he said. "Right now, there's someone out there I need to talk to."

"Does the someone have tits?" She lifted one finely plucked brow. "Because tonight I don't want to share you."

"Don't worry," he said, looking back toward Jane. "You won't."

She was looking back at him as well, her beautiful face completely unreadable. He wanted to run to her. To hold her.

But all he could do was look at her.

He couldn't even touch this woman and pretend that it was Jane. He couldn't tease them both by using another woman as a proxy the way they had before. They'd just talked about it, and he knew damn well that she didn't want it. Hell, he didn't want it, either.

Right then, all he wanted was Jane.

As if she could read his thoughts, she met his eyes defiantly.

And then, with equal moxie, she turned on her heel, and walked away, disappearing through the French doors and onto the pool deck.

A moment later, his phone buzzed, signaling a text. "Sorry," he said to Fiona. "I need to check this."

He pulled it from his pocket, careful to hide the screen from view.

I know you have to, but I can't be here.

His gut twisted just from reading it, and all he wanted to do in that moment was go after her. He couldn't let her go. A bone-deep fear was rising in him, telling him that if she left—

Well, dammit, she just *couldn't* leave.

He pressed his hand to Fiona's waist, urging her toward the pool deck. He wasn't sure what he intended to do, but at the very least he needed to see where Jane had gone.

Once on the flagstones, though, he didn't see any sign of her. He did, however, see Henry Darcy.

"Dallas. Good to see you," the older man said, extending his hand. "Appreciate the invitation."

"Glad you could make it, Henry." He gripped the man's hand, knowing that he had a job to do. He needed to suggest they take a seat. Keep Fiona close for camouflage. Chat Darcy up, steering the conversation in practiced circles as he tried to find out what, if anything, Darcy knew about the details of Deliverance.

That's what he was supposed to do. That's why he'd organized this entire party.

Instead, he apologized for needing to duck inside and make a call. "I just got a text about a matter I can't ignore. But, Fiona, maybe you and Henry could grab a table, and I'll come back in a few minutes and join you?"

"Sure, baby," she said, though she looked less than thrilled by the prospect. Henry, on the contrary, looked delighted by the plan. "Hurry back," she added, then pulled him close and kissed him hard.

It took all his willpower to keep from wiping away her kiss until he was safely back inside the house.

He'd almost made it to the front door when Liam caught up to him.

"I don't even want to hear it."

"Hear what?" Liam countered, his arms crossed over his muscled chest. "I haven't said a word. Not a single thing."

"Whatever Darcy was going to tell WORR or the UN or the FBI, he has." The World Organization for Rescue and Rehabilitation wasn't a government agency, but it consulted closely with agencies all over the world, including the FBI, and its power and influence was significant. More than that, Bill Martin—Jane's ex-husband—was one of the organization's movers and shakers. "And since we haven't been handed our asses recently, it's a safe bet that they know nothing. That Darcy knows nothing."

"A safe bet isn't a certainty."

For a moment, Dallas almost told Liam to back off. Deliverance was Dallas's brainchild, his operation, and he'd run it however the hell he chose.

But that was idiotic. For one, Dallas may have started the group, but it was only as good as the team he put together. A team he respected, made up of men who were his closest friends.

"I can't do it," he said. "Not right now. And I know it's a risk, but I think it's a small one. I'll still talk to Darcy—I'll find out whatever is left to find out—but right now, I need to find Jane. So dammit, Liam, get the fuck out of my way."

5

A Hasty Retreat

I'm shifting my weight from foot to foot, trying not to be pissed off at the hired valet guys for stupidly parking the guests' cars in front of the garage. I'd thrust my keys into his hands and told him to please just hurry.

But you can only move so fast when you have a dozen or so cars to rearrange, and that means that I'm stuck here until he manages to work out that little puzzle and bring me my car.

And, dammit, I really want to get the hell out of here.

I know Dallas has a role to play, I get it. For that matter, I even understand that it was only partially a role before. I mean, he wanted those women in his bed. Hell, he got off on it. Doing things with them. To them.

It was a release. A way to satisfy himself.

He didn't literally fuck them—I know that—but he sure as hell enjoyed them. And I don't begrudge him that. I really don't.

I mean, hell, I got married. So it's not like I was living the life of a nun. And even after my divorce, I wasn't celibate. There've been guys. Not a lot, but enough. After all, I'm rather fond of orgasms. And although I'd wanted Dallas, I'd believed I could never have him. So why not drown my sorrows in other men?

But the last guy I fucked was a long time ago, and I sure as hell haven't been with anyone since Dallas.

I know he's putting on a show—*I know it*. But I had assumed he would pick some anonymous girl from the crowd. Not Fiona, a girl he's gone out with more than once, which means that she's more than just a throw-away.

And I'd assumed that he'd simply pat her ass and put on the touchy-feely show. I hadn't expected to see her grab his cock. And I sure as hell hadn't anticipated watching him get hard from another woman's touch.

I realize that I've clenched my fists, and right then I think I'd punch Fiona in her pert little nose if I saw her. For that matter, I just might punch Dallas.

He, however, isn't nearby. Most likely because he's taken her upstairs to his bedroom.

Oh dear god. His bedroom.

I remember the day not too long ago when I'd come to this house to see him—and found him in his room with two very naked women in his bed. I'd missed the actual show, thank god, but I'd gotten an eyeful of both the girls and a collection of toys lying around.

I close my eyes and wrap my arms around myself, thinking about those black satin sheets where he'll soon be taking her. Sheets that have touched my bare skin. That I've clawed, trying to hang on to reason while his beard stubble scratched my inner thighs and his tongue worked magic on my clit.

Cool sheets that soothed my red, stinging skin after he'd spanked me, then finger-fucked me, taking me to the edge over and over again, tormenting me incessantly before letting me find release.

That room is ours now, and I hate the thought that Fiona—

that any woman—will share that bed with him while I'm at my house eating ice cream and drowning my sorrows in chocolate syrup and too much red wine.

I'm so wrapped up in my pity party that I don't realize that the valet has brought my car around until he taps the horn. I open my eyes, but not even the prospect of putting my darling little Vanquish Volante through her paces knocks me out of my funk.

The valet holds the door open for me. But as I take a step forward, I'm held back by a firm hand on my shoulder. I jump, surprised, but when I turn, the surprise fades.

Dallas.

Of course he's there.

Of course he's come to me.

"Stay." His voice is low. Steady.

"I can't. Seriously, Dallas. I need to go."

But he just lifts his arm, then signals the driver to take my car away.

"What the hell?"

"Wait." He takes my elbow and leads me away from the temporary valet stand so that we can talk more privately.

I jerk my arm free and glare at him, irritated as much by the whole damn situation as I am by the fact that now I'm going to have to send for my car again. "Dammit, I know what you have to do. I don't know all the details, but I get that your persona's important. And—"

He is shaking his head. "We talked about it. I thought you were okay with it. I thought *we* were okay."

I've been looking anywhere but at him, but now I lift my chin and defiantly stare him down. "You are so fucking dense sometimes. Yes, we had a conversation. But do you really think I want to just sit around while you're upstairs in your bed with your mouth on some other girl's cunt?"

My voice is so low it's barely a whisper. Even so, the words come out like a lashing, and I glance around quickly to make sure no one else has heard them. Part of me doesn't even care. Because honestly, he's pissing me off. I mean, he really doesn't get why I might want to get the hell out of here?

Apparently he's also clueless about how annoyed I am, because the son of a bitch is actually grinning at me.

"What?" I demand.

"You don't have to leave."

"You know what, Dallas? Fuck you." I've had enough, and I turn to head back to the valet stand.

He catches my hand and tugs me back. "What you're worried about—it's not happening."

I cock my head, then yank my hand free and cross my arms. "In case you've forgotten, Mr. Sykes, you have a reputation to protect. Or destroy, depending on your point of view. Do not even try to convince me that you won't have a girl in your bed tonight."

"I will," he says, looking at me with the kind of intensity designed to make me melt. "You."

"What?" My legs suddenly feel a little weak, even as my head feels a little confused.

"I want you in my bed, Jane. You. Because you're the only woman with the right to be there. Go," he adds. "Go now."

"Dallas." My voice is a protest. He knows as well as I do why me heading to his bedroom right now is a very bad idea.

He steps closer, all power and control and intensity. "Now. Or I'll spank your ass right here and if any one looks at us funny I'll tell them it's a big-brother prerogative."

Now I actually have to fight a smile, and the tears are the happy kind. "You're only four months older than me."

He just points toward the house.

"How the hell do you expect to pull off your Playboy of the Western World routine without a girl who's not your sister in your bed?"

"Go," he repeats. "I'll be right behind you."

"Fine." I take a step toward the door. "But we'll talk when we get upstairs."

"Sweetheart, talking is the last thing on my mind."

Oh.

I pause just long enough to take in his words.

Then I do as he says, and go.

6

Bitch in Satin Sheets

I can't deny that I'm in a good mood as I head to the bedroom. I don't know what he thinks he can possibly do, but if he says that he has a way to keep the playboy reputation without getting naked with any of those women, then I'm all for that plan.

I take the back stairs, just as I did earlier to get to my old bedroom. This time, though, I go all the way to the third floor and enter at the far end of the residential section of the hallway.

From this perspective, the master bedroom is on my right and Dallas's home office is on the left. I consider skipping the bedroom and going to his office—not only because the idea of disobeying him amuses me, but also because the thought of fooling around on top of his desk has a certain appeal—but I decide against it. Maybe one day I'll suggest we play secretary and boss. Right now, I want to be between those sheets where I belong.

I'm actually reaching back for the zipper of my skirt as I push open the door—and I stop cold when a female voice says, "Hey, baby. I've been waiting for—*Oh!*"

I freeze, confused. But my confusion is quickly being replaced by anger. And humiliation. And hurt. And a whole load of other emotions that I can't easily identify, but they sure as hell don't feel good.

"Jane?" From the bed, a woman gapes at me. And as soon as I realize it's Fiona, I gape back. Because she's *here*. And also because she's naked. "What are you doing here?" she asks, pulling the sheet up to cover her breasts.

I realize my mouth is hanging open. I close it, then swallow before answering. I need the time to remember how to form words. "I—I didn't realize Dallas had anyone with him. I was—I mean, I just got a text from our parents that I need to talk to him about, so I thought I'd wait for him here."

I clear my throat, thinking the lie sounds pretty reasonable. "I, um, didn't think he'd be with anybody, but considering my brother's reputation, I guess I should have known better."

She doesn't look offended at being labeled one of very, very many. On the contrary, she just laughs. "Isn't that the damn truth? But like I told you downstairs, we've had our share of good times. Now I'm just waiting for another." She cocks her head and smiles prettily. "I'll tell him you're looking for him. Or are you planning to just hang here. With me."

She doesn't look pleased by the possibility. I'm not crazy about it, either. Frankly, I want to get as far from this room—and from Dallas—as it's possible to get. Because right now, I'm angry enough that my fist might just break that very pretty face of his.

"No." My voice is shaky, and I clear my throat. "No, I don't need to wait. I'll just go back to the city. I'll call him tomorrow. That's soon enough." And maybe that'll give me time to cool off. Frankly, I doubt it.

I head back to the door, yank it open, and find myself staring right at the man himself.

At any other time, his wicked smile would melt me. Right now, it infuriates me. But before I can say anything, he starts to slide his arm around my waist.

Some sort of self-preservation instinct kicks in and I slam my elbow into his gut, making him both release me and groan.

"Jesus, Jane. What the—"

"Hey, baby."

He goes completely still, then looks at the bed. Then looks at me. "What the fuck?"

I'm so tense I think I might shatter. "Actually, I think that's my line."

I grab his arm and yank him into the hallway, then turn back to Fiona with what I hope looks like a genuine smile. "Actually, I'll just talk to him now about that text our parents sent, and then I'll get out of your hair so you two can have your fun."

"Take your time," Fiona says easily. "I'm comfy, and your brother's most definitely worth the wait."

I do not race back to the bed and smack her for that. I also don't punch Dallas in the jaw. On the whole, I think I'm showing remarkable restraint.

What I do instead is drag him across the hall and into his study.

I slam the door behind us, then smack him in the chest with the heel of my hand. "What the fuck?" I yell. I know for a fact that this office was professionally soundproofed. I can yell as loud as I want and no one will be the wiser.

"You stupid, fucking son of a bitch," I rant. "Do you think sex games are going to prove some sort of point to me? Was that just a flat-out lie about not having them in your bed anymore? Or did you mean you weren't going to have them alone? Is this where you want us to go, Dallas? Is a threesome the kink you need? Is Fiona—*Fiona*—the dark you're going to take me down into?"

I see emerald fire flash in his eyes, and know that I've pissed him off. Well, good. At least that makes us well-matched.

A muscle in his jaw tightens, and when he speaks, his words are a little too crisp. "What happened to you'll go anywhere with me? Or did you only mean that you'd go if it was comfortable?"

I stumble back, his words shocking me. I'd expected an apology. Instead, what? He's *admitting* it? He really did intend to have Fiona and me in bed together?

I feel bile rise in my throat even as tears sting my eyes. I swallow in defense against the first, and look down at the floor so he can't see the second. I need a moment to think. To adjust. Because I did tell him I would go wherever he needs—and I meant what I said.

I just hadn't expected this.

Finally, I feel confident enough to speak. But, dammit, my voice still shakes. "I will go wherever you want me and do whatever you want. But I guess I thought you'd do me the courtesy of telling me what to expect."

"Jane."

His voice is tender and I can't handle that right now. I toss up my hand to silence him, then continue speaking because I need to get these words out.

"I mean it," I say. "I will go into the dark with you. But I just think—hell, Dallas, you blindsided me. You told me you only wanted me." I meet his eyes now, sure that mine are bloodshot and weepy. "That's what you said, and I believed you."

"Oh, baby." He pulls me against him before I can react, and I stand stiff in the circle of his arms. "I do only want you."

I tug free of the embrace, hating how vulnerable I feel. Hating that this man has the power to hurt me so very deeply. "Do you think I don't have eyes? I saw her touch you. Even from where I was standing I could see how hard you were."

"Shit." He turns away from me, then goes to sit in one of the guest chairs in front of the huge mahogany desk. I watch him, thinking that I've won this round of the argument and wondering why the hell I don't feel victorious.

It seems to take forever for him to speak, and when he does, it's low. Almost monotone. As if he has to hold in the emotion, because if he lets go the words will burst out of him. "Do you think getting hard is only about desire?" he asks. "Goddammit, Jane, do you think I wanted to get a fucking erection with Fiona? How about back when the Woman touched me?"

I suck in a breath, his words conjuring memory and pain. And regret, because I pushed this, and I know how tied up sex is with the kidnapping for him. I may have suffered in captivity, but it was Dallas who truly went down into hell.

"Look at me," he demands, and I realize that I am studying the pattern in the carpet. I lift my head, and feel a tear snake down my cheek. "Do you think I wanted her? That bitch who tormented us? Do you think that I wanted to be aroused?"

The monotone is disappearing, giving way to a hard edge honed by pain.

He pushes himself out of the chair, then sweeps his arm violently over the desktop, sending papers and pens flying. "I fucking hated my body. Hated myself."

He crosses to me, his strides long, then grabs me by the shoulders. "I was fifteen, and I thought that if my cock was hard then I must want sex. Must want *her*. I thought that I was royally fucked up because she was turning me on."

"No." I clutch tight to him, as if I can make him believe the truth simply by holding on. "God, Dallas, no. You can't believe that."

"I don't," he assures me. "Not anymore." I feel the rise and fall of his chest as he gathers himself. And then, very gently, he tilts my chin up so that I am looking right at him. "But you do."

"What? No, I don't." I'm shocked he could even think such a thing. I know that what the Woman did to him was torture, even if he hasn't told me all of it yet. And there is no way in hell that I would ever believe he wanted it just because she got him hard, made him come. "I don't believe that at all."

"And yet you thought I wanted Fiona."

It actually takes me a moment to figure out what he means, but the moment I do, the only thing I can say is, "Oh."

I'm mortified. I'm ecstatic. And I'm desperately relieved.

I'm also pretty damn confused. "But if you don't want her, then why did you invite her into your bed when you knew I was coming?"

"*Our* bed," he corrects. "And I didn't."

I raise my brows. After all, the woman is right across the hall, naked between his sheets.

He chuckles and drags fingers through his hair. "Jesus, Jane—do you really think that I set this up? That I want to share you?"

"But you said—" I frown, because just a few minutes ago he'd lashed back at me, reminding me that I'd promised to go anywhere with him.

"Well, you pissed me off," he admits, then drags me to him and kisses me hard. "I want you, you little idiot. I don't want her. And I'm not going to say it again—I didn't invite her."

I believe him, but I don't answer for few seconds anyway, simply because I want to savor the truth of his words.

Still, I can't deny the oddity of the situation, and so I ask the most obvious question I can think of. "If you didn't invite her, then why is she naked in your bed?"

"I really wish I knew." He reaches into his back pocket and pulls out his phone, and I watch, baffled, as he sends a quick text.

I flash a lopsided smile. "Are you texting to ask her?"

"Funny, but no. I have a few ideas. And we have about five minutes until I tell you what they are." He steps back and leans casually against the desk, then slowly looks me up and down, my senses firing beneath the weight of that heavy, heated gaze.

When he finally meets my eyes, his are dark with passion, and this time I'm certain that the reason his cock is straining against his jeans is because he wants me. "Five minutes," he repeats. "I wonder what we can do in five minutes. Unless you're still mad at me?"

"I'm getting less mad," I admit, taking a single step toward him.

"You should trust me."

I take another step. "I do."

"Recent events would suggest otherwise."

I stop walking, leaving me about one long stride away from him.

"I guess I was a bad girl," I say, then reach back and slide my hands down over my rear. "Maybe I should be punished." I draw my hands back up, lifting the skirt as I do, exposing my bare ass—but not to him. I'm facing him. So all Dallas has is imagination, and if the expression on his face is any indication, he's using it.

"Maybe you ought to bend me over your knee." I take a step closer so that the front of my skirt brushes his knees. "Maybe you should spank me, slide your finger inside me, and see if I like it when you punish me."

I hold his gaze as I take one hand and slide it between my legs. I sigh with pleasure, and it is most definitely not an act. I'm hot and slick and I want him desperately. And when I pull my hand free, I lift my finger to his lips. "Yeah," I say. "I think I like it."

I ease my finger into his mouth, and he sucks so hard I feel the thrum of it all the way down to my now throbbing pussy. He pulls me closer, his hands squeezing my ass as his mouth teases my finger, and right then all I want to do is scream for him to move that finger to my clit and please, please make me come.

Instead, I jump at the sharp rap at the door.

He yanks his hands away, then brushes my skirt down into place.

Five minutes my ass, I think, and I'm feeling pretty damn cheated when the door opens and Liam steps in.

His eyes go straight to us. Me between Dallas's legs. Dallas's arms around me.

"You invite me up here for a peep show? 'Cause as pretty as both of you are, I'm still not keen on watching my two best friends go at it."

I give him a wry look. "I know exactly how you feel. I wasn't at all interested in watching a show tonight, either."

Liam frowns. "What am I missing?"

Dallas pulls me closer, his arms circling my waist. "My side-piece ended up in my bed."

I see Liam's mouth twitch as he looks at me.

I roll my eyes. "Don't even say it."

"Uninvited," Dallas clarifies.

"So, what? You brought me up here to be the bouncer?"

"Actually, yeah. Jane told her she'd gotten a text from our parents. I thought you could go in and tell her I had to leave."

Liam shakes his head as if amused by the deception. Then he shrugs. "Why the hell not? Darcy's already left."

Behind me, I feel Dallas cringe.

I frown, then turn in his arms to gape at him. "But I thought talking to Darcy was the whole point. Of this party and every-thing."

He looks at me steadily. "My plans changed."

"You came after me." I exhale as I realize what he sacrificed to reassure me. "Shit. I'm sorry. I—"

"So make it up to us," Liam interrupts.

"What?"

"Why don't you talk to Darcy?"

Dallas scowls. "What the hell are you talking about?"

"It makes sense," Liam says. "She can tell him it's research. Hell, she can ask questions a lot easier than you can. She's writing a book, so of course she'd want to pry out every bit of information about Deliverance that she can."

The moment he says it, I know that he's right. I've made a living writing true crime articles and books about kidnapping victims. My most recent book is even going to be a movie, and the one I'm currently researching and writing is about the dangers of vigilante groups such as the one run by a violent mercenary, Lionel Benson, and, yes, Deliverance.

Granted, at the time I started writing the book, I'd been unaware of who was behind Deliverance. I'd simply known that the organization existed. And I'd gotten the idea for the title of my work-in-progress from Henry Darcy's revelation as to the group's name—*Code Name: Deliverance.*

I'm still writing the book, but I have to admit that my perspective has changed. Benson is undoubtedly motivated by the money. The prick would happily sacrifice one victim to save another whose parents are paying his bill. But Deliverance is different. I know, because I know Dallas. I know Liam. And I know what drives them.

But that doesn't mean I'm one hundred percent on board with the idea of a vigilante group at all, even one with a conscience. There are still rules. There are still procedures. And Deliverance skirts all of them.

Sometime soon, Dallas and I are going to have to sit down and talk more fully about what he does—and about how it works. He's promised me no secrets, and he's told his team he's bringing me into the loop. So far, I haven't pushed. For one thing, it's only been about a week since I even learned the truth.

But for another, I'm not entirely sure that I want to know the details. Because at my core, I'm afraid that if Dallas really does find our kidnappers, I'm not going to give a fuck about due process. Because all I want is to see them dead.

Right now, though, none of that matters. Right now, it's all about Henry Darcy. "Well?" Liam presses.

"I don't know if she should—"

"Of course I will," I interrupt.

"You shouldn't be involved in this," Dallas says.

"Bullshit. I *am* involved."

He starts to protest, but I hold up a finger to silence him. "Yes, I am. Of course I am. Because I love you. And I love you, too," I say, glancing back at Liam. "And if there is even the slightest chance that Henry Darcy is going to expose my lover and my best friend and the rest of your guys, then you need to know. *We* need to know. And if I'm the best person to figure that out, then I'm damn well going to do it."

"She's right," Liam says. "And it's not dangerous. It's just a writer talking to a witness."

"Fine," Dallas says, but I can tell from his expression he doesn't like it.

"All right then," Liam says. "One mission accomplished. Now I guess I'll go get rid of the woman in your bed." He grins. "The things I do for you . . ."

"Wait," Dallas says as Liam turns toward the door. He moves around the desk and opens a drawer, then pulls out a stack of blue envelopes.

I frown, confused, as he holds them out to Liam. "I've been getting these for a while."

Liam approaches, looking as clueless as I feel. He takes the letters and skims over them one by one. I read over his shoulder, words and phrases seeming to reach out and punch me in the gut.

my darling
passion
mine
patience
me
only for you

I glance up at Dallas. "What the hell?"

His expression is hard. "They started coming about a year ago. About a dozen so far. No fingerprints. No return address. Most by messenger, some left at the door or under the windshield wiper of my car."

"Why the hell didn't you tell me about this before?" Liam asks, voicing my thoughts.

"Doesn't have anything to do with Deliverance."

"Hello? Lifelong friend here. Some crazy chick is sending you psycho letters—"

"Possessive, maybe. But I didn't think the sender was dangerous. At least not at first."

I look from him to the door, imagining the girl across the hall in his bed. "But now that Fiona let herself into your bed . . ."

"You think it's her?" Liam asks.

"I don't know," Dallas says. "But the timing's right. The first time I went out with her was about a year ago. Could be that she thought my attention tonight meant that everything she wrote in those letters is true."

Liam exhales. "Fair enough. I'll chat her up when I walk her out. See if I can get a read."

Dallas nods. "There's another letter in the bedroom on the table by the door. Came Monday, but I didn't open it until earlier today." He glances at me. "I was distracted before."

"I'll make sure she sees me pick it up, then watch her reaction. If we're lucky, the woman doesn't play poker."

"Sounds good. And pass everything on to Noah. Maybe he or Quince can work some magic. God knows Archie and I haven't had any luck."

"Will do." Liam gives me a quick hug before heading out of the room, though I'm not sure that I even hug him back. My mind is in too much of a whir, my chest tight with memory and fear, and it's all I can do to keep quiet until the door shuts behind him.

The second it clicks into place, I turn my attention back to Dallas. "What the hell do you mean this has nothing to do with Deliverance? You need to tell him. Even if you haven't told him the details, he needs to know." I'm talking too fast, my words tumbling out.

Dallas stares back at me as if I've lost my mind, and I blink, suddenly realizing that he hasn't a clue what I'm talking about. He honestly doesn't see the connection between these letters and our kidnapping. "You really have no idea who's sending them."

It's a statement, but he takes it as a question. "None of the women I've—"

"Open your eyes, Dallas. It's not one of your bimbettes."

"What are you talking about?"

"I'm talking about the woman sending the letters. I'm saying it's obvious who she is."

7

The Usual Suspects

"Obvious?" Dallas repeated, not entirely sure he was comprehending her words. Because it sure as hell wasn't obvious to him. "Just from glancing over the letters, you know who's sending them? Fiona?"

"No." She shook her head. "Not Fiona."

The tightness of her voice belied the way she perched casually on the edge of his desk. And he couldn't help but notice that her hands were clutching the mahogany desktop so tightly her knuckles were white.

Not Fiona, he thought, as a chill crept up his spine. *And not good.*

"Who?"

Her throat moved as she swallowed, then glanced toward the door. "Does Liam know what happened to us inside? What the Woman did to you?"

He frowned, trying to follow her thoughts. "No. I've told him enough that he knows they fucked me up. But only you know what she did."

She shook her head, then looked back at him with a sad smile. "Some, maybe. But not everything. Not yet."

He pinched the bridge of his nose, wondering how the hell they'd gotten back on this topic. "It's not because I don't trust you, or because I don't want to tell you. I do. Hell, I need to." He hoped she knew how much he meant those words. But it was so damn hard, because every time he thought about what happened in that dark room with that psychotic bitch, he got pulled back in. Lost the little pieces of himself that he'd reclaimed.

Remembered just how fucked up he was—and why.

"Dallas, we—"

"Christ, Jane," he snapped. "Why are we talking about this? What the hell does the Woman have to do with—"

He cut himself off and stared at her. "The Woman? You can't possibly think that the Woman is sending these letters."

But she was nodding, so clearly she did think that. Which would be absolutely ridiculous except for the fact that it actually made some sense.

"It's been seventeen years." He realized that he was simply stating a fact, not raising the years as an argument against her theory. Because, goddammit, if he weren't so close to it—if the Woman hadn't messed with his head so damn much that he'd do anything to keep her the fuck out of it—maybe he would have seen the possibility, too.

"I know how long it's been." She spoke softly and steadily, as if she knew that every word hurt him. "But we were both in that cell, Dallas. We both know these people. They were cold. Calculating. Tenacious. Smart. Prepared. More than that, she was a psycho. A seventeen-year wait is nothing to someone that warped."

"I don't know," he said, but the words were only for show. He knew, all right. Even if she was wrong, it was a damn good guess.

"We need to at least consider it," she said. "And—and we need to talk about her, too. About what happened."

"No." This time the protest was real. "Not now. I don't want her in my head."

"You need to talk about it."

He thought of the memories that had been haunting his dreams since Liam gave him the news about Colin. "I said no."

She threw her hands up, her fingers curled like she wanted to punch the air—or him. "Dammit—you always do this. Anytime it looks like I'm winning an argument you dig in. It drives me nuts."

"I dig in? You're the one pushing and pushing."

"God, you're infuriating."

"Are you talking to me as my lover or as my sister?"

She whirled on him, her expression ferocious. "Are you trying to push me away? Because it won't work. You think you're the only one trying to deal with all this? That's bullshit."

She marched right up to him and poked him in the chest so hard he winced. "You're the one who kept me here, remember? I was trying to get the hell away from this place so that maybe—*maybe*—I could get my head around the fact that we have to live in this gray plastic bubble where we can't touch or even look at each other in the real world because you're my brother and we're fucking—"

"*No.*" Her words had been pounding on him like a hammer, but that one finally broke him.

He grabbed her shoulders and shook her. "No, that is not what's between us." He pulled her close and captured her mouth, then shifted his hands to her back and pulled her tight against him. He wanted to absorb her. Consume her. And when he broke away from her, he felt the loss like a physical blow. "That is not all there is," he said breathlessly, "and you know it as well as I do."

She was breathing as hard as he was, her chest rising and falling, her skin flushed, her eyes wild. "I do. Of course I do. It's so much more."

She fisted her hand in his collar and used that hold to lever herself to him. "And I want even more, Dallas. I told you. I'm greedy. Where you're concerned I'm the greediest woman on earth." She reached out and brushed his cheek with the side of her hand. "I want every bit of you. Even the scary parts. Even the part she touched."

"Jane." He couldn't find words. He wanted to argue. He wanted to run.

He wanted to pull her close and kiss her again just to shut her up.

And because he wanted it so damn much, that's exactly what he did.

8

Glass Houses

His mouth closes over mine, hot and demanding, and every thought in my head disappears like dandelion fluff in the wind. Somewhere in my mind, I know that I should press him—that we have things to talk about—but I don't have the willpower.

Where Dallas is concerned, I have no strength at all.

"I need you," he says, breaking the kiss and cupping my face with his hands. "I need you to understand. To know."

I start to ask what that means—what he thinks I don't understand—but the words stall in my throat when he unzips my skirt, takes the two halves of the waistband, and rips it completely off my body.

I gasp, and some small part of my brain tells me that I should be angry. I love this skirt, and it cost a small fortune. But I'm not upset. On the contrary, I'm so desperately turned on that I feel the muscles of my core clenching with need. And I'm incredibly wet. That one violent, wild act of possession has completely stripped me of my defenses and I'm open and desperate and wanting.

"The shirt." His voice is as hard as his expression. "Take it off or I'll take it off for you."

I lick my lips, and part of me wants to challenge him. There's something unfamiliar and dangerous in his eyes. Something possessive and primal. I want to push—I want to taunt him into going as far as he wants and needs—but some instinct tells me to hold back, and so I quell the urge and very slowly peel my shirt off and toss it on top of my tattered skirt.

I never put on fresh underwear, so now I am standing in nothing but my bra and three-inch strappy sandals. I reach back to unfasten the bra, but he shakes his head.

"Don't even think about it," he says. "You look too damn delicious."

"Do I?" I step closer, then slide into his arms, my essentially naked body pressed against his still fully-clothed one. "Then maybe you should eat me?"

"Believe me, it's on the agenda." He takes a step back, and I frown as the distance between us grows. "To the window," he says, nodding at the floor to ceiling window that looks out over one of the side lawns and across the dunes to the ocean.

I walk slowly, not sure what he's up to.

"Hands on the glass," he says, coming up behind me. "Spread your legs."

I stay perfectly still, not making a single move to comply as he tugs the cups of my lacy bra down to expose my breasts.

"Breasts, too," he says. "Think how nice the cool glass will feel against your warm nipples."

"Dallas." My voice is hoarse. "Someone might see."

"They won't. The guests are mostly on the pool deck and by the band and the bar." He pushes me forward, then lifts my hands and places my palms against the glass. Then he spreads my legs and eases me forward. I whimper as my nipples touch the cool window, and then I suck in a sharp breath as he traces a fingertip down my spine, over my ass, and then slides his warm hand between my legs.

He is standing right behind me, and I can see the reflection of his face in the glass, and beyond that the foam on the cresting waves glowing in the moonlight. "No one will see us," he murmurs in my ear. "But even if they did," he adds as he slides his fingers deep inside me, "all that would mean is that they know you are mine. That you're the woman I want. Not Fiona or Christine or any of them. Only you."

I want to argue. I want to remind him that there's a whole hell of a lot that people would know. Like what Dallas and I are to each other, and how we are breaking the rules.

But I can't say it. Hell, I can barely think it. He has completely undone me, and right now I am nothing but sensation and need and desire.

"That's it, baby," he says, and I realize that I'm grinding my hips, trying to find release as he teases me so intimately. "Do you like this?"

"Yes."

"Then beg for it."

"Please. Please, Dallas, make me come."

He's touching and stroking and teasing, and I'm so close. I shift, trying to find release, but it's always just a little bit off, just a little bit further away. I'm so turned on and so frustrated, and all I want is for him to take me the rest of the way, fast and hard and wild.

"Tell me you're mine," he urges. "Tell me you understand that it's only you. That it's only ever been you."

"I do," I say. "I understand."

"No," he says, as he spins me around and then presses my back against the glass. "I really don't think you do."

I'm breathing hard, and so is he. I'm wet, and so wildly turned on, and the sensation thrills me. I'm completely out of control—I've surrendered everything to him—and I'm okay. *I'm okay.*

"Dallas." I hear the plea in my voice. "Make me. Make me understand."

One of his hands is against my shoulder, pinning me back against the glass. The ferocity—the hunger—is so clear on his face that I expect him to take everything I'm offering and more. And I want it. Oh, dear god, I want it.

I'm breathing hard, and I feel the perspiration bead at the back of my neck, on my upper lip, between my legs. I'm nervous with wanting, fired with anticipation. I'm ready. I'm so, so ready.

I lick my lips, and that simple gesture seems to spur him to action. He looks back over his shoulder toward the desk, and I feel a wildness circle inside me, remembering my earlier fantasy about him taking me on that very desktop.

I expect him to jerk me toward him. To force me to bend over the desk.

I imagine him spreading my legs wide and holding my head down while he spanks me, then teases and strokes me with his cock before thrusting deep into me with his fingers.

Or maybe this is it—maybe this is what he needs—and I'll finally feel him slamming hard into me. His cock filling me. His fingers clutching my shoulders so hard he marks me as he takes me fully and completely.

I want it—and at the same time I hate myself for wanting it because I know it might not happen. But the passion—the wildness—*that* I know is coming.

I really cannot wait.

And so I'm more than a little befuddled when his gaze shifts back to me, and the feral look is gone, subjugated to a slow-burn of passion and the face of a warrior who's just fought the battle of his life.

I shake my head slowly, not wanting to understand, but I do. I get it, because I get him.

And I don't like it.

"Dallas—"

"Shhh, baby." His forefinger presses against my lips, quieting me, as he moves closer, then presses his hands lightly over my breasts before trailing his fingertips down my body, the contact making me tremble with a desire that is significantly more tame, but no less real. His fingers move lower, teasing the fold of skin between my thigh and my torso, stroking the soft skin of my vulva. Driving me deliciously wild because he is taking such care to completely avoid my clit.

With his other hand, he cups one breast, his thumb playing lightly over my nipple even as he bends forward and closes his mouth over the other.

I gasp, my body shaking with desire. With need. I feel as though I am on fire, like every millimeter of my skin is a sensual playground.

He has reined himself in, but the effect on me is no less dramatic. His touch is a garden of erotic delights, but when he pulls back, his teeth grazing my nipple in the process, I open my eyes and look at him. That's when I see that his soft caresses are belied by the fire in his eyes.

He wants more, damn him. And yet he's holding back, cheating us both.

"Dallas," I say again.

"What, baby?"

I start to protest that he needs to stop protecting me when I've told him I'll go with him wherever he needs me to go. But then I realize this isn't about protecting me, but about protecting himself.

He's fighting hard to hold it all in. To push it all back. His memories. His fears. The dark desires that he loathes.

I want him to stop fighting—to let it out—to share with me all of what happened in there, in the dark. To tell me what it is he craves.

I want that—even more, I need it. And I know that he needs it, too.

But I don't say a word. I can't push him on this. Not now. Not when we're both still raw.

"Jane?"

I hear the concern in his voice and force a smile to my lips. "I love you," I say. "I just wanted to tell you that I love you."

"Oh, baby."

He pulls me to him and kisses me gently, then eases me down onto the area rug. It's soft and thick, and I stretch my arms above my head as he straddles me. Slowly, he kisses his way down my body, then gently parts my thighs.

I feel the whisper of breath on my clit and arch up, my hands over my breasts. My palms brush my sensitive nipples in time with his tongue laving my clit, sending waves of pleasure crashing through me with such wild brutality that my entire body is trembling.

His fingers are inside me, his mouth playing me. I'm lost in pleasure, and I want to explode even as much as I want this sensation to last, but I have no control at all. I've surrendered entirely to Dallas. His touch, his demands, his teases and caresses, and it's all too much. Building and building until finally it is as though reality is yanked out from under me, and I burst apart, with Dallas right there to hold me and put me back together.

I gasp and shudder, my body lost in pleasure as he slides up my body and holds me close, telling me he loves me. Telling me that I'm his. Telling me that everything is going to work out.

"Promise?" I whisper when I can form words again.

"Always."

I smile, then slide my hand down to stroke him. I'm pretty much bare, but he is still very clothed. And very hard.

I meet his eyes as my hand cups his steel-hard cock. "You really should do something about that. Or perhaps I could volunteer my services? Take over until you want to finish?"

But he only shakes his head as he presses his hand on top of mine. "I like this," he says. "I like feeling what you do to me."

Oh.

"When you put it like that, I like it, too." I kiss him lightly and curl against him, and for the first time since the party began, it feels like we're us again. I sigh, thinking of what happened. Of my fears and doubts. Then I tilt my head back to look at him.

"I'm sorry I didn't trust you earlier. Thinking that you wanted a three-way with Fiona. I'm just—I saw that you were hard and I got jealous."

He brushes a kiss over my forehead. "We said no secrets," he says softly, "and I already told you that I didn't want her. That I don't want her. And that's the truth. But I did hold something back."

"You did?" I shift a bit, not because I want to put distance between us, but because I want to see him better.

"She is attractive," he says. "And I know she's a good time in bed."

I scowl. "Gee. Now I feel better."

He chuckles. "I'm not finished. The thing is, the kidnapping has been on my mind lately what with—well, us. And this thing with Darcy and Deliverance. But it was unfair of me to compare getting hard because Fiona touched me with what the Woman did." He twists a lock of my hair around his finger. "Unfair to her and unfair to you."

I swallow, trying to dissipate the lump that has settled in my throat. "So, are you saying that you do want her?"

"Now? Oh, baby, no. But I won't deny that she's hot. Or that I've had good times with her in bed before. I meant what I said, sweetheart. Only you. But I play this role and I have to be . . . receptive. It's hard not to—"

I lift a brow. "Method act?"

"You could say that."

I sit up so that I can hug my knees as I look at him. "This is going to be hard, isn't it?"

He doesn't answer, but he really doesn't need to.

"You know, if I was another woman—" I say airily, as if the words mean nothing. "If I wasn't your sister, I could join you. Be the second girl in your bed."

His brows lift. "Would you like that?" he asks, his eyes studying my face.

"Would you?" I counter, because I'm still trying to figure out what the line is for him. What he wants. What he needs. I know because of his reputation and because I've seen it with my own eyes that he often entertained more than one girl in his bed. Is he going to miss that dynamic with me?

He is silent for so long that I think he is going to simply avoid the question. Finally, though, he answers. "I've had two women at a time. Often, actually. Most of the time, frankly."

"Oh." He's not really doing a good job of soothing me here. I mean, I'm reasonably confident of my skill in bed, but I can't be two girls. Just not physically possible.

"Do you know why?"

"Because you're an insatiable manwhore?"

He laughs out loud. "It definitely feeds the reputation, but no. Because of the distraction."

I shake my head, not understanding.

"Oh, baby, don't you get it? Not one of the women who has ever shared my bed is the woman I truly wanted. And rather than share so much intimacy with a woman I didn't really want, I'd bring in a second—or sometimes a third. But with you—oh, god, Jane, don't you know that I only want you in my bed?"

I exhale, my relief so intense I feel light-headed. He leans toward me and kisses me softly. "Okay?"

"Very much," I say, and realize that I am grinning like a fool.

He grins, too, and I see the moment his expression turns mischievous. "Now, to be clear, just because I don't need another woman in my bed doesn't mean that you can't invite one. I mean, if you want to romp naked with one of your girlfriends, possibly with whipped cream . . ."

He trails off, and I smack him lightly in the arm. "You are such a guy."

"I'm very glad you think so."

"Oh, I more than think so. I can prove it." I move to straddle him, then stroke my hands over his shirt, tugging it up as I move down his body. It's untucked by the time I reach the waistband of his jeans, and as my fingers go to the button on his fly, my kisses trace the arrow of hair that leads from his abdomen to his cock.

As I'm following that trail to heaven, his phone rings in his back pocket. He reaches for it, pulls it out, and silences it with a firm touch of a button.

I smile and ease his zipper down, watching with satisfaction the way the muscles in his lower abs tighten, evidencing his effort to keep control.

"See?" I say. "This bit of hair, these very nice muscles. Definitely a guy kind of thing."

"I do appreciate a woman who searches out the evidence."

I laugh and start to tug his jeans down, gratified when he lifts his hips to help.

He's wearing black boxer briefs, and I tug them down to reveal his very hard cock. And then, with one quick glance at him, I slowly lick him from balls to tip.

He arches up, and the sound of his moan fills me up and turns me on. I start to tease the tip, and his damn phone starts to ping, signaling a text.

"Fuck," he says, then glances at the screen. "Well, shit."

"What is it?"

He starts to answer, but the phone rings. "What it is, is that

I have to take this call. It's Adele. She texted to say I need to answer. That it's important."

I lift a brow, wondering what the hell my birth father's ex-wife could be calling about that's so important. "Go ahead," I say. "Don't mind me."

"Jane . . ."

But I ignore him, drawing his cock into my mouth and fighting a laugh as he groans, "Oh, fuck me," before picking up the phone and managing to croak out, "Yeah, I'm here. What is it? . . . Actually, no. I'm hosting a party, and at this particular moment I'm having a conversation with Jane . . . Very funny. Yes, we're being very civil to each other."

At that, I gently nip the tip of his cock, making him gasp. As far as Adele knows, Dallas and I still mostly avoid each other.

"Why did I need to answer the phone?" he asks. "I have guests here."

It's clear from the conversation that they know each other pretty well, better than I know her, actually. I know that Colin—my birth father—and Dallas repaired their relationship when he was in college, after the kidnapping. That was about the time Colin met and married Adele, and I know Dallas and Adele stayed friends after she and Colin divorced. Apparently, pretty good friends.

I think—though I don't know for sure—that Dallas has even talked to her a bit about the kidnapping. She's a professional therapist, and I've actually considered seeing her. But the family connection makes it too weird. Probably unethical, too. Plus, I've never really clicked with her. She's always been nice enough, but I still never felt like it would be easy to open up to her.

Right now, though, Adele is the last person I want to think about, and I wish she'd tell Dallas why she called so he can get off the phone.

"Yeah," Dallas is saying. "I made plans to have dinner with

him later this week. He mentioned that he'd finished some of the remodeling on the house and . . . well, of course you're welcome to join us . . . Adele, do you really think—fine. Fine, I'll ask and I'll let you know. Was that it? . . . Okay then, I'll talk to you later. Bye." He tosses the phone aside, then twines his fingers in my hair as I run my tongue over the length of him.

"That was seriously surreal," he says.

I lift my head long enough to look at him. "Having a woman go down on you while you talk to her former stepmother? What is it you always say? How you like it fucked up?"

A shadow seems to cross his face, and I regret the joke.

"Hey," I say. "I was just being glib. You okay?"

"I'm great." He tugs my hair, urging me up to him. "Come here."

"Don't you want—"

"You. I want you."

I ease in next to him, trying to find a comfortable position on the floor. "What was so important?"

He rolls his eyes. "She wants to join me and Colin at dinner next week, but didn't want to include herself without asking. And she said I should invite you, too. Since we're being civil."

"Oh." I consider that. "Well, I guess I could come. That's the civil thing to do, right?"

He nods, but he doesn't look happy, and in the back of my head, a few little alarm bells start to tingle. "What's wrong?"

"Nothing. I'm just incredibly tired." He stands, then picks me up, cradling my naked body against his chest. His jeans are still open and hanging on his hips, and despite our relative nakedness, he heads straight for the door.

"Time for bed," he says. "And I hope to hell Liam's got Fiona out of the bedroom, because if he hasn't, they're both about to get an eyeful."

9

Starry, Starry Night

I wake alone and stretch out my arm to find Dallas, but find only the cool sheets instead. I sit up, groggy, and peer around the dark room, but he's not here. I frown, then remember the party.

We'd been so caught up in ourselves that we'd forgotten about the soiree going on downstairs. Maybe he couldn't sleep. Maybe he went down to say goodbye to the last of the guests.

It's a possibility, but when I go to the balcony and look down at the pool area, I see that all the lights are off, and there's no sign of lingering guests. My first thought is to ring for Archie, but then I remember he's gone. And, anyway, it's four in the morning and even if he were here, I wouldn't want to wake him. Besides, Dallas is only missing from our bed, not from the world. It's his house, and a big one. He must be around here somewhere.

I know that he fell asleep, because he drifted off before I did, and I'd laid in his arms for at least fifteen minutes, comforted by the sound of his steady breathing, before I'd finally succumbed to sleep as well. But he'd obviously awakened at some time during the night. And when he couldn't fall back asleep, he probably went to another room to read or watch television so as not to wake me.

I think about going back to sleep—he's certainly entitled to privacy—but it has been a strange night for both of us. I tell myself that I need to check on him, but as I pull on one of his T-shirts and head for the door, I know that's a lie. My motives are selfish; I need to find Dallas for me.

He's not in his study or in the den. I check the kitchen next—empty—then continue on to the basement room that Deliverance uses as an operations center. I have the code to enter, but when I do, I see that it is empty as well.

I lock it back up, lean against the closed door, and wonder where to look next.

I check the garage, because maybe he decided to go out, but his cars are all parked in their slots, and his motorcycle is, too, so he didn't go joyriding down Meadow Lane in the middle of the night.

I head out to the pool, using my phone as a flashlight to il-luminate the deck chairs, but he's not there. I'm certain I'll find him in our cabana, but I lose that bet because he's not there, either.

Finally, I'm out of ideas, and I return to the house to check the alarm system which monitors all the public rooms. *Empty.* There's also a setting that allows me to see if any of the closed rooms have been recently entered. None.

I'm about to give up, when I think to switch over to the sys-tem that monitors the windows and attic access. And that's when, finally, I find success.

When Dallas and I were growing up, we used to sneak up to the attic, then climb out through one of the windows so that we could sit on the roof and look out at the Atlantic. Sometimes we'd just talk. Sometimes we'd count falling stars or look for ships on the horizon. When we were older, we held hands, each telling ourselves that it was innocent. A way to make sure we didn't tumble off the roof.

But it wasn't innocent, not for him and certainly not for me. After our rooftop excursions, I would return to my room, climb into my bed, and slide the hand that had held his between my legs. I didn't really know what I was doing, but I knew it felt good. And I wanted him to be part of that feeling.

I've loved Dallas Sykes my whole life. And I don't think I ever believed in curses or bad luck until Eli decided to adopt me—just like he and my mother had adopted Dallas—and made us full-blown siblings.

The attic is easily accessed by a set of stairs behind a door in Dallas's office, and I go there now. As I'd expected, the door is cracked open—I should have noticed it when I peeked in the office earlier—and I climb the stairs slowly, careful to avoid the fifth one, which always creaks.

As attics go, it's huge, and full of old furniture and boxes of holiday decorations and all the usual things that get stored instead of tossed. My childhood memories are here, but I don't even glance at the boxes with my name printed in my mother's neat handwriting. Instead, I head straight for the open window and the man who I can see sitting on the flat roof where we spent so much time as children.

"Hey," I say as I climb out next to him. "Hiding from me?"

I'm joking, but for a moment I think he's going to admit that he is. But then he shakes his head, his smile little more than a contraction of the muscles around his mouth. "Never," he says. "I've just—I've just got a lot of shit running through my head."

I exhale, a little concerned. A little afraid. For a moment, we both just sit there looking at the ocean, but then I take his hand. I don't look at him, though. I don't think I can say what needs to be said if I'm looking at him.

"I thought it would be easier," I begin. "Us being together."

He turns sharply. "What are you talking about?"

"Together, we're not fighting anymore," I say. "This thing between us. So I thought it would be easier." I lick my lips, hating what I'm about to say, yet knowing that I have to at least put it out there. "But now I'm thinking that we're making it harder on you. Forcing you to see what you'd rather forget."

I can see from his expression that he doesn't understand me. Or maybe he doesn't want to understand me.

I draw a breath. "Memories," I say. "Nightmares. I know you're remembering stuff, Dallas. I sleep right beside you. And I'm afraid that all of this—you and me—has made it harder on you."

"No. Never."

I glance at him, but don't respond. Instead, I draw my knees up to my chest and hug them, staring out at the ocean beyond. "We had great talks out here as kids. And this was the no bullshit zone, remember? If we talked about something, we told the truth." I hold up my hand and wiggle my pinkie. "You, me, and Liam. We pinkie swore."

"It's not harder," he says. "You seem to have me confused with someone who has forgotten. I don't remember because I'm with you, Jane." He puts his arm around me, and I lean my head on his shoulder. "But because I'm with you, I want to get past it."

I sigh and nod, and right then all I want to do is stay quiet and let the moment take us. But I can't, because there's more. "Then tell me what is bothering you."

"There's nothing—"

I sit up straight. "Do not even *think* you can bullshit me. I know you way, way, way too well. You're out here before dawn, so there's a clue. Plus, you held back in the study. That started out a lot wilder than it ended up. And I'm not complaining because it was pretty damn awesome, but it wasn't what you wanted—no, don't deny it. I know you, remember?"

"Jane." My name sounds like glass, about to break on the sharp edges of his voice.

"Please, Dallas. Talk to me. Maybe I'm wrong and looking for problems. But I feel like there's something going on with you. Something you're not telling me."

He says nothing—just sighs and looks out at the night. I'm about to break down into full-blown begging when he finally says, "I know we promised each other no more secrets, and I want to live up to that. But there are things . . ."

"Like what she did to you?" I ask when he trails off.

He drags his fingers through his hair. "That's sure as hell part of it."

"And the rest of it?"

"Jane, can we not do this right now—"

"We need to talk. You need to talk. I know something's bothering you and I'm sorry if I'm pushing, but—"

"Yes, you are pushing." He turns to me, his eyes dark. "You are most definitely pushing," he repeats, then sighs. "Christ, you always do this. It makes me crazy, like that time when you were in Girl Scouts and—"

I can't help but laugh.

He looks at me like I'm insane. "What?"

"I was just wondering how many couples break down into sibling arguments in the middle of a lovers' quarrel."

His mouth twitches. "You have a point." He narrows his eyes at me. "I still win the argument, but you have a point."

"You do not win," I say. "You can't win if you don't finish, and you are so totally avoiding the—"

"Jane?"

"Yeah?"

"Shut up and kiss me."

Since that's something we don't have to argue about, I do, and it's long and hot and tender and sweet all rolled up in the perfect rooftop kiss.

I sigh and curl against him as he slides his arm around my shoulders. "I don't want to have secrets," he says softly. "And I'm trying my damnedest not to. But some things I have to work through first. Does that make sense?"

I nod. "Yeah. It does."

"Good."

We sit like that for a while, just holding each other, wrapped in the dark of the night.

"We've got this right?" I finally ask, my voice a whisper, my eyes on the ocean that churns in front of us.

"Yeah," he says, pulling me closer. "We've totally got this."

10

What the Butler Saw

I wake up curled against Dallas and think that there's really no place I'd rather be, and nothing else I will ever need. Except for coffee.

I definitely need coffee.

"Good morning." His hair is deliciously mussed, and there's a very obvious invitation in his eyes. An invitation that he backs up with the slow trailing of his fingers up and down my bare arm.

"Don't even think about it," I tease. "The only way you're getting any this morning is if I get some coffee."

"I can do that." He stretches, yawns, then sits up on the side of the bed, giving me a very nice view of his well-muscled back and broad, strong shoulders.

"Mmmm," I say, and he peers at me over his shoulder.

"Something on your mind?"

"Just enjoying the view."

His eyes graze over me, bare except for the spread of black satin draped over my calf. "I know exactly what you mean." He leans down and kisses me gently. "Give me a minute to go down to the kitchen," he says as he stands. He grabs a pair of sweatpants from where he'd left them over the arm of a chair a day or so ago, then tugs them on.

"And this is why I have a Keurig in my bedroom."

"I'm not the addict you are." He flashes a wolfish grin. "You're all the buzz I need."

I counter by throwing a pillow at him. "Go," I say, pulling the sheet up to my neck and then pointing toward the door. "No looking or touching until I'm properly caffeinated."

He inclines his head in a subservient bow. "As you wish."

I roll my eyes, but I'm still smiling after he's gone. And when he taps lightly on the door a few minutes later, I say in my most authoritative voice, "Enter."

Except it's not him. It's Archie. And he's carrying a tray with a coffeepot.

The sheet, thank God, is still under my chin—I'd been planning on tormenting Dallas a little upon his return. But that fact barely makes a dent in my overall level of mortification.

Archie, however, is his usual professional self.

He crosses the room without even rattling the cups and sets the tray down on the bedside table. "Shall I pour?"

"I—um." I struggle to answer, not really certain how to act in this situation. As I'm fumbling, Dallas comes in through the open door. He's carrying two mugs, and he didn't bother with a tray.

"Thanks," I say wryly. "But you're a little late."

His eyes meet mine, and I honestly can't tell if that's an apology or amusement coloring his expression. Probably a little of both.

"I didn't intend to disturb you so early," Archie says smoothly. "But you have a guest. Mr. Martin."

He's looking at Dallas, but I'm the one who replies. "Mr. Martin? Bill? My Bill?"

"Yours?" Dallas says sharply, then looks as though he wishes he'd bitten his tongue instead.

"Miss Jane's ex-husband, yes," Archie says.

"Oh," I say, peering around the room for clothes, then remembering they are across the hall in the study. And mostly ruined. Thankfully, I'd ordered a few things online during our four days of bliss—including my now-destroyed skirt—and that new wardrobe is downstairs in my old bedroom. "Well, I just need to get dressed and—"

"He's here to see Dallas, actually. I've put him in the first floor den," he adds. "With coffee and orange juice."

"Right. Well, I'll go see what he wants," Dallas says, looking as though he'd rather do anything but.

As I watch, he pulls on a pair of khakis that Archie hands him from the closet, then matches them with a loose knit shirt and loafers. He's gone from looking like he just woke up to someone who could model for *GQ* in approximately twelve seconds. And when he takes the next step and smooths his sex-mussed hair, then rolls back his shoulders and stands tall, he looks like a man who could run an empire.

My man, I think, and hug the little nugget of pride close even as a disturbing question occurs to me. "Why is he here? Do you think he's found out about—" I'm looking at Dallas, but I don't finish the question because it occurs to me that I have absolutely no idea if Archie knows about Deliverance. But I'm terrified that Bill has come on behalf of WORR—the World Organization for Rescue and Rehabilitation.

It's a group with a mission I believe in—assisting government agencies in the rescue of kidnap victims. But it has another purpose, too, and that's to locate and shut down vigilante groups. A former assistant United States attorney, Bill is one of the top people at WORR. And Deliverance is very much on his radar.

"If that's why he's here, we'll deal. But I'm going to start with the assumption that this is family business." His gaze cuts toward me. "After all, the man used to be my brother-in-law."

I scowl, not liking that reminder.

He heads for the door, pausing long enough to glance at me, his smile thin but reassuring. Then he's out the door and out of sight.

I expect Archie to leave. I hope he will, actually, because I really want to get out of this bed and get dressed.

But he's not going anywhere, and I'm pretty sure I know why.

"We've shocked you," I say.

His mouth curves just slightly, making the wrinkles at the corners of his eyes deepen and softening his usually dour, professional expression. "No, Miss Jane. At least not in the way you mean."

"'Not in the way I mean'? I don't understand."

"Deliverance," he says flatly, and my eyes go wide. "I'm surprised he told you."

I think back on the conversation. "How do you know he did?"

"Because you're worried that your Mr. Martin is here to interrogate him. That he's learned that Dallas created Deliverance, and that he's on a mission to bring him down."

"Well, yeah," I admit. "That about sums it up." I consider him thoughtfully. "I guess I should have assumed that you'd know. You know pretty much everything that goes on in this house."

"I do indeed." This time, I don't have to search to see that he's amused. It's all over his face. "Surely you didn't think that I find job satisfaction in throwing decadent parties for a useless playboy."

"I—no." I frown, remembering. I've seen the pride on Archie's face when he looks at Dallas, heard it in his voice. But Archie isn't the kind of man who would be pleased by the lifestyle that Dallas projects. On the contrary, he helped raise us, and I know he feels proprietary about us. A wasted life isn't something he would be happy about.

"And Mrs. Foster?" I ask, referring to Liam's mother.

"She knows about Deliverance. Dallas and Liam decided early on that it made sense to tell her. She supports it, though she doesn't work for it."

"And you do."

"As much as I'm able."

I exhale loudly. "So many secrets . . ."

"But fewer today than yesterday, Miss Jane."

"You call Dallas and Liam by their names. Why am I Miss Jane?"

"Because I'm an old man set in my ways."

I actually snort. "Not hardly."

He chuckles. "I'll let you get dressed now. Shall I pour first?"

It takes me a minute to realize he means the coffee. I've managed to wake up just fine without a single cup. "I'll get it myself in a bit."

He nods, then starts toward the door.

"Archie?"

He turns back.

"Thanks."

He hesitates. "I should clarify—when I said that I was surprised he told you about Deliverance, I meant the timing, not the revelation. You two couldn't be what you are to each other with something that significant hanging between you."

"He told you that?"

"No, but as you said, there's not much I miss that goes on in this house. Last week, I knew you two had a disagreement. I had hoped you would make up, of course, but I didn't anticipate that revelations about Deliverance would be part of that equation."

"Deliverance was at the heart of the argument," I confide. "I learned about it accidentally and kind of freaked out."

"Ah," he says, as if all the pieces are falling into place.

They're falling into place for me, too. "You don't really have a sick aunt in Pennsylvania, do you?" I recall how he'd left without even speaking to Dallas. We'd simply come back into the house from the cabana and found Archie's note.

"I have a cousin in Chicago who's feeling slightly under the weather, but no. I thought the two of you needed some privacy."

"And, um, it really doesn't bother you? What Dallas and I are to each other, I mean." It's an awkward question, but I'm compelled to ask it. If Archie's not freaked out, then maybe my parents will come to accept it, too.

It's a nice little fantasy, and so I cling to it gratefully, but I also know it's not true. My mother, maybe. But Daddy? Not in a million years.

It takes a moment for Archie to answer, and in the silence, I can read nothing in his face. Finally, he speaks. "Do you intend to give him up?"

"No." My answer is firm and immediate.

"Then it doesn't matter what I think. It doesn't matter what anybody thinks," he adds, as if he understands exactly where my mind has been going.

"I guess it doesn't." I want to be satisfied with his answer, but I can't deny that I crave the words—the reassurance that he doesn't judge us harshly. I want that, and at the same time I hate how insecure that need makes me feel.

"Jane," he says gently, "I saw the connection between you two more than twenty years ago. I'm not upset at you, but for you. You have a hard road, but you can make it. You're strong," he says. "You were forged in fire . . . You're a fighter."

And he's right. Dallas and I both are.

But the problem with a fight is that there's always the chance you'll lose.

11

The Other Man

Dallas paused outside the den, his hands on the polished brass knobs of the massive double doors. He didn't know why the hell he was hesitating. It's not like William Martin intimidated him. And if Bill had come to arrest him, there'd be a shitload of Virginia farm boys dancing all over the mansion's front lawn.

Except, of course that was bullshit.

Not the part about the FBI, but about not knowing why he was hesitating.

He knew.

He was still standing out here in the hall because he simply didn't want to see the man whose ring used to be on Jane's finger. The man who'd laughed with her, lived with her. Made love to her.

Intimidated? Not even close.

On the contrary, he was seething with jealousy, and he hated himself for it.

With one final breath to steel himself, he pushed open the

door, then extended his hand to the man rising from one of the leather armchairs.

"Bill, good to see you again. It's been too long."

"It has." Bill met him midway across the room and took his hand in a firm shake that only irritated Dallas more. In his mind, William Martin was a skinny, quiet pansy who had never deserved a woman as vibrant as Jane.

In real life, Bill was not only a brilliant and respected attorney, he was a decent-looking guy with ginger hair and the all-American features that had certainly helped him climb the government ranks. Not only that, Dallas happened to know that the man could hold his own on a basketball court.

Were Jane not in the picture, Dallas would probably like him.

As it was, he barely tolerated him.

Right now, he was doing his best to not flat-out ask the man what the hell he was doing in Southampton. In Dallas's house in Southampton, to be more specific.

"You're probably wondering why I'm here," Bill said, and Dallas had to laugh.

"To be honest, I was. Not that I don't welcome a drop-in from you at seven in the morning . . ."

Bill had the good grace to look sheepish. "I need to get back to DC for a lunch meeting, but I wanted to talk to you. This was the first and only chance I've had. Frankly, I considered myself lucky you were here. But I guess you had a party last night?"

Dallas flashed his most charming smile. "If I'd known you were in New York, I would have invited you. There were quite a few single women who I'm sure would have been very interested in meeting a well-placed attorney." He studied Bill's face. "Or are you seeing someone?"

"No," Bill said. "No one special." He shoved his hands in his pockets. "Is Jane?" As soon as he said the words, it was obvious he regretted them. He waved his hand, as if trying to call them back. "Sorry. That's not why I came. Besides, I know you two don't talk much. I didn't mean to bring up a sore subject for either of us."

"Not a problem," Dallas said. He turned away, then went to the sideboard and began to pour himself a glass of juice. "I don't think she's seeing anyone in particular," he said, hating every word. "But I thought you two kept in touch. Wouldn't she have told you?"

He turned back in time to see Bill's bemused expression. "Strangely enough, ex-wives tend not to discuss their dating lives with their former husbands. Continuing friendship not withstanding."

"I suppose not," Dallas agreed. "Did you come here to talk about my sister?"

"No. No, of course not." He gestured to the juice. "Do you mind?"

Dallas poured Bill a glass then passed it to him before taking a seat on the small divan across from the armchair that Bill had returned to.

"Thanks." He swallowed half the juice in one gulp. "Honestly, I'm not sure how to begin."

"I'd suggest the beginning," Dallas said, leaning back and extending his feet even while keeping his eyes on the other man. "But that's just me."

"Are you familiar with the name Silas Ortega?"

Dallas sat up straighter. Apparently when Bill decided to cut to the chase, he went right to the heart of it. "I am. Jane told me about him." That much was true. What he didn't tell Bill—and what Bill certainly didn't know—was that Deliverance had learned about Ortega as well.

"I told her she could," Bill said. "His incarceration was classified, but considering the information he provided—"

"A Sykes kidnapping," Dallas said coldly. "Yeah. I heard about that, too."

"Dallas, we can find who did that to you."

To you. Dallas drew in a relieved breath. Jane had once told him that she'd never revealed anything about her kidnapping to Bill. Apparently, that still hadn't changed. As far as Bill knew, Jane wasn't taken at all.

"Dallas," Bill urged. "We can help." Bill's voice was soft. Soothing. And Dallas wanted to smash his face in.

"I haven't asked you to do that." Dallas tried to sit still. To keep his hands on the arms of the chair and just sit calmly.

To hell with that.

He got up, paced the length of the room and back. "I haven't asked it," he repeated. "And I don't want you to."

"It's not your call," Bill said, his voice irritatingly level. "It's not even Eli's call," he added, referring to Dallas and Jane's father. "Although I'm going to talk to him, too. Professional courtesy. Family courtesy, too."

"*Courtesy*? You think it's courtesy to insert yourself where you don't belong? It's been seventeen years, and Ortega—" He snapped his mouth shut before he jammed his foot right into it. Dallas knew damn well that Ortega had been killed in custody— and that his death had been labeled a suicide. He also knew damn well that the government was keeping the death quiet. It was locked up tight and classified, sealed with a nice shiny bow.

Which meant that the playboy department store heir Dallas Sykes couldn't know about it. And Bill couldn't know about Dallas Sykes, the founder of Deliverance, who had his own means of obtaining that kind of information.

"What about Ortega?" Bill pressed.

"Just that—you have him in custody. He's going to say whatever he thinks you want to hear," Dallas improvised. "And since it's been seventeen years, the odds are pretty damn good he doesn't know anything useful. But he can make all sorts of shit up and send you on a wild goose chase. And that may keep your agents earning their paychecks, but it's going to wreak hell with me and my family." He took a beat to calm down. "Just let it go, Bill. I have."

He closed his eyes, thinking that every single word was a lie. A deception. And that he damn sure hoped that it worked.

"You're right that it's a risk," Bill agreed. "Ortega might not have anything relevant to reveal. But I think he does."

Dallas narrowed his eyes, trying to figure out Bill's angle. The man knew Ortega was dead, so what kind of game was he playing?

He debated between feigned disinterest and another plea for Bill to just drop the issue on the one hand, and a request to know exactly what information the supposedly still alive Ortega might have on the other.

He knew he should try to push the topic of the investigation away. But he was too damn curious. "What? What do you think he knows?"

Bill sighed. "This is top secret, Dallas, but Ortega was murdered in prison. Murdered right after revealing that he would disclose information about a Sykes kidnapping in exchange for leniency. That's a bold stroke, and highly risky."

"Which is why you believe what Ortega said—that there really was a Sykes kidnapping."

"Exactly," Bill said. "But there's more. Security was tight around Ortega. Damn tight. No one outside of WORR, the FBI, or UNODC should have been aware of the information he was providing," he added, referring to the United Nations Office on Drugs and Crime, with which WORR worked closely.

"So you have a leak," Dallas put in. He didn't say that Bill himself was the leak, albeit an unknowing one. Dallas hadn't realized it at the time of Ortega's death, because he hadn't known about Colin. Now that he did, Dallas understood what happened—Bill had told Jane. Jane had told Colin.

And Colin had arranged the kill.

Dallas fought the urge to close his eyes against the truth

that was pressing in against him. Sure, he could be wrong about Colin. About all of it. But more and more he feared that Colin was at the heart of it. And when Jane learned that her conversation with Colin led not only to Ortega's death, but had also triggered WORR's investigation into the Sykes kidnapping . . .

Well, it would rip her apart.

He had to tell her. But how the hell could he tell her?

Bill let out a frustrated breath. "A leak? Yeah, it sure as hell looks that way. And whoever wanted Ortega dead must have a solid network of eyes and ears looking for leaks about the kidnapping even after all this time. A network," he reiterated, "and a powerful one at that. He was able to insert an operative to kill a witness. That's someone dangerous."

He met Dallas's eyes. "And that's someone that neither my group nor the FBI nor any of the agencies that WORR works with is willing to have on the street. Your kidnapping is our best lead to finding this person. Maybe we prosecute for the kidnapping, or maybe we prosecute for Ortega's murder. But we are going to follow the evidence. And, Dallas, the evidence starts with you."

"I guess this wasn't ever intended to be a friendly chat," Dallas said, his temper rising. He wanted his kidnappers caught—no question. But he fully intended to be the one who had the pleasure of bringing the Jailer and the Woman down.

He took a step toward Bill and felt a sharp stab of satisfaction when the other man sank back in his chair. "You just came here to tell me you'd shoved a knife in my gut and now you're going to twist it."

"I'm not trying to hurt you, Dallas. But I do want to find the person who did this."

Dallas pointed to the door. "You know what, Bill? Why don't you get the hell out of my house?"

Bill levered himself out of the chair. "Now wait a minute, Dallas, you're being—"

The door opened, and they both turned as Jane stepped into the room, her eyes going wide as she assessed the situation.

Dallas started to move toward her, craving the comfort of simply touching her. But he couldn't claim that now. Not in front of Bill. And so he stopped in place while the man he wanted off his property went to greet the woman Dallas loved.

The woman who had once belonged to Bill.

The woman Dallas had no right to have.

Dallas pressed his fingertips to his temples, fighting a building headache. The certainty that it was Jane who had tipped off Colin. The thought of Bill knowing the details of the kidnapping. Of learning that Jane had been a prisoner, too. The memories of what the Woman did to him—and the horror of knowing that Bill might learn that as well.

And on top of all that, the thought of Bill touching Jane. Of knowing her body as intimately as Dallas did.

And even more intimately, too. How many times had Bill been inside her? Filled her up and heard her moan. How many times had he—

Fuck.

"Bill was just leaving," he said, forcing the words out through a clenched jaw and even more tightly clenched hands.

Jane glanced between Dallas and Bill, finally settling on the latter. "I'll walk you out. Come on."

Bill looked back at Dallas. "We'll talk more later."

"I have no doubt."

Bill frowned, but turned away. Jane looked back at Dallas, though, and he saw the pain in her eyes.

"Why are you here?" Bill asked, drawing her attention to him and away from Dallas.

"Oh, they're fumigating the townhouse. Apparently I have ants. And I'd heard that Dallas was having a party last night, and I wanted to see the debauchery for myself . . ."

Her voice faded as they stepped through the doors and out

into the hallway. He heard their footsteps echo across the entryway, and then the sound of the front door opening and closing.

And only when he was surrounded by silence, did Dallas let himself drop down onto the sofa, lean forward, and bury his face in his hands.

12

Deliver Us from Evil

"Why didn't you tell me Dallas had been kidnapped?"

We're outside the house, standing beside the ornate ceramic pots filled with colorful flowers. His car is parked less than ten yards away on the circular drive, and all I want is for him to get in it and go far, far away.

But I know Bill. He's dug in now. He wants answers.

Hell, he wants answers to questions he doesn't even realize he should be asking.

"Jane," he presses.

"I did tell you," I say. I walk a few feet farther, leaving the front porch and taking a seat on the marble bench that is one of the focal pieces of a large flowerbed that lines the curving driveway and leads all the way down to Meadow Lane. "I told you the same day you told me about Ortega."

"You know what I mean," he says as he takes a seat beside me. "When we were married. Why didn't you tell me then?"

I stand again, unreasonably irritated with him for making me give up my comfortable perch. "It wasn't my story to tell,

Bill." Which is a true answer, but not the full answer. I had my own story I could have shared with my husband. But I never once told him about my kidnapping, either.

He sighs, then pinches the bridge of his nose. "I wish you would have." He looks at me.

I lift a shoulder. What the hell am I supposed to say to that?

"It's just that I always liked your brother, but he always kept his distance, you know. Not rude, not usually anyway, but . . ."

"But what?"

"Like he was holding on to some big secret."

"He was," I say, thinking that Bill doesn't know the half of it. The kidnapping, sure. But the other secret was me. How could Dallas and Bill ever have been close when I was married to one man and in love with the other?

I shiver and hug myself, and Bill stands up and puts his light jacket over my shoulders.

"It's chilly out," he says. "You should have grabbed a wrap."

I just nod. It's not the morning chill that has made me tremble, but the simple fact that this is all on me. I never should have married Bill. Hell, I never should have fallen in love with my brother.

Even though Dallas and I weren't together then—even though we both believed we would never, ever be together—the bottom line is the same: I'd kept huge secrets in my marriage.

I'm keeping them still.

"Anyway, I'm glad I know now. I understand him better. And I understand you better, too."

At that, my eyes snap to him.

"Your fascination with kidnappings. The books, the articles." He nods, as if to himself. "It makes sense. Dallas is messed up, but you are, too, Janie. And writing is your way of working through what happened to your family."

"It is," I say, because that's one hundred percent true, even if it's not the full truth.

"Does it help?" His voice is gentle, reminding me of why we'd started dating. Why I'd thought that maybe a marriage could work.

"Yeah," I say. "It does."

"Dallas needs to work through it, too. Finding his kidnapper will help."

I don't answer. Mostly, because I don't disagree. But for the first time, it truly hits me that Bill is absolutely right. Finding who took us really will help Dallas put it behind him once and for all. But it needs to be Dallas who finds them. It needs to be Deliverance.

Bill sighs. "Look, I get that this is hard, but talk to him, okay? Because this thing is bigger than me, and even if I wanted to stop it, I couldn't. The investigation into the Sykes kidnapping is officially moving forward. You should try and help him realize that's not a bad thing."

"The funny thing about Dallas is that he tends to see things for himself."

"He sees you, too," Bill says, not understanding just how right he is.

Once again, I say nothing. I just pull his jacket off my shoulders, then pass it to him in a not-so-subtle signal that he should go.

Thankfully, he takes the hint and walks toward his car. He pauses by the driver's door. "I still love you, you know."

"Bill—" There is no disguising the pain in my voice.

"Just tell me—did you ever love me? And don't lie. I'll know if you're lying."

I almost smile, because he wouldn't. I'm far too practiced a liar for him to be able to tell. But we shared a life, even if only for a short time, and he deserves the truth. "I did," I say. "Or, at least, I thought I did. You're right about one thing, I'm messed up. It's nothing to do with you. You're a wonderful man and I am so grateful that you didn't write me out of your life. But we weren't meant to be married."

He comes back around the car, pausing at the trunk but looking like he wants to continue on and close the distance between us. "How's the screenplay coming? The new book? I'm heading back to DC today. You can come anytime if you need to do more research. And you know you can stay at my place."

My chest tightens at the thought. "Bill—don't push me."

He taps his fingers idly on the trunk. "I was devastated at first when you wanted to leave me. Then I thought fine. She wants to go, I'll consider it an opportunity." He shakes his head, chuckling softly. "But that turned out to be a load of bullshit. I've been dating on and off for years now but I've never found anyone who moves me the way you do."

I say nothing. I just stand there wishing he'd stop saying these things that I really don't want to hear.

"Dallas says you're not seeing anyone."

I almost laugh at the irony. "Yeah, he'd say that."

"Maybe . . . maybe now that I know the truth we could try again. Maybe whatever distance you felt was because of those secrets."

"It wasn't the secrets, Bill. We just never . . . *fit*."

"Maybe what you think you want doesn't exist," he presses. "It's not as though you're making wedding plans with someone else, right? It's not like you've found the right guy."

"No." I force out the lie. "I haven't found him."

"So you're sacrificing something solid for something you might never really have."

My heart hitches, because without even understanding what he's said, he's hit a little too close to the truth.

"Yeah," I finally say. "I guess I am."

* * *

When I go back inside, Dallas is still in the den, and I notice right away that he's switched from orange juice to bourbon.

"Little early, don't you think?"

He looks at me, his face a mixture of fury and exhaustion. "You know, I really don't." As if to drive home the point, he tosses back the drink, then pours another.

I'm at his side in an instant, my hand covering his before he can raise the glass. "Dallas. Don't."

He ignores me, pulling his hand from under mine and holding tight to the Waterford highball glass. He starts to raise it to his lips, hesitates, and then hurls it against the far wall where it shatters into a million pieces, littering the polished wood floor with some of Kentucky's finest liquor and Ireland's best crystal.

"*Goddammit,*" he says, then reaches out as if to grab another glass.

I take his hand, sliding in front of him. "I like those gla—" But I don't finish. He pulls me hard against him, his mouth on mine, wild and rough and desperate. Claiming me. Teeth and tongue warring and tasting as he holds my head in place, his fingers twined tight in my hair so that I have no choice but to submit to this assault that is melting me, burning through me.

When he pulls back, I lick my lips and taste blood. I'm breathing hard, my body singing with desire. He is looking at me, his eyes wild, his expression hard. He's taken a step back so that he is leaning against the sideboard, his hands gripping the edge of the antique piece as if it is the only thing that is anchoring him.

But I don't want him to be anchored. He's on the edge, so close to going under, and dammit, I want to go there with him.

"Dallas—"

"*No.*" He pushes away from the sideboard, and comes to me, his hands going to the hem of my tank top. "No talking. Right now I can think of much better uses for that very pretty mouth."

He yanks the shirt up over my head, then tosses it onto the floor. I'm not wearing a bra—I'd only pulled on yoga pants and a tank—and now I'm bare from the waist up, and the sensation of the cool air against my hot skin is delicious. All the more so when Dallas cups his hands on my breasts, and teases my nipples with his thumbs.

"Mine," he says, and though I start to say yes, I'm silenced by his sharp look reminding me that I'm to stay quiet.

He hooks his arm around my waist, and then pulls me to him, arching me back with a firm tug on my hair before he bends over and takes my breast in his mouth, sucking and teasing until my nipple is so hard it's painful, and I can feel each bite and suck and lick all through me, making me so wet and needy that I have to bite my lower lip in defense against the urge to beg and plead for him to touch me, stroke me, make me come.

When he finally pulls back, I whimper, wanting and needing more, and I can't help myself when I whisper, "Dallas."

His mouth curves up in what looks like a smile of victory, and he tightens his grip on my hair and forces me down to my knees. My blood pounds through me, wild and hot. I like this—being at his mercy, knowing that my only purpose in the moment is to please him. To obey him.

I peek up at him through my lashes just long enough to see him looking back down at me, his expression stern, but his eyes filled with the same desire I've seen all my life. Then he tugs on my hair and says, "Now, dammit. Your mouth, my cock," and I feel a shiver of pure pleasure cut through me with such intensity that it rivals an orgasm.

I unbutton his pants and ease out his cock. He's hard—so damn hard—and absolutely perfect. I cup his balls with one hand and fist his cock with the other, then tease the tip with my tongue, gratified when a tremor cuts through him and he moans, low and deep. I want more, though. He thinks he's the one in control, keeping me silent and on my knees, but right now, I want to break him. I want to take him all the way.

And even though I know he says he can't, I want to feel him explode in my mouth.

I take him in, slowly at first, teasing and sucking. Letting the sensation build and gauging his reaction by the way he holds my head. The almost pained noises he makes. I take him deeper, reveling in feminine power as he holds me tight with one hand and reaches back to balance himself against the sideboard with the other.

He's close—his body trembling, his cock tightening. And oh, god, if I can just take him there. If I can just get him off that would be one step closer—one bit of proof that we *can* make this work. That we can work past all the loss and horror—all the crap—that's followed us around for seventeen long years.

As if he realizes it, too, he releases the sideboard and grabs my head with both hands, holding me motionless. So that now it's not me going down on him—it's not me in control—but Dallas. Dallas fucking my mouth. Using me. Taking himself to the edge, and me with him. Because I'm on fire. Every inch of my body tingling. My yoga pants soaked. And all I want is release. All I want is for him to break, to come.

He's thrusting hard into me, his cock pounding into the back of my throat so that I have to concentrate to breathe through my nose, to not gag, but I want this. I crave it. I fucking love it, because it's wild and it's *him* and he's not holding back.

But even as the thought cuts through me, he gasps, the sound choked. He roughly pulls out of me, releasing my hair and pushing me back at the same time, so that I fall backward, my arms out to keep me from landing flat on my back.

I'm breathing hard from my position on the floor, and he's doing the same from above me. Our eyes lock, and I can see both frustration and need on his face. At first I think that he's frustrated because he couldn't reach release, but then he lowers himself to me and tugs off my pants. My chest tightens as I realize what he wants—what he's willing to try.

"You're mine, Jane," he growls as he straddles me. "Mine," he says as he kisses me. As he reaches between us and strokes me, his fingers slick as he thrusts inside, readying me.

"Say you want me."

"You know I do," I whisper, then feel the head of his cock at my core. I bite my lower lip as he pushes against me, as his eyes meet mine, and I see the flair of victory as he enters me—and then the gray shadow of defeat as he goes soft.

I press my lips together, my heart breaking for him. "Dallas, it's—"

"Okay?" His eyes flash. "Is it? Is it really?"

I start to answer but he shakes his head, and I stay silent, uncertain if we're playing the game again or if he just needs the silence. I expect him to get up. To pace and fume and work out his frustration. But as his hands start to stroke along my body, hard and possessive, I realize that it is not the world that will bear the brunt of his frustration, but me.

Slowly, sensually, he traces his fingers over my body. Grazing my shoulders. Circling my breasts. Teasing my nipples so relentlessly that I arch up in a silent, demanding claim for more.

He moves lower, his hand rubbing my belly as his mouth sucks each of my fingers, the sensation rocking through me, making me squeeze my thighs together in defense against the growing pressure building at my core.

He's pushing it aside—the failure to fuck me. He's turning it around and turning me on. Owning me. Claiming me. Proving that he deserves his reputation, and that whether he can penetrate me or not, he can still take me all the way to heaven and back.

I don't know what's going on in his head—I don't understand what triggered this or why he tried to fuck me now. And at the moment, I don't care. I'm content to lose myself in sensation. In the feel of him. Sucking. Stroking. And then his hands are working lower and lower until he thrusts two fingers inside me and orders me to ride him.

"Tell me," he says, teasing just around my clit, but not quite touching where I so desperately want pressure. "Tell me you're mine."

"I am."

"Mine," he repeats, and this time the demand is coupled with the deep, rhythmic thrust of his fingers and the relentless tease of his thumb against my clit. "Not Bill's. Not any other man's."

I can barely think, much less talk, but I understand now. *Bill.* My ex-husband. A man Dallas knows has fucked me. Has been inside me.

I want to tell him that he's an idiot. That I love him, not Bill, and I always have. That I want him inside me—*I do*—but if it never happens I'm okay because I want him more. As much of him as he can give me, in every way he needs me.

I want to say all of that, but my body is too overwhelmed, the pressure rising too fast. And when I finally tumble over the edge, sound bursts from my lips and I can say only the words he wants to hear. "Yes," I scream, hoping that he understands I mean everything. "Yes, I'm yours."

Afterward, we lay together, breathing hard, holding each other. I'm not sure what to say—or even if I should say anything at all. But this is Dallas, and I can neither lie to him nor keep things from him, even though I know that there are still things he is keeping from me.

I roll over and prop myself up on an elbow so that I can face him. "I am, you know."

"What?"

"Yours," I say. "I'm yours now, and I've always been yours."

I lean forward and brush a kiss over his lips. "I was never Bill's. And maybe that's horrible because it's so unfair to him, but it's true. I wasn't his. I couldn't be his."

"And yet he's had a part of you that I never have."

"But you have." We were together countless times in captivity.

"I had the girl," Dallas says. "Bill had the woman."

I roll my eyes. "Don't be a Neanderthal, Dallas. I've slept with more guys than you and Bill. And you've slept with enough women to populate a small country. But you're the only one who has my heart."

"And you mine." He sighs deeply. "And I'm sorry. I am. I know I'm acting like a fucking caveman. I just want—well, I want everything."

"I know." I curl up beside him again, idly stroking my fingers over his chest hair. "I do, too."

He presses a kiss to my temple, and the moment is warm and sweet and wonderful.

Naturally, I can't just keep my mouth shut. "That wasn't all that upset you, though."

He chuckles. "No. I'd say that nothing your ex brought with him sat well with me."

"There's no stopping it, you know."

"I know."

I have to smile, because I'd been more than a little cryptic, but I knew Dallas would understand. We may have been out of sync earlier with the whole Fiona fiasco, but we're back now, and he's followed my thoughts perfectly.

"Bill and WORR and the UN and the FBI are all going to do what they're going to do," he says, then shifts position so he can press a kiss to my forehead. "And Deliverance has to do what it has to do."

"I get that," I say, then frown. "Have you found anything?

The team, I mean. Ortega was a huge lead. Even dead he can help, right? So have you found anything about our kidnappers?"

I shift in time to see his expression go hard. "Dallas?"

"No," he finally says, his voice oddly firm. "We haven't found one concrete thing."

I study his expression. "What is it? What aren't you telling me?"

He drags his fingers through his hair. "What aren't I telling you?" he repeats. "For one thing, I'm not telling you how frustrated the whole thing makes me."

I nod; that makes sense. Deliverance had gotten so close—hell, *Dallas* had gotten so close. And Ortega's death stopped the investigation cold. "Maybe you should work together. Deliverance. WORR. You're both hunting the same people."

"No." His tone leaves no room for argument.

I press anyway. "Why not?" I know the answer, but I need to hear him say it.

"Deliverance doesn't operate like WORR. They want to prosecute."

"And you?" My mouth is so dry I can barely get out the words.

"I want to execute."

I swallow, then nod slowly as I push myself to my feet. I'm naked, and I grab his shirt off the floor and put it on, feeling just a little too exposed at the moment.

This room has an adjacent private garden, and I walk toward the curtained French doors and push the drapes aside enough that I can slip through. I'm sandwiched there, my hand to the glass and my back to the curtains, when he joins me.

"I know it upsets you," he says as I keep my eyes fixed on the morning glories blooming outside the window. "I know you think it's reckless. Stupid. That we don't have the right to play judge and jury. I understand all that," he says as he softly presses a hand between my shoulder blades, "but I have to. I can't find them and look at them and not destroy them."

I say nothing.

He sighs, and in the glass I can see the pain reflected on his face. "Even if it hurts you, baby, I have to. They stole part of our lives. I need to take it back. I have to," he repeats. "I need you to understand that."

I close my eyes, draw a breath, and then turn to face him. "You know what I went through. How those men Daddy hired went in and tried to rescue you. How the place exploded and we thought you were dead."

"It was a setup, Jane. We know that now."

"Doesn't change the way I felt. Doesn't erase the wound in my heart that just kept bleeding for those weeks I thought you were gone forever."

"I'm standing right beside you." He takes my hand and twines his fingers with mine. "And I'm not letting go."

"I know you are. That's part of what I'm trying to say. I've thought about things one way for years. Vigilantes are danger-ous. Men like Benson—they put innocent people at risk in order to chase a dollar. And that's bad. Hell, it's evil. And even Deliverance is cutting corners. Stripping away due process. Stepping in where it doesn't have the right and playing jury and executioner."

"Jane—"

"*No.* Let me finish." I draw a deep breath. "That's been my core premise for so long, Dallas. And it's so, so hard to let it go. But now . . . I think about what they did to you—I don't even know what all they did to you—and I want . . ."

I trail off, blinking back tears. And then, finally, I force out the words. "You're right," I say instead. "You shouldn't work with WORR."

The tears spill out, and I brutally swipe under my eyes. "Dammit."

"Jane?"

"Don't you get it?" I turn on him, my voice as sharp as a slap. "I want whoever did this to us dead, too. I want to watch you put a bullet in his head. In her head. I want them to fucking suffer."

My voice hitches, and I swallow back tears as he pulls me close and holds me tight. "I want that," I manage to say, finally admitting the truth that has been dancing in my head. That talking with Bill finally drove home. "I want it so badly, and I'm not sure I like the person that makes me."

I'm shaking, but in his arms I feel safe, and I cling to him as he strokes my back and kisses my head. "Oh, baby. Sweetheart, it makes you human." He shifts so that he can look at my face, then gently strokes my cheek. "It will be hard on you," he says softly. "Christ, it's going to be so damn hard on you."

"Because I'm not as strong as you are?" I can't help the sharp edge in my voice.

"God, no. You're strong—you're even stronger than you know. And no matter how hard it gets, I'll be beside you."

I nod, considering his words. "I need to know the rest of it, Dallas. I need to know what you and the guys find out about who's behind our kidnapping. I need to feel like I'm part of the process. But even more than that, I need you to tell me what that bitch did to you. I need to hear the truth of it. All of it."

"So that you feel justified in wanting to eradicate that slime off the face of the planet?"

"Damn right. They're evil. They're pure, walking evil." I draw a breath. "But it's not just that. I want to know because I don't want there to be any more secrets between us. I need for there not to be any more secrets. Please tell me you understand that."

His hesitation is so brief it's barely noticeable. But I notice.

"I do, baby. I understand. I know that you need it. And I understand why."

He's saying all the right things, and yet his words chill me. Because saying that he understands isn't the same thing as promising to tell me.

I start to call him out on his evasion, but some instinct holds my tongue. Instead, I tilt my head back and force a smile, needing to lighten the moment, even if just a little. "I want to know everything about you. Sexually. Emotionally. All your secrets." My voice is teasing, but my words are serious. And Dallas knows me well enough to realize that.

"I will, you know," I say with certainty. "The whole story of Dallas, body and soul."

"I know," he says. "And you will. Eventually you'll know everything."

The words are exactly what I need to hear, but there's something in his voice that scares me. Sure, he's acknowledging that he's holding something back, and that's a big deal. But I'm no longer sure that this secret he's keeping is about what the Woman did to him.

All I know is that it's something important. Something huge.

And for the first time, I'm terribly afraid that I don't really want to know.

13

Dirty Little Boy

All your secrets.

Dallas paced the basement ops center, Jane's words still running through his head.

It was still early, not much past eight, and when she'd suggested going to the kitchen for some breakfast, he'd lied and told her he had to take care of a couple of things first.

He didn't have shit to take care of. Or, rather, he didn't have anything to take care of that wasn't inside his own head.

Secrets.

God, they just kept piling up. She'd flat out asked him what they'd learned by investigating Ortega. And though he'd told her the literal truth—because they had nothing concrete on Colin yet—it was still a goddamn lie.

And although she hadn't pressed when he'd essentially admitted that he was holding things back, that didn't mean that she'd be okay with his silence about Colin once the truth came out. Hell, even if Colin was innocent, Dallas was going to catch

shit for staying quiet. And he could only hope that she'd understand his reasons for keeping her removed.

But he was holding back more, too. Things she deserved to
know because they affected their physical relationship. All the
shit in captivity that had fucked him up. That had ripped away
any possibility that he'd have a normal sex life, a normal relationship.

Those were the big ones. But there were other things, too.
Like the letters—he should have told her before about some
crazy female sending him stalker letters. At least he'd rectified
that last night. But he still hadn't told her about Adele; about
the strange attraction they'd shared, and the way Adele had understood his need for kink, for the dark. She'd gone there with
him willingly. Maybe even too enthusiastically—because eventually she'd crossed the line, and Dallas had been so disgusted
with her and himself that he'd called it off.

But that had ended months ago, and it wasn't as if Jane
needed a rundown of every woman who'd shared his bed. But
where Adele was concerned . . . well, the woman was practically
family.

He bit back a derisive laugh. *Family.*

Apparently sleeping with his family was his goddammed MO.
Christ, he was screwed up.

He was standing at one of the workstations, and now he
pressed his hands to the cool metal and bent over, giving himself a moment to just breathe.

He heard her the moment she stepped into the room, and he
expected it when she came to him. When she put her arms
around him and held him close, her face pressed against his
back.

She said nothing, just held him, and it was her touch that
gave him strength. This was Jane, after all. The woman he
loved. And even though it would hurt, he knew that he could

tell her the truth. Not about Colin. Not yet. Not until he was certain.

But he had to tell her about what happened to him. He owed her that. More, he wanted her to know, even if he didn't relish the thought of actually talking about it.

But oh, Christ, where the hell did he begin?

He didn't know—for that matter, he was still pondering the question—when he heard himself saying, "She raped me. Over and over, and in so many ways."

Jane's arms tightened around him, silently giving him support. But she said nothing, and he was grateful. If she'd offered him even the tiniest of condolences, he thought he'd clam up for sure.

Instead, he spoke into the quiet of the room, knowing that she was there, but still speaking for himself. For the sensation of once and for all, finally, expressing what happened.

"That wasn't the first thing she did, but it sure as hell stands out the most. She had a dildo. She said I'd like it. I didn't. But damned if I didn't come. And damned if she didn't tell me she knew I'd enjoy it. That it would make me hard."

He sucked in air and closed his eyes, fighting back the memories. He could handle them singularly, but not the flood. Not everything rushing at him at once.

"She'd stroke me, too. Get me hard. Sometimes she'd use a cockring. Keep it on." He almost turned to look at her then, but didn't. Instead, he said, "I won't use them, you know. Won't even try, even if it would keep me hard. Even if I could be inside you. I can't. Just the thought makes me sick." Hell, he felt ill just thinking about it.

"I understand," she said, her voice low and soft. "I do."

"I didn't have a choice then. She'd do whatever she wanted, but in the end, I'd be hard. And she'd get on me. Ride me. She said I wanted that as well. That I wanted to fuck her. That she was a woman and you were a girl and that with her I was a man."

Behind him, he felt Jane's body shake, and he knew that she was crying. He closed his eyes, trying not to think about her pain. About his. Trying to just force the words out, because if he let emotion get to him, he wouldn't be able to go on.

"Those were the good days. On the bad ones, she'd stroke me and make me hard, then slap my face and tell me I was nasty. That I was thinking about you and that I was a sick little boy. She'd pour ice water on my genitals. She'd use electric shock on my cock and hold a knife to my balls. If it was vile and painful, she'd do it.

"And if I was hard, she'd tell me I was a pervert. If I was soft, she'd tell me I was a pussy. And every time she made me come, she'd tell me to close my eyes and imagine it was you touching me." His voice was hard, the words coming fast, heavy with fury. "You hitting me. You jamming some goddamn dildo up my ass."

"Dallas, I—"

She broke away, and he mourned the loss of her warmth against his back. He wanted to turn to her. To comfort her. But he was terrified of the disgust he'd see in her eyes when he turned around.

He had to, though, and when he did, he saw her curled up on the concrete floor, her body shaking with tears. He froze—he just fucking froze.

But when she looked up at him, it wasn't disgust he saw, but rage. Not at him, but at the Woman.

"That fucking bitch," she whispered, and the words were like a trigger. He sank to the ground, and when she crawled to him and held out her arms, he collapsed into the comfort of her embrace.

"The fucking bitch," she repeated.

"Not disagreeing," he said.

She released him long enough to lean back and study his face. "Are you okay? Right now, I mean. Is this—do you want to stop talking about it?"

He considered saying yes, but he shook his head. "I can't say I want to talk about it," he admitted. "But I think I need to. I think I've needed to for a long, long time."

She nodded, then bit her lower lip uncertainly.

"It's okay," he said. "If you want to ask me questions, it's okay."

"Did you try to fight?"

"I tried. I couldn't." He sighed. "You know how you crave control now?"

She nodded. "Avoiding crowds. Taking my self-defense classes." Her smile when she met his eyes was tremulous. "You're the only one I let go with. The only one I really feel safe with."

He knew that, of course, but still the words were like a knife. *Safe.* Safe with him was a goddamn joke. If he let himself go too far—

Stop.

He pushed the thought away. He needed to move, and so he stood, holding on to the worktable until he had his bearings again, then he started to pace. "You surrender that control to me," he finally said. "I don't. I don't surrender it to anybody. Not anymore."

"I know. I get that."

"You don't. Not really. I don't think you can."

"That's bullshit, Dallas. But you have to tell me. You have to lay it out for me."

"But that's just it. I don't know if I can. She changed me, but I'm not sure even I understand how. I mean, Christ. Why the hell can't I fuck a woman? What's the correlation between what that bitch did to me and the reality I'm now living with? I thought it was you, Jane. I thought that if I ever had you in my bed, that little problem wouldn't be a problem anymore, because she'd tied sex up so tightly with the thought of you that I figured you must be the goddamn cure. But you weren't. You aren't. *Shit*."

He gritted his teeth and turned away. He hadn't meant to blurt it out like that. To cover her with all that bile.

Across the room, she climbed to her feet and came to him, then gently laid a hand on his shoulder. "What do you mean she tied sex up with me?"

A shiver cut through him—he didn't want to go there. Didn't want to talk about it. Didn't want to bring her down into all of that. But goddammit, they were already halfway there. "Like what I was saying earlier. She'd touch me. Do things to me. And she'd tell me to close my eyes and imagine it was you. She'd tell me you liked it. Wanted it. But then later she'd flip it around and she'd say you were a nasty girl who liked nasty things, and on another day she'd say that you were an innocent, and I was tainted now, and why the hell would you want me?"

"I do want you. Desperately."

"She changed what I want sexually. What I need. I like it rough, baby, and that's on her—"

"A lot of people like rough sex. Including me. Don't tie everything you feel back to that bitch. Don't give her the power."

"She already has it. She's between us every time we're together because she planted you in the middle of every fucked up need she created in me. So how the hell can we ever be normal, Jane? How can we ever do this right?"

"Normal?" she repeated. "Right?" She stepped back from him, and damned if the compassion hadn't faded from her face, replaced instead by anger. "You like it rough? You like it dirty? Well, guess what, Dallas, that's your normal. And that's okay. I mean, seriously, what's normal anyway? Because all I know is that you make me feel good. You make me feel better about myself than I ever have. And all I really care about is do you love me? Do I make you happy?"

"Yes," he said, reeling a little from the force of her speech.

"Well, then what more are you looking for?"

He shook his head, not sure how to explain. He believed her words, but also knew that she didn't really know what she was talking about. How could she when he didn't even know how far down he wanted to drag her?

"I'm serious, Dallas. What else do you need?"

He drew in a breath. "I need her out of my head."

"Then do it. You couldn't fight back then—but now you can. Overpower her. End her."

"Why do you think I founded Deliverance?"

"Not like that. Right here. Right now."

"What the hell are you talking about?"

"Go back. In your head. In your memories. Let me be her. Fight me. Fight me, then fuck me. She took control? Take it back."

His blood ran cold, and he remembered the times that Adele had suggested Dallas pretend that she was Jane. That idea had horrified him. So did this one, but for a completely different reason. "Do you have any idea what you're asking? What kind of door you could be opening?"

"Yeah," she said. "I do."

"You're basically saying that I need to rape her. I need to act out my fantasy, overpower the bitch, and hurt her the way she hurt me."

"Pretty damn politically incorrect, I know. But that about sums it up."

"With you playing the role of the Woman. No. No fucking way." He couldn't. It was a screwed up idea. But that wasn't what scared him. No, what terrified him was how much he wanted to do exactly that. Not because she was a stand-in for the Woman, but because he wanted to claim Jane fully and completely. He wanted to make her his. He wanted to be that damned Neanderthal and drag her by the hair around after him.

Because how else could he be certain she wouldn't pack up and leave the moment she finally got through her thick head just how screwed up he was?

He heard her voice in his head telling him that she'd give him whatever he needed. But how did he know what he needed until he went there? Even in The Cellar, he hung back. Didn't matter that it was a full-on kink club and he could indulge any whim there. He still pulled it in, because those weren't the women he wanted on their knees. That honor belonged to Jane, and until he had her—until he took her—how would he know how far he would go? How much he would crave?

And the thought of going too far—of breaking her limits, of scaring her, of having her look at him like he was broken beyond repair—he couldn't risk that.

He had to hold back.

Had to fight for normal.

Had to draw a line in the sand and not cross it.

Everything they'd done had brought them together.

But everything they couldn't—that he *wouldn't*—do would keep them that way. Crossing the line just might rip them apart.

He needed time to think. To regroup. This was too much too fast, and he was reeling.

He pressed his fingers to his temples and rubbed, fighting a building headache. And then, regretfully, he raised his eyes to hers. "Anything I need, right?"

"Of course."

"All right." He swallowed, hating what he was about to say, but knowing that he needed to say it. That he needed it. For a little while, at least, he needed it.

He drew a breath, then said, "I need you to go."

The hurt that cut across her face was like a physical punch to the gut. "Dallas, no. I didn't mean—I didn't want—" She sucked in air. "I pushed too hard. I should never have suggested—"

"*No*. We said no secrets, right?" God, he was a hypocrite. He was keeping some damn juicy secrets. But that secret was about Colin. That secret was to protect her. But this? This, he had to tell her.

"No," he said again, forcing the word out. "What you said makes sense. I just don't—"

"Want to try it," she put in. "I get that. But—"

"Jane, no." He drew a deep breath. "That's not the problem," he said flatly.

"Then, what?"

He met her eyes, certain his were as cold as ice. "The problem is that I do."

She'd been gone for less than fifteen minutes, and already the house seemed desolate. He'd watched the pain cross her face, and then seen the true depth of her strength as she'd schooled her features and nodded.

"You want it," she'd said. "You want to play out the fantasy. You want to use me as a stand-in for that bitch. You want to take her. To win."

He'd nodded, feeling sick even as he did. "Yes. I do."

"But you won't do it? Even though I've told you it's okay? That I understand? That I'm consenting, fully and completely? All that, and you won't, even when we both know this is important? Critical, even."

He'd met her eyes, and he'd held fast. "I won't," he said. "I can't."

She'd nodded slowly. "Okay, then. I'll drop it. We can just forget I said anything. But I don't have to go."

Once again, he'd held firm, even though all he'd really

wanted was to pull her close to him. "You do. I need time. An hour. A day. I don't know. But I need to clear my head. Besides, things will have piled up at the Sykes offices that I need to take care of. And you have a screenplay to finish."

She'd scowled at that, but it was true. She'd done no work for almost a week, and he knew she had to be pushing up against a deadline. "Go home," he'd insisted. "You have work, and so do I. We should both step out of the bubble for a while. You know I'm right."

She hadn't agreed, but she had gone. And now he was alone in the house and missing her already.

He may have suggested that he was going into the city to work, but that was utter bullshit. He was too ripped up to be around other people. Better to stay in, go through some loose ends for Deliverance. Maybe watch five or six hours of mindless television so he wouldn't have to think about how maybe he'd just made the biggest mistake of his life by sending her away.

It was all true—he needed to think. He needed time. He needed to figure out what he wanted, what he needed.

Because right now, he only knew one thing—he needed her. He just didn't know how to have her without hurting her. Without dragging her down to a place she said she was willing to go, but he knew damn well she didn't belong.

Dammit all to hell. He was a fucking mess.

A fucking mess, and at loose ends.

He'd meant it when he said he needed to clear his head, and the best way he knew to do that was to take a walk on the beach. He was back in his bedroom, and now he looked for his headphones, finally finding them on the bedside table. He pulled up a playlist on his phone, then started toward the door.

He paused, then stripped off the slacks he'd pulled on to go meet Bill. He crumpled the damn things, tossed them in a corner, and then searched out the jeans he'd worn at the party. He picked them up, then breathed in the scent of her, grateful that Archie hadn't come through to gather up the laundry.

After telling himself he was being ridiculous but not much caring, he pulled on the jeans. Because, dammit, if he couldn't have the woman, he at least wanted the memory.

He hurried downstairs, then out the French doors to the pool deck—then stopped short when he saw the woman on one of the deck chairs.

Not Jane—*Adele*.

"Adele," he said, forcing himself not to frown as he crossed to her. "I didn't know you were here."

She tilted the brim of her hat back and smiled up at him, still stunning even past fifty. "Didn't Archie tell you?" Her mouth pulled down into a frown. "He must still be looking for you."

"So what's up? Why are you here?"

"I'm meeting a real estate agent in forty minutes—there was hardly any traffic coming in and I got here so early I thought I'd drive over and see you and Jane." She turned to sit up. Her dress was short, and hitched up as she shifted, revealing a glimpse of pink lace. Dallas looked away, certain the casual reveal had been intentional.

"Buying?"

"Considering." She glanced around. "Isn't Jane around?"

He shook his head, trying to look casual. "Why would she be?"

"She was here when I called," Adele reminded him.

"Oh, that. She just came to gawk at the party," he said, copying Jane's earlier story to Bill. "She left well before it ran its course."

"Did she?" She took a step toward him, and he saw the small beads of sweat in her cleavage. She reached for him, taking his hand in hers before he could pull away. "Did that upset you?"

Her voice was low. Soothing. "Had you fantasized that she would stay? Maybe sneak into your room late at night?"

He tugged his hand free and stepped back. "Don't even go there."

She lifted a brow. "So that would be a yes, then. Poor little rich boy, can't have the girl he wants."

He clenched his mouth closed so tight it almost hurt. Adele knew he wanted Jane. But wanting and having were two different things, and no way was he telling her that he and Jane had crossed that line. She might keep it confidential—hell, the woman was a therapist, so she was trained to keep secrets—but she might also tell Colin. After all, she wasn't Dallas's therapist, but she'd once been his lover. If she learned about Jane . . . if she turned out to be jealous . . .

The thought made him frown. At one point, he'd actually considered that Adele might be his letter writer. But he'd dismissed the idea quickly enough. The timing was wrong, for one thing. He'd finally and fully broken off with Adele about four months ago, but the letters had started long before that.

Besides, Adele was hardly obsessed with him. She had a long string of lovers, including her ex-husband, Colin.

"Must have been hard." She tilted her head to one side as she studied him.

"What's that?"

"Having her in your house. Being civil to her. And not having her the way you want to."

He kept his face passive. The woman had no idea how much she spoke the truth.

"I could ease some of that tension." She stepped closer. "I'm sure that agent won't mind if I'm a few minutes late."

He had to chuckle. "I don't think so, Adele. I don't want fucked up. Not today."

"No? What do you want?"

Wasn't that the question of the hour? That was exactly why

he'd sent Jane away, so he could figure out just what the hell he wanted. And, more important, how he could have it.

And now, standing here with Adele, he realized that it wasn't fucked up that he wanted. Needed, yes. Craved, absolutely. And maybe they'd have to go there if they were ever going to get clear of all the emotional shit that surrounded them.

But what he wanted went deeper. What he wanted was normal, pure and simple. Dinner. A movie. Dancing and hand-holding. Something to ground them, to hold them steady and prop them up when he and Jane inevitably careened toward the precipice. Something solid to pull them back if they went over.

But he didn't tell Adele any of that. Instead, he nodded toward the front of the house. "I think I want to walk you to your car."

He headed that way and she fell in step beside him. "So we'll see both of you next week?" Adele said. "Jane agreed to come to dinner?"

"She did."

"Lovely." Her smile was overly bright. "I look forward to seeing the two of you together. It's so much fun watching a man with blue balls."

"Anyone ever tell you that you're a raving bitch, Adele?"

She laughed. "All the time."

They'd reached her car, and she pulled her keys out of her bag. She was heading toward the driver's door when Dallas reached out and caught her elbow. "Quick question. Who was Colin with between my mother and you?"

Lisa had divorced Colin when he and Jane were little kids. And Colin had married Adele when Dallas was in college. If it turned out that Colin was the Jailer, then somewhere in that gap, he met the Woman. And it was just possible that Adele had heard her name.

"What on earth makes you ask that?"

And wasn't that a damn good question? "I was thinking about my mom. You two are so different. I was wondering if there was a progression or if Colin just went from Georgia belle to European vixen."

"Vixen? Well, aren't you sweet." She pursed her lips in thought. "Honestly, I have no idea about his other women." She seemed entirely uninterested. "I suppose you could ask him at dinner."

"Maybe I will," he said as Adele got in her car, even though he knew full well he wouldn't. But he did have another idea, and as soon as he had the chance, he'd give his mom a call. With any luck, Lisa had kept an eye on Colin after the divorce.

With even more luck, she'd lead Dallas straight to the Woman.

He turned to head back toward the beach, then stopped cold, realizing the import of his words. Somewhere along the way, his thinking had shifted. He was truly seeing Colin as guilty now. As one half of a team.

The possibility made him queasy, not just because Colin had become a friend. But because he knew that if he was right, he'd end up putting a bullet through the head of the man that Jane once called Daddy.

14

Reality Bites

Despite the fact that I've parked myself in front of my computer, I am completely incapable of getting any work done.

I tell myself that I understand why Dallas wanted me to go. It isn't my fault—not really. It's not that I pushed too hard. Instead, it's that he needs space to get his head around everything he's feeling. To battle with everything he is fighting.

I tell myself all that, and maybe I even believe it. But that doesn't soothe my hurt. For seventeen years we'd separately battled our past, and I'd let myself believe that we'd conquered the hard part. That we were together now, and whatever came next we would face as a couple, holding tight to each other and sharing our strength.

I was wrong. I didn't really know what the hard part was. Not for Dallas, anyway. And now I'm here and Dallas is there, and I'm going crazy wondering what he's doing, what he's thinking, what he's feeling.

I sigh, wishing I could turn off my churning thoughts. I'd arrived back at my townhouse over an hour ago, and I'd thought that diving back into work would help, but clearly I'm insane. The scene on my computer screen is intense and full of action, and I think it's one of the best scenes in the screenplay. It's unfinished, however. All that drama and angst and roiling emotions coming to a dead stop because I don't know what to do next.

Honestly, it's a metaphor for my life.

I push back from the kitchen table where I've set up my laptop, and for what must be the hundredth time that morning, I pour myself another cup of coffee and start to pace the kitchen, back and forth in front of the table.

I'm antsy and out of sorts, and all I want is for things to be right between me and Dallas. I'd thought we were moving in that direction—hell, I'd thought we'd arrived—but then he'd sideswiped me, and now I feel as if he'd physically knocked me off the planet and I'm tumbling wild and out of control and off into space.

Out of control.

That's the real kicker, isn't it?

Because as much as I want to hold on to control, I've let it slip with Dallas. I'd surrendered every ounce of control that I'd held so tightly to for years. Now I'm at loose ends, and don't know what to do, because I don't know how to fight, much less how to help.

I glance at my phone, toying with the idea of calling him like the needy, insecure woman I am.

But then I realize that as much as I need to hear his voice, what I really need is to feel in control again. For the last seventeen years I've religiously studied everything from kickboxing to various martial arts to police certified self-defense classes. I've even hired an ex-cop to teach me how to shoot and got my dad to pull strings so that I could get a New York City license to carry a handgun.

But it's been forever since I've taken one of my self-defense classes or gone to the range. I've let my training slide. It's as if in surrendering to my need for Dallas, I let go of my grip on everything else. And now I have to get it back.

I glance at the clock on the mantel. I'm pretty sure the studio on Eighty-Fourth has a class at four today, and if I go change right now, I can easily make it.

I'm about to do just that when my gaze catches my phone, and I hesitate. Because the one thing that will make me feel even more in control is if I can help Dallas. And seeing the phone makes me remember how I can.

I snatch it up, ecstatic to be *doing* rather than waiting.

And what I'm doing is calling Henry Darcy.

It takes me a few minutes to track down Darcy's number, but he's done business with my father on and off for years, so I end up calling Dallas's assistant.

"Ms. Martin," she says. "How lovely to hear from you."

"Sorry to interrupt your day. I'm sure you're swamped what with Dallas back in the office after a week's vacation, but I need a favor."

"No interruption. Dallas took today off, too, so I'm catching up on filing."

"Oh." I hesitate, because I thought he was coming into the city and to his office.

"I'm sorry, what did you say you needed?"

"What?" It takes a moment for her words to penetrate my numb brain, then I rattle off my plan to interview Henry Darcy for my book and ask her to text me his number.

I'm frowning when we end the call, and still frowning when the number comes across my phone's screen. Did Dallas think that he had to pretend that he was going to the office in order to get rid of me? Did he want me gone so badly that he had to make up excuses?

I clutch my phone tighter and tell myself not to think about it. I have a plan, after all, and worrying about Dallas's machinations isn't part of it. Instead, I need to call Henry Darcy. That's the next step, and that's what I do.

And even though I'm tempted to hang up after the first ring because I'm just feeling so damn shaky, I force myself to hold on, then ask the woman who answers if I can speak to him. And then I hear myself saying, "Mr. Darcy, this is Jane Martin, Eli Sykes's daughter and Dallas's sister. I was hoping you had a moment to chat?"

He's surprised to hear from me, of course, but when I tell him that I want to talk about his daughters' kidnapping, he says that he probably should have expected my call. After all, the press has been covering my books lately, and gossip about the casting for the movie of *The Price of Ransom* has been all over social media.

"I've heard about the title of your upcoming book," he says. "I saw you on *Evening Edge* last Saturday."

"*Code Name: Deliverance,*" I say. "I guess I should start by saying thank you. It's a great title, and it pretty much came from you."

Darcy had told Bill about the vigilante group that had orchestrated his daughters' rescue. And in the telling, he'd also mentioned that he'd heard something he probably shouldn't—the internal name that the group used. *Deliverance.*

"That's actually why I'm calling," I say. "I was hoping to interview you for the book. Get a few details about how it worked. My thesis is all about the aftereffects of vigilante involvement, of course, but I think that providing the reader with an overview of the process, contact protocols, that sort of thing would really help the book as a whole. Do you think we could meet?"

Thankfully, he agrees. Unfortunately, he can't do it today. But I get him on my calendar for a lunch in just a few days and consider myself lucky.

I'm basking in the pleasure of a mission accomplished as I grab my phone and start toward the stairs to change for my class. I'm halfway up when it rings, and I pause to look at the caller ID.

Dallas.

I consider not answering—after all, if Dallas needed a break to get his shit together, I ought to help him stick to that.

But the truth is that I don't have the willpower. Not where Dallas is concerned, and so I hit the button and answer the call.

"You call it the dark?" Dallas says without even waiting for me to speak. "I call it hell. A pit. A chamber of horrors. And I hate myself for wanting to go there with you." His voice is hard. Unflinching. And almost monotone in its precision.

"I told you, Dallas. I'm there for you however you need me to be. All you have to do is believe me."

"I do." His tone has softened, and I hear a touch of gentleness. "And we'll go there. But not yet. Not the first thing."

I'm actually smiling a little when I say, "Well, it would hardly be the first thing . . ."

I'm not even sure he's heard me, because he presses on so quickly. "I want to go out on a date. I want something normal."

I frown, not sure that this is a good step. "Nothing between us is normal, Dallas. And maybe that's okay."

"Maybe," he concedes. "But I want it anyway. I want hand-holding and stolen kisses and candlelight." There's a beat, and in the silence I feel as though I'm floating simply from the impact of his words. "What are you doing tonight?"

"Oh." The question takes me off guard, and my head is suddenly flooded with all sorts of reasons why I should tell him I'm busy. I'd have to miss my class. I need to finish writing this scene. He tossed me out of his house, so maybe I should reject him as well, if for no other reason than to be contrary.

But then I think about the sensation of his skin against mine. Of how much I want his kiss. Of how I want to see his features lit by the glow of a candle.

And I think about how safe I feel just being near him.

"I don't know," I finally say. "What am I doing tonight?"

"Going out with me. I'll pick you up at seven. Dinner. A movie. Maybe drinks after."

I'm grinning like an idiot, but my smile soon dies. "A real date? In public? Dallas, are you insane? You know we can't. What if people figure it out?"

"Trust me," he says.

And because I do, I say, "All right."

15

Dinner and a Movie

Honestly, you'd think I'd never been on a date before.

I take a long bath with lavender scented bath salts, taking my time to soak and shave and generally relax. After I get out and towel off, I use some of the luxurious body butter that Stacey gave me for Christmas last year, rubbing it in so that my legs and arms are soft and subtly scented.

I brush my teeth—twice. Do my makeup with more care than usual. Then get dressed in a sheer black blouse and Agent Provocateur bra paired with a stunning cotton jersey skirt that features a slit so high up my thigh it would have revealed the leg band of my underwear had I been wearing any.

I'm not sure if Dallas is planning a hands-off, old-fashioned date or if he intends to rip my clothes off and have his way with me. If it's the first, he'll never know I'm going commando. And if it's the second—

Well, I really hope it's the second.

He said he wanted hand-holding and kisses—and while

that sounds lovely, I want more. With Dallas, I always want more. And the truth is, I know he does, too.

So while I'm excited for the date, I'm also a little afraid that this is part of a bigger slide backward. That he's going to keep dangling the carrot of kink without ever actually getting there. Which would be fine if we were a regular couple, but we're not. At some point he has to take me into the dark with him. He says he knows that; he even sounds like he really believes it.

I'm just not completely confident in his follow-through.

I draw a breath and tell myself it's okay. He needs time, and he needs to work things through for himself.

Hopefully, tonight is about doing the work.

I check my hair and makeup one last time, then slip on my shoes—strappy sandals with four-inch heels that do wonders for my legs and ass. I'm ready. And I still have twenty minutes before he's scheduled to arrive.

I frown, my mind in a whirl, the seconds ticking away so slowly it's painful. With a shock, I realize I'm nervous, as much at loose ends as I'd been for my very first date with Danny McBride when I was thirteen. I hadn't really been interested in Danny—even then, I knew deep down which boy I really wanted—but I was genuinely flattered by his attraction to me. I'd been a wreck waiting for him to show up, not knowing what to expect or if I'd like it.

With Dallas, I know I'll like it very much. But I still don't know what to expect. And the not knowing is making me just a little crazy.

Still, it's better than him sending me away, and me crying on Brody's shoulder. So I tell myself it's all good, then change my earrings twice just to have something to do. When I glance at the clock again, I realize that only two minutes have passed.

Great.

Finally determined to shake off my ridiculous case of nerves and uncertainty, I head downstairs to the kitchen, pour a glass of wine, and take a long sip.

By the time Dallas rings the bell fifteen minutes later, I've finished the glass and am on my second. I take a final swallow, then hurry to the door. I hesitate only a second, telling myself that it's stupid to be nervous. That this is Dallas, and that we will get through this. How can we not when we've conquered so much already?

I say it—and then I tell myself that I have to believe it.

Finally, I pull open the door, intending to casually invite him inside. Instead, I draw in a sharp breath and simply stand in the doorway staring at the man.

He dominates my front stoop, so poised and perfect that I'm amazed that pedestrians aren't stopping to stare, drawn to him as if to some stunning natural phenomenon like the aurora borealis or a majestic mountain.

He's wearing a tailored gray suit with a crisp white shirt and a pale blue tie. The tie, however, is loose and the top button of his shirt is undone, giving him a bad-boy-playing-good vibe that is wildly sexy. His caramel hair is slightly mussed, as if he tried to tame it, but either the wind or his habit of dragging his fingers through it has foiled his efforts, and the slight messiness only adds to the sensual allure of the man standing in front of me.

The fact that he is holding a dozen roses makes me smile. But what makes me go weak at the knees is the look of pure desire I see on his face as he skims his gaze over me, his emerald eyes finally meeting mine.

"You look gorgeous," he says, and his voice holds so much heat and passion that it takes every ounce of willpower for me not to press my body against his and beg him to hold me and talk to me and tell me that we are going to be just fine.

Instead, I manage to choke out a sincere thank you, then

step back to let him enter. He does, but he pauses just over the threshold to study me, as if he hasn't yet gotten his fill.

"You're stunning."

"I'm glad you think so." And then, because I've had a glass and a half of wine, I turn for him, modeling the outfit and the way the figure-skimming material clings to my rear and the slit exposes a long expanse of leg.

"Stunning," he repeats as he reaches for the edge of the door that I've stupidly left open. He shuts it with a bang, his eyes never leaving my face. "And right now, all I want to do is tear that outfit off you."

My entire body clenches as his words rip through me like fire, melting me. Burning me.

Dallas.

I try to say his name aloud, but can manage only a breathy gasp, and as I watch, the corner of his mouth curls up in satisfaction. He sees my need, and he knows that it matches his own.

"I want it," he says, his voice softer now and heavy with longing. He reaches out and traces my lower lip with the pad of his thumb. "I want to lay you out naked on this floor. I want to kiss every inch of your body. I want to tease your nipples with my tongue, then slide down between your legs and suck your clit until you scream.

"I want to," he continues with a wicked grin, "but I'm not going to. Not yet."

I swallow. "Why not?"

"Because I want what we've never had. I want you at my side out in the world, even if I can only go so far as to open the door for you or chastely press my hand against your back to guide you through a room. I want normal."

I shake my head, just a little. "We can't have it. Not that kind of normal. Not now. Not ever." I want to kick myself for saying it, because I am relishing this moment. The power of his desire for me is intoxicating, and I want to lose myself in it.

"I know," he says. "But right now, I want the fantasy."

My heart twists, and I nod. "All right," I whisper.

"Then come with me."

I hesitate only long enough to put the flowers in water, and then let him lead me out of the house to where a chauffeur holds open the door to a limo. I turn to him and raise a brow. We both have access to limos, of course, but we rarely use them, opting to drive our own cars or use one of the company's Town Cars.

"I like to impress my dates," he says with a small shrug.

"Consider me impressed, Mr. Sykes."

I have to laugh when we pull up at the Film Forum on West Houston. *Bringing Up Baby,* I say, reading the marquee. I turn back to him and realize that he's just a little blurry because I'm looking at him through sentimental tears.

"Good?" he asks.

I manage a nod and a watery smile. "Oh, yeah," I say, my voice a little hoarse. "It's great."

Bringing Up Baby is not only one of my favorite classic films, but it's the last movie that Dallas and I saw together. We were fourteen, and it was the week before Dallas was sent off to London for boarding school. We'd snuck out of the house, just wanting to be together, and had ended up at a Katharine Hepburn film festival.

Nothing had happened, but there'd been so much tension buzzing between us that if I hadn't already seen the movie a half dozen times with my mom, I never would have figured out what was going on. And to this day, I remember the way my entire body hummed when our fingers brushed in the popcorn tub. And how very, very aware I was of the way his knee bumped into mine and our elbows touched on the shared armrest.

That afternoon counts as one of the most sensual times in

my life, and yet we didn't do a single thing. Nothing, that is, except want each other.

Now, almost two decades later, I still want him.

Inside, we stop at the concession stand for a bucket of popcorn and two sodas, then head into the dimly lit theater where classic cartoons are playing on the pre-show screen in lieu of modern commercials and trailers.

I expect Dallas to sit dead-center in the theater as he always did when we were kids. But instead he takes my arm as we head to the very back row.

I lift a brow in question and he shrugs. "I want to take you out in public," he says. "But that doesn't mean I don't still value our privacy."

"Oh." I think about that, my body tingling from all the delicious implications as I step into the row and walk carefully to the center seats.

Dallas sits beside me, his hand holding mine, and I realize I'm actually feeling a little bit shy. Like this is a real first date and not a game that we're playing. At least, I think it's a game.

I hope it's a game.

I'd like to say that my mind is more on the movie this time than it was so many years ago, but that would be a lie. I keep my eyes on the screen, true. But nothing seems to stick in my head. I'm too aware of the man beside me. The way his hand feels against mine. The sensual caress of his thumb against my skin.

And then, just when I start to fear that he really did bring me here only to hold hands and watch the movie, he releases my hand and moves his to my thigh. The thigh exposed by the very high slit of my skirt.

He is touching me only above the knee, and the contact is entirely innocent. Doesn't matter. It still burns through me, as fiery as cheap whiskey and at least as intoxicating.

"I love this part," Dallas says, leaning over to whisper in my ear. And I don't know if he means the part of the film where the dog steals the dinosaur bone or the part of the evening where he skims his fingers up my thigh.

I can't ask him, though, because I'm having trouble wrapping my mind around words. We've done so much more, and yet I am so wildly aroused by the simple progression of his fingers up my leg that I'm thanking the fashion gods that my skirt is black, because I'm quite certain it's soaked.

When his fingertip is almost to the juncture of my thigh and pelvis, I place my hand over his. "What exactly are you doing, Mr. Sykes?" I whisper.

He leans closer so that his breath teases my ear when he replies. "That's up to you. I can be a man who's bold and takes what he wants, or I can be a gentleman. Your call."

I lick some of the popcorn butter off my lips, trying to decide. "I guess that depends on your definition of a gentleman," I finally say. "Isn't a gentleman the kind of man who takes care of his woman?"

The corner of his mouth curves up. "Oh, yes," he says, as his finger continues the slow, inexorable path to my core.

I tilt my head back as I draw in a shuddering breath. "Be a gentleman," I demand as his fingers slide over my slick, wet clit and I spread my legs, wanting more, trying to stay silent, and desperately thankful that he brought us to the back row. "Please," I beg. "Fuck me like a gentleman."

"Whatever the lady wants," he says as he enters me and I pivot my hips, rocking against his hand, getting fucked in a movie theater in front of Katharine Hepburn and Cary Grant as my orgasm crashes over me, fast and hard and wonderful.

After making me explode during the Golden Age of Hollywood, Dallas sweeps me away to another era. We're at the Balcony for dinner and cocktails while we listen to the Glenn

Miller-esque sounds of a big band and watch at least half a dozen dancers on the floor in front of us.

It's wonderful and lovely and sweet and classy.

It's also frustrating as hell because he hasn't touched me once since we left the theater. On the contrary, we wasted a forty-five minute drive in the limo sitting politely next to each other while he talked about Hepburn and Cary Grant and Howard Hawks, the director.

I can't tell if he's pulling some sort of mind fuck on me or if he regrets the way he'd stroked and filled me during the movie, and almost made me scream louder than the damn soundtrack.

Something's up, though, and it's driving me batshit crazy.

"Do you want to dance?" he asks as I take a sip of my martini.

"No," I say, more sharply than I intended. "I really don't."

"You don't like it here?"

"No—I mean yes." I exhale loudly. "Oh, fuck, Dallas. This place is amazing and you know it. It's like we stepped into a different age. The band. The cocktails. The lighting. The whole ambiance." I push my chair back and rise. "It's like we're not even ourselves anymore."

"Jane?" He's out of his seat, too, but I gesture him back down.

"No, no, stay. I just—I just need to go to the ladies' room."

I turn without waiting for his reply, and follow the signs to a restroom that is just as elegant as the rest of the Balcony. The door opens onto a lounge area, beyond which are individual stalls each complete with a toilet, sink, vanity, lighted mirror, and an upholstered stool to make reapplying makeup that much more comfortable.

Since I don't actually need the restroom, I loiter in front of the mirrored wall in the lounge, ostensibly checking my outfit, but really trying to figure out what the fuck I'm doing. Or, more accurately, what the fuck Dallas is doing. It had been so incredibly hot in the theater, but now he's reined it in so far that I can't help but think he regrets it. That he's trying to prove some point to himself or to me, and that he believes that making me come during the movie was a huge mistake, contrary to some idiotic plan that he's outlined in his head to turn us into a normal couple.

Well, dammit, I don't want to be normal.

Or, rather, I want *our* normal. Mine and Dallas's. Just like I told him at the house. Just like he'd understand if he'd just listen to me and actually let my words penetrate his goddamn thick skull.

Resolved, I turn away from the mirror, planning to head for the door. I'm going to go back out there, plunk myself down at the table beside him, and demand that Dallas tell me every single thing that is going through his head. That he explain what he's doing, why he's doing it, and why the hell he didn't lay me out and fuck me hard in the limo.

At least, that's my plan. I don't get very far because the second I turn around, the door opens, and Dallas strides in.

I open my mouth to speak, but he shakes his head and the words die in my throat. Before I even have time to think, he's across the lounge, his hands on my shoulders pushing me back against the mirror, his mouth crushing against mine, his hand sliding up my thigh to cup my bare sex.

I moan against his mouth, and he takes full advantage, deepening the kiss, his tongue exploring, his teeth clashing with mine. He takes my lower lip and sucks on it even as his fingers stroke me, then he bites my lip as he thrusts two fingers hard inside of me, and I try to cry out, but I can't because he is claiming all of me, so much that I can't even make a sound.

I'm melting in his arms, and I don't even care that we're in the ladies' lounge of a popular nightclub. All I need is what he's giving me. All I want is to revel in the sensation of Dallas—his touch, his scent, *him*. The man I've been craving all night. Because he's back. Oh, thank god, he's back, and I just want to get lost in him.

At least until I hear the toilet flush in the back part of the restroom, and my body grows stiff and cold as I realize we're not alone.

I try to push away, but he only holds me closer, his mouth hard and hot against mine, his fingers stroking inside me as his thumb teases my clit. I hear footsteps, and I squirm, needing to get away. He raises his hand to the side of my face, blocking me from view of whoever is coming. But that's not enough. We're still here, and someone is going to see, and it's so fucking out of control and I'm so damn wet—and so damn scared that we'll be found out. That whoever it is won't just avert their eyes and walk away, but will confront Dallas. Will see me. And then the world will know and—

And—

Oh, Christ, what then?

My mind is whirling and it feels like a million hours have gone by, but then I hear the stall door open and the click of high heels on the marble floor and I realize that hardly any time has passed, and I can still push away. I can still end this. I could thrust my leg up—I could knee him, break his hold. God knows I've done it enough in self-defense classes. But damn me, I don't want to.

I don't want to.

The realization sweeps over me, and I relax, surrendering to his touch, growing wetter and hotter and wilder as the steps continue, then soften on the carpeting.

His fingers are inside me, thrusting hard, and I hear the startled gasp from across the room, and then the woman's quick steps followed by the sound of the door opening and closing. And then, as if the knowledge that we were seen but not caught is a trigger, I explode in Dallas's arms as he continues to stroke me, milking every drop of pleasure from my wild, re-lentless, fucked up, awesome orgasm.

When my body finally stops trembling, he eases his hand away, then downshifts the pressure of his mouth against mine to gentle—not to mention deliciously sexy. Finally, he pulls away, his expression a mixture of heat and tenderness so potent I have to clench my hands against the temptation to grab his collar and pull him close again.

He steps back, then smooths my skirt before brushing his finger over my lower lip. "I'll see you back at the table," he says. And before I can even process his words, he turns and leaves the lounge as swiftly as he'd entered.

I watch as the door closes behind him, then lean back against the mirror, ripped up, sated, and utterly content.

I am, I realize, smiling.

I revel in the lingering pleasure for a moment before heading back to our table. He rises as I approach just like a proper gentleman. I meet his eyes, certain he can see the smile in mine.

"I'm sorry," he says, once we're seated.

I tense, thinking for a moment that he's apologizing for what happened in the lounge. Then I realize that's not right at all. Instead, he's apologizing for what came before. For the way he pulled back in the limo after such sweet wildness in the the-ater.

He's apologizing for pretending to be something we're not.

"Apology accepted."

The booth is semi-circular and designed for two, which puts us close together, the idea being that both people can see the dance floor. There's a drape on the table, and when he rests his hand lightly on my thigh, I moan just a little.

"Be careful," I whisper. "You have me so on edge that if you push me over I don't know if I could be quiet."

"Tempting," he says, with such heat that I fear I've just chal-lenged him to do exactly that. He doesn't, though. Instead, he softly says, "Hey," and I turn to face him more directly. He tilts his head, his eyes taking in the whole ballroom. "I know this isn't your thing."

"You're my thing," I say, then match his answering smile with my own.

"And big band music?"

I love music, and he knows it. All music, actually. But I lean toward either sixties rock, heavy metal, or opera. I'm nothing if not eclectic. "I confess it wouldn't have occurred to me to come here tonight, but I really do love it. It wasn't the place that was bugging me. It was—"

"I know. I blew it." He rubs his thumb over my thigh. "Do you have any idea how much I wanted to lay you out and fuck you hard in that limo?"

"Dallas . . ." My voice is breathy. Needy. "Do you know how much I wanted you to?"

"In that case, I apologize for disappointing the lady."

"Well, you made it up to me in the ladies' lounge."

His fingers ease higher up my thigh. "I'm very glad to hear it. And, baby, I understand what you've been saying. We have our own standard for normal. But that still doesn't mean that I can—"

I press my finger to his lips to silence him. "What I suggested—you pretending that I'm the Woman—that was extreme, Dallas. That's not our normal, and never could be. If you need it, I'm here. I'm always here for you. But it's up to you, and I won't mention it again." I smile as I reach under the table and slide his hand up higher even as I spread my legs. "Believe me," I say, "there are plenty of things I'd rather do with you."

He strokes his finger over my clit and I tremble with anticipation, trying hard not to be obvious about the fact that I'm in the middle of a nightclub on the verge of a stunning orgasm.

"I can think of things I'd rather do, too," he says as he gently pulls his hand away. "Lots of different things, actually. Including this." As he speaks, he reaches into his interior jacket pocket and pulls out a narrow box about five inches long.

I'm intrigued enough that I almost forgive him for withdrawing his touch, and I wonder for a moment if he's bought me a necklace. But when he hands me the box there is almost no weight to it at all, and no rattle when I gently shake it.

"What is this?"

"Happy birthday," he says, and I light with pleasure.

"Thank you, but that's not for four more days."

"Open it."

I can hardly argue with that, and so I pull off the lid, then squeal when I see the two tickets. "Dominion Gate?" It's a Finnish heavy metal band I adore. "Dallas, that's incredible! I thought about going but their New York dates have been sold out for ages. When did you—"

"It's not New York. It's LA. Westerfield's in West Hollywood. A small venue for a concert, but a friend of mine owns the place and so I managed to score a couple of tickets." He grins, looking more than a little pleased with himself. "I figured you wouldn't mind going to LA for the concert since you've probably been putting off things out there anyway."

"Smart man," I admit. "I've been trying to decide if need to go back for a few weeks." I shrug. "Before, it was no big deal to go to LA for a while. Now, I prefer to be in New York."

"Is that so?" He lifts a brow. "Why?"

He knows perfectly well why, of course, but I tell him anyway. "I used to like being out there because it kept me away from you." I smile, then take a sip of my martini.

"I'm shocked," he says as he slides his hand back under the table. Once again, he gently strokes my thigh, the sensation making me want to curl up and start purring. "Why on earth would you want to be away from me?"

I sigh a little, but finally manage to form words. "Because when I was near you, all I could think about was touching you."

"And now?"

"Now I want to be here. In New York. Wherever you are."

"Why?"

I look at his face and see the heat I feel reflected right back at me. "Because when I'm near you, all I can think about is touching you."

"I think it's time to go home."

"Yes," I agree. "It absolutely is."

He texts our driver and the limo is waiting for us as we step out onto the street. Unfortunately, so are two men with cameras.

"Dallas! Hey, Dallas! What's the story? You and your sister patch up your rift?"

I freeze, my body going completely cold as the driver holds the door open for us. I expect that Dallas is going to hustle me into the limo and ignore them. But he doesn't. Instead, he looks straight at them.

"Rift? No idea what you're talking about. My sister and I just wanted to spend some time together before she heads back to LA. We both lead busy lives and don't get to hang out often enough."

"So the rumors you two have been feuding for years are false?"

Dallas flashes his most photogenic smile. "Come on, guys. Do you know how many rumors there are about me out there? How am I supposed to keep up?"

"Dallas! Dallas! Jane, can you—"

But the last is cut off as Dallas finally does take my hand and urges me into the limo, then follows, shutting the door behind him.

I collapse into the seat, breathing hard, my heart beating wildly, and all I can think is that we were almost discovered. What if Dallas had been holding my hand? What if he'd forgotten himself in the moment and kissed me? What if the woman from the lounge had recognized him? Had figured out exactly who we were and what we'd been doing?

Oh, god.

Oh, god, oh, god, oh, god.

He pulls me close, and I realize I'm trembling. "Shhh. It's okay. It's fine. We covered and it's all good."

I cling to him. "You covered. I froze. I completely froze."

"Doesn't matter," he repeats, kissing my hair. "They didn't see anything. They didn't suspect anything."

"But—"

"Jane?"

"Yeah?"

"Look at me." When I do, he continues, his voice firm. "I wanted this. I think we needed it."

"To be hounded by the press?" I can practically hear the hysteria in my voice. "Our affair almost revealed?"

"No," he says calmly. "To go out in public. To act like we're just a couple on a date. To feel like we're part of the world, and not still in a concrete cell in London."

His words push through my fear, because I understand that. How many times have I felt like he and I are still trapped, social taboos and laws and our family's disapproval keeping us as firmly imprisoned as the Jailer and the Woman once did?

"I don't regret, tonight," he says. "I didn't intend for the media to notice us, but I don't even regret that. Okay?" He takes my chin and turns my head so that I have no choice but to look at him again.

"But what if they push the story? What if Daddy hears about it?" The idea of our relationship trending on Twitter scares the crap out of me. But not as much as the ire that will come down on us when our father gets wind of what is between me and Dallas.

"Then we'll deal," he says reasonably. "If it happens, we'll survive. We've survived worse, Jane. We've survived hell." He holds my gaze, his so tender I feel like weeping.

"Okay?" he asks gently.

I nod, and before I can add a spoken yes, he slants his mouth over mine, kissing me long and deep, making me forget my lingering fears. Soothing me. Saving me. Letting me lose myself in the pleasure of this man who has sworn so many times that he will always protect me.

He will, I know, and I melt gratefully into his arms for the short drive home.

When we arrive, we hurry up the steps, both of us wanting to get inside. Wanting to touch and kiss and finish this night lost in the warmth of each other's arms. I'm giddy as he unlocks the door and leads us through the main door to the small al-cove that doubles as a mudroom.

But my laughter fades when he stops cold and I slam against him, not expecting him to freeze so suddenly.

"Dallas, what's wrong?" I ask, but I don't need him to tell me. I see the answer well enough—a blue envelope sitting men-acingly on the floor. It's in a clear plastic bag and was obviously pushed through the mail slot. "Oh, shit. Here?" I ask as he bends to pick it up. "Oh, god, if she sent it here, then she must know about us, and—"

"No, it's okay." There is relief in Dallas's voice. "There's a messenger slip in the envelope. It came to the mansion. Archie sent it over."

"Oh." I'm ashamed at how relieved I am. I don't want Dallas receiving creepy stalker letters, but I really don't want the creepy stalker to out the two of us to the world.

"Come on," he says, leading us the rest of the way inside before opening the note.

I read over his shoulder, then murmur, "Bitch," as I see the words:

When will you understand? When will you touch me? When will you see that there is no woman except me? They are all just noise coming between us.

I meet Dallas's eyes. His are hard. Mine, I'm sure, are full of worry. "Give it to Liam," I say. "Tell him to pull out all the stops. You have to figure it out before she does something."

"You think she's unstable."

"I think she's a fucking nutcase," I admit, and I see Dallas's shoulders drop as he nods.

"Liam's on it," he says. "He doesn't think it's Fiona, by the way. She could have an excellent poker face, but he told me he didn't see even a hint of a reaction when he showed her the envelope in my room and led her out of the house."

"I already told you who I think it is. And Fiona's way too young to be the Woman."

He sighs. "I know." He pulls me into his arms, then kisses my forehead.

I cling to him. "If it is the Woman and she saw us together—" I tremble, because the Woman is one of the few people in the world who knows what Dallas and I are to each other.

Apparently Dallas is thinking along the same lines, because he asks if I noticed anyone watching us at the movie or at the Balcony.

"No one. You?"

He shakes his head, then kisses me again. "No more worrying about this tonight. Come on," he says, taking my hand. "I want to take you to bed."

I smile, forcing myself to shove aside all the fear and worry. "Do you?" I ask as we head for the stairs. "How very bold. And here I thought you were a gentleman."

"I am," he says. "I will absolutely make sure that you come first."

I burst out laughing, then pause on the stairs to look down at him. "I love you."

"Now who's being bold on a first date?"

"That would be me." I step down one so that I am right beside him. "By the way, Mr. Sykes, I intend to take advantage of you tonight."

"Oh, really?"

"Just fair warning. I'm going to use you. I'm going to take what I want." I smile, imagining all the delicious possibilities. "I just thought I should let you know."

16

Wrecked

Despite my bold pronouncement to take complete advantage of Dallas, we'd made love slowly and sweetly, then curled up in each other's arms. He never said a word about my apparently unfulfilled promise, and I hadn't mentioned it, either.

But I hadn't forgotten.

Now, I lay propped up beside him on an elbow, watching his eyes move behind his lids as he dreams. I'd dozed briefly as he'd slept, but then I'd climbed out of bed to go work a bit on my screenplay, too charged up emotionally to succumb to slumber.

Besides, I had a plan, and that required making sure that I didn't sleep through until morning.

Now, I'm back in bed and my plan is at the forefront of my thoughts.

Gently, I tug the sheet down, exposing all of him. He's semi-erect, and I smile to myself, wondering what he's dreaming and planning to make it so much better.

I stroke my hand over his belly, then watch as his body reacts. His muscles tighten in response to my touch. I'm gentle—

I'm not ready for him to wake up just yet—and I'm enjoying watching the pleasure of my touch work its way into his dreams.

He turns his head, his lips parting. And as my hand slides lower—as I press a gentle kiss to his breast and lick his nipple— I feel the movement in his hips and a tightening of the muscles throughout his body. I look down and see that he's harder now. Almost fully erect. And I hope that he's dreaming of me.

Slowly, I work kisses down his abdomen, along the trail of hair, and then I run my tongue along the length of his cock. He groans in his sleep, and I freeze for a moment, because I'm still not ready for him to wake. I told him that I was going to take what I wanted, and I meant it.

Tonight, I want his cock.

I smile as I move to straddle him. We've done this before, and I essentially told him I was going to do it again, so I feel perfectly justified in taking what I want—especially when I know that he wants it, too.

He's hard, so damn hard, and we fit together so perfectly. I sigh with pleasure as he fills me. As I raise and lower myself, taking him. Pumping him.

He feels it, too. I can tell by the incredible sensation of him inside me as well as by the way his body writhes beneath mine. He is close, and I think that if I can just take him all the way—if he will just come inside me even in this dreamland—then it will break the spell. Like the princess kissing the sleeping prince and waking him once more.

I think that I am succeeding. Beneath me, he begins to move more wildly, and just when I think that he is there, he opens his eyes and stares into mine.

I gasp because he is still hard, and for a moment I am overwhelmed with the power of everything that is between us. But that changes in an instant. He moves fast, rolling us over until he is on top of me and no longer inside of me. He yanks me to my feet, his hands clenching painfully tight around my upper arms.

I gasp, trying to read his expression, but he's not with me—I can see that clearly enough now. He's dreaming. He's fifteen. And I'm certain that in his dream he is doing exactly what I told him to do.

He is fighting.

He is fighting me.

With a groan, he slams me against the wall, one hand around my neck, the other between my legs. His expression is hard, his eyes wild, and I gasp, trying to breathe as he roughly spreads my legs and thrusts inside me, wild and untamed.

I'm scared—goddammit, I'm really and truly scared—but not of him. I'm scared of the dream. Of the fact that he doesn't see me. He sees her. The Woman. I know that he wants to hurt her. And right now, I don't know how far he will go.

I whimper as he tosses me back on the bed, as he forces me up on my knees, then tugs my arms behind me so that my shoulders feel ripped out of me and my weight is on my head. He still has me around the neck, and I'm completely unable to move, and he's inside me, thrusting hard. Not his cock, but his fingers, and he's lost in the intensity of the moment, so far gone with pain and fury that I can barely make out the words he mutters: *Bitch. Pain. Never again.*

I'm light-headed, and though part of me says I need to let him do this—I need to be the stand-in for the object of his rage—I cry out, the sound muffled because I can't draw air and the room is turning gray. A darker, colder fear washes over me and I force my name out, *Jane,* I cry. *I'm Jane.* But I don't even know if I've actually made sounds.

Then his grip loosens and he flips me over. His hand is still around my neck. He's still fucking me, thrusting deep. But now it's slower, more methodical. His eyes are still glazed, but I see the man I love behind the shadows, and when he whispers, *Mine,* I know that he sees me, too, even from somewhere in his dream.

With each thrust of his fingers, he's moving over my pelvis. Grinding himself against me. And I can see that he's close. I feel it when his body tenses, when he tightens his grip around my throat again, when he explodes over my belly, my breasts, and then throws his head back and groans.

For a moment, I think it's a victory, but when he opens his eyes and looks at me, all I see is horror.

Within seconds, he's released my neck. He leaps off the bed and is flat against the wall, his chest rising and falling. His eyes wide. His face so full of pain and self-loathing it breaks my heart.

I sit up, trying not to show how sore I am. How hard it is to breathe. "Dallas," I say, but he holds up his hand as if he can't stand the sound of his name.

I don't silence myself though. "It's okay," I say. "I told you to. You didn't hurt me. I consented. A hundred times, a thousand times. I wanted this. You needed it."

"Needed to fucking *rape* you?" His voice is thick, and I think he is on the verge of breaking down.

"You didn't," I repeat. "I wanted it. I told you."

"I could have hurt you."

"I'm right here. I'm not hurt."

"No." He shakes his head, then brings his hands up and squeezes his skull. "God, no. What the fuck? This isn't—I can't. *Fuck.*"

His eyes find me. "I was a fool," he says, his voice low. "We can't ever have normal. We can't ever be normal. I'm a danger to you. Physically. Emotionally. And I can't do this. I can't stay with you and watch myself destroy what I love most in the world."

He starts for the door.

"Dallas!" I call, but he just keeps going. And he doesn't look back.

My body aches to go after him, but I hold myself still, clutching tight to the sheets as if to anchor me. I tell myself that he just needs time. After all, that was seriously intense.

I tell myself that, but I'm not convinced. Because I know that he believes that tonight is proof that he can't do normal, whatever the fuck that is. That at his core he's a man who needs pain. Who needs danger. Who needs to hurt to get off and, maybe, needs to be hurt, too.

The one thing that Dallas has consistently told me throughout all of our life together is that he will protect me, no matter what it takes.

Right now, I know, he thinks to protect me he has to leave me.

And I have no idea how to convince him otherwise.

I stay curled up in bed, alternating between dozing and crying, until almost noon. Then I can't take it any longer. I have to talk to him. He may need time, but I need to hear his voice, and right now, my need is the one that's winning.

I hit the speed dial for Dallas, then hold my breath as I wait for him to answer. And wait.

And wait.

And wait.

Then I get voicemail.

Shit.

I don't bother leaving a message. Instead, I call the house line, which Mrs. Foster answers on the first ring.

"Hey there, sweetheart," she says, as soon as I say hello.

"I didn't realize you were back," I say.

"Just an hour ago."

I grin. "And naturally, you're already dug in and putting the house back to rights."

"Now don't you say that like you're surprised," she retorts, making me laugh outright.

"Fair enough. I'm not surprised at all. But I was hoping to speak to Dallas. He must be away from his cell. Can you grab him for me?"

"Of course I can. You just hold on for a second."

She means that literally, and hold music starts to play, and when it clicks off, I expect to hear Dallas come on the line, so I'm completely surprised to hear, "Miss Jane. What can I help you with?"

"Archie? I—I thought Mrs. Foster was getting Dallas."

"I'm afraid he's not available right now."

"Not available," I repeat, as cold chills race up my spine, caused as much by my own fear as by the stark, unfamiliar formality of Archie's voice. "Did he ask you to say that to me?"

"Miss Jane . . ."

I close my eyes in defense against the truth that I hear now in Archie's voice. The warm, paternal voice that used to comfort me and put Bactine and bandages on my skinned knees.

"If you want to leave a message—I'm sure he just needs some time to get back to you."

"No." I'm fighting not to cry. "No, that's okay."

I hang up. I actually hang up on Archie, and then I realize that my knees are weak, and that's because I'm not breathing. I'm too busy choking on the tears caught in my throat to catch my breath.

I slide down the cabinets until my ass is on the tile and my back is against the wood, and I'm holding my phone tight and feeling lost and needing Dallas.

But Dallas isn't here for me—and god only knows when he will be again.

Oh, shit. Oh, fuck.

Maybe he really is going to walk away from me. Maybe he wants us to go back to the way we used to be, desperately wanting each other, but not having. Not touching. Hardly ever even seeing each other because it was just too damn painful to be together and not give in to passion.

I would hate him for that—and he damn well knows that.

But Dallas would rather I hate him than hurt me, and the more I think about it, the more I fear that this is the end.

That he is going to leave me in order to save me.

But all that will really do is destroy me.

I have to do something—I have to get through to him somehow. I have to make him see me—really *see* me—and believe me when I tell him that I can handle whatever he needs.

But I don't know how to do that. I'm lost, so damn lost.

And I can think of only one person who can help me find my way.

Brody.

I pull on loose-fitting jeans and a Moschino T-shirt and tie my hair back in a messy ponytail. I jam my feet into a pair of ratty Converse skids, grab my purse, and head out into the real world. The sun is bright, the clouds are fluffy, and the temperature is pleasant in the low seventies. It's an absolutely gorgeous day—and I'm not enjoying it at all. Instead, I'm on auto-pilot. Standing in the street. Hailing a cab. Closing my eyes and letting the rhythm of the vehicle soothe me as the taxi speeds toward the Village.

Except, of course, I'm not sootheable at all.

I pay, get out, and then climb the stairs to the main door of Brody's building. He and Stacey rent the entire third floor of the converted townhouse, along with the roof garden that's accessed by a private staircase. I'm about to ring the bell when the door opens and Stacey says, "Oh!"

"Sorry. I didn't mean to startle you." She's wearing workout gear and carrying a gym bag. "Is Brody—I mean, is it okay if I go in?"

She studies my face, and I'm sure she can see that I've been crying. "Of course you can. He was in the shower when I left, but he'll be out soon. There's coffee in the kitchen and some croissants in a bag. Make yourself at home."

I'm eating a chocolate croissant when Brody comes into the

kitchen wearing absolutely nothing. And, with the kind of aplomb that is so very Brody, he doesn't even blink when he sees me sitting there.

I, of course, am completely flustered.

"Oh, please," he says, dropping into a seat opposite me at the table. "Like you haven't seen my junk before."

"But now your junk belongs to Stacey."

He shrugs. "And yet I still rent it out."

I roll my eyes. Brody may be a professional dom, but he's also my best friend. And I happen to know that he's very limited in the clients that he actual fucks. Still, there are a few. And Stacey is actually cool with that, which impresses the hell out of me.

Right now, I'm just glad that he's seated. He's still shirtless, but at least the rest of him is hidden from view.

"Considering the early hour, I'm guessing this is either the apocalypse or you're still having Dallas issues."

"It damn sure feels like the apocalypse," I admit, then cringe when an unexpected tear trickles down my cheek.

"Oh, kiddo, I'm sorry." He reaches across and squeezes my hand. "Tell me."

I start to do exactly that—and then I realize that in order for Brody to give me the advice I crave, I have to tell him everything. I have to share my secrets. More to the point, I have to share Dallas's.

I take a breath. "I need to tell you some things. Lots of things. But they're private—even more than what you already know about—but I need help." I lick my lips. "I—I thought about talking to one of my therapists, but this is—it's sex. Except it's more than sex. And I—"

"Hey, whatever you need. You know I won't break your confidence."

I nod, because I do know that.

"So tell me what's going on."

I try to gather my thoughts. Brody already knows a bit of what happened during our captivity. He knows that Dallas and I were together, and he knows that Dallas was tortured. But he doesn't know the extent of it—hell, I only just learned that myself. He doesn't know that Dallas is afraid of physically hurting me. And he doesn't know that Dallas hasn't been able to penetrate a woman since he and I were fifteen.

But he needs to know all of that if he's going to really help me. So I grab another coffee, sit back down, and start at the beginning.

When I finish, Brody looks a little shell-shocked, which says a lot about how fucked up everything is with Dallas and me. Because Brody has seen a lot.

"And now you're afraid it's over?" he asks. "Because of the way he freaked out and left."

I nod. Then I shake my head. Then I nod again. "I guess I'm afraid that what I thought was the beginning was really just us ending with a bang."

Brody leans back, his arms crossed over his chest as he studies me.

"I'm scared," I admit.

He nods slowly. And then he leans forward and puts his elbows on his knees, never taking his eyes off me. "Bullshit," he says, and the word is so unexpected that I shift to sit more upright. "Yeah, I said bullshit."

"What the fuck?"

"You're not scared. At least, you're not scared of it ending. You're scared of where it's going. Of how hard it might be. You're confused because he's not acting according to script and you don't know what to make of that."

I hug myself. "No, I—"

"Oh, come on, Jane. You're vulnerable; I get that. And maybe you two really are sliding backward, but backward doesn't mean it's over, just that there's more work to be done." He reaches out and takes my hands. "Listen, kid. As hard as it was for you seventeen years ago, it was even harder for him, right? And everything you two do together brings it all back for him. There's a connection in his mind between you and that place. That time. That torture. He's used to that—hell, he's even been handling it in his own way. Then you go and suggest that he put you in the role of the woman who tortured him and, yeah, that's gonna fuck anyone up."

I nod slowly, because he's right.

"And except for this hitch, you two were moving forward, right?"

"Yeah. We've stumbled a bit, sure. But this is the first time I've been really scared."

"So, that's good. That's progress."

"I guess so." I frown. "Except he's been holding back all along, keeping me on that damn pedestal. I mean, we still haven't done anything in the playroom," I add, referring to a converted maid's room in my townhouse.

His brows rise. "Well, that was a huge waste of my considerable talents." After Brody told me in confidence that he knew that Dallas belonged to a kink club called The Cellar, I'd had him help me redo the room with a BDSM flair in an effort to convince Dallas that he could trust me to go with him as far as he needed.

Apparently that's a battle I'm still fighting.

"So what do I do?" I press. "I love him. And I'm so damned afraid I'm going to lose him."

"Like I've said all along, you have to prove to him you can handle it. That you can take whatever he gives."

"And like I've been saying all along, I've been trying. So far, not succeeding."

"Honestly, kiddo. I'm not sure what the best approach is. But I'd start by going to The Cellar."

"Seriously?"

"Hell yeah. If you go and tell him you're there to play, I promise you he'll show up, if only to keep you away from anyone else."

"But I wouldn't do anything with anyone else. And he knows it."

Brody lifts a shoulder. "Knowing it and *knowing* it are two different things. He'll come."

I nod. About that, Brody's probably right.

"You need to make it clear that even though he's the one in control, he won't hurt you. Pick a safe word. I can't guarantee it would have made a difference, but if you'd yelled a safe word— something offbeat—I bet it would have crashed through his dream, zen state, whatever the fuck it was. And if he knows you're thinking in those terms—"

"Then maybe he'll understand that I can handle it. That I want to handle it."

"Maybe." He sighs. "Honestly, this is out of my league. But that's my best advice. We're not talking a normal dom/sub relationship, here. You get that, right? This is all Dallas. All pain and past, and I don't really have a road map for you."

"I know. I don't need a map. I just need—I don't know, I guess I just need help."

"I'll always give you that in spades."

"I know. And I love you for it." I exhale, then nod. "Okay. So, back to The Cellar. Do I just . . . show up?"

"I'll arrange it for you. And I'll make sure you two have a private room available, too, because—hang on." He tilts his head, obviously considering something. "You know what? I take it back. Forget The Cellar."

"What? Why?"

"This is not a man who wants to share you, and we already know he's afraid of freaking you out or humiliating you."

I lean forward, listening. "Go on."

"Dallas wants the kink, sure. Hell, he needs it. But he doesn't want to need it. And he sure as hell doesn't like that he wants it. He goes to the club to fill a need, not because he likes it there or is comfortable being there."

I nod, because all of that rings true. "So where does that leave me?"

"You need privacy. And we've already set up pretty much what you need back in your townhouse."

"Except I told you that he seems entirely uninterested in christening that room. And, honestly, after the way he bolted from me, how the hell would I get him in there, anyway? I mean, after last night, I'm not sure he'll set foot in my house again."

Brody's grin is devious. "Oh, I can get him there. He may end up being pissed as hell and a little freaked out, but I think you can manage him."

"Pissed and freaked?" I repeat, then widen my eyes when I realize what Brody's thinking.

I almost start to protest, but then I close my mouth tight. It just might work. And, honestly, I'm desperate enough to try anything.

17

Master of Illusion

Dallas pretty much hated himself. Worse, he was damn sure that Jane hated him, too.

He was a fucking mess, and it's a wonder she didn't just kick him in the balls. He sure as hell deserved it.

With a groan, he bent forward and lowered his head, letting the spray from the shower pound against his aching back, wishing that it could wash away all his mistakes.

His body ached as he remembered the way she'd felt on top of him, his cock hard inside her warmth. But he'd only been half there. The rest of him lost in a dream.

A dream of darkness. And torment.

A dream where he was at her mercy—Jane's, the Woman—it didn't matter because in the dream they'd been all mixed up. They'd been one. They'd been taunting him, torturing him, *using* him.

The first time he'd awakened to find himself hard and inside of Jane was like a fantasy come true. It had rocked him to the core, and the way she had taken control had aroused him so fully that for the first time he had hope that he might actually be able to finish inside her.

And now the memory of the Woman was destroying that pleasure. Taking something he cherished and turning it around on him, twisting it up now, seventeen years later, just like she'd done when he was a boy.

Fucking bitch.

He couldn't take it any longer. He couldn't live with the memories. With the fear. He couldn't live knowing what she'd done to him.

And all he could hear was Jane's words in his head. *She took control? Take it back.*

Well, fuck if that wasn't exactly what he'd tried to do.

Except it wasn't the Woman who was riding him. It wasn't the Woman he'd tossed to the ground, slammed against the wall. A damp concrete wall, hidden away in an underground fortress.

It wasn't the Woman he'd grabbed by the throat, holding her tight—so damn tight—as he'd thrust his fingers hard inside of her. Claiming her. Taming her. Proving that it was he who held fast to control.

It wasn't the Woman he was punishing. It wasn't a cell he was inhabiting.

It was Jane. It was her bedroom.

But he hadn't stopped. Goddamn him, he'd kept holding her. He'd kept fucking her. He wanted to claim her, needed to have her. Completely. Fully. Needed to know that she meant it when she said she would go with him as far as he wanted to go.

Then he'd looked at her—really seen her. More than that, he'd really seen himself. His hand on her throat. The brutality with which he was taking her.

He'd thrown himself off her, then scrambled back, horrified, leaving her to sag to the floor, limp and coughing.

She'd told him it was okay. She'd told him that she was fine.

But he knew better.

It wasn't okay.

And so long as she was with a guy as fucked up as he was, she wouldn't ever be fine.

Once again, he closed his eyes, then shivered as he realized the water in the shower had gone cold.

With a curse, he turned off the water, then pushed open the door and reached for a towel. He was wrapping it around his hips when Archie's voice crackled over the intercom.

"Liam is here. He's waiting for you in the ops center."

"Thanks." His voice was hoarse, and he realized he'd been crying.

Well, why wouldn't he have been? First he'd lost himself. Then he'd lost Jane.

God only knew what he'd lose next.

Dallas paused outside the door to the op center, breathing deep, trying to erase any last hint of Jane from his face. It wouldn't work, of course. Jane was part of him and always would be, even if he knew damn well that walking away from her was for the best.

It was—he was certain of it. But right now he wasn't in the mood to justify his decision to Liam. They needed to focus on Deliverance. On Colin.

And he didn't need his best friend to tell him what he already knew—that Dallas and Jane were meant to be together, and it was only his own goddamn inability to get his shit together that was keeping them apart.

Maybe if he found the Woman. Maybe if he could fucking erase her then he could erase his fears and needs, too.

Or maybe he'd sprout wings and fly over the Statue of Liberty. Because that seemed about as likely.

Forcing himself to focus, he took a deep breath, punched in the code to unlock the door, and strode into the ops center.

Liam looked up, waving from where he stood in front of one of the computer screens talking to Noah and Quince, whose faces peered out from the monitors.

"So that's the plan, then," Quince said. "I've got a briefing in the prime minister's office in an hour, but Noah and I will get going on our end." His eyes cut to Dallas. "Good to see you, mate. Liam can get you up to speed."

"Sounds good," Dallas agreed, as Noah said his goodbyes, too, and the monitors winked to black.

"So what's the plan?"

"We're going to send Colin anonymous texts from a burner phone. Vague, but suggesting we know his secret. With luck, it'll spur him to action."

Dallas nodded, considering. "Ballsy. But dangerous, too."

"True. But we need to make a play. After seventeen years, he's not doing anything that's going to spontaneously lead us back to the kidnapping."

"I've been thinking along the same lines, actually. Thought I'd mention my conversation with Bill when I'm at Colin's for dinner. Let him know that WORR and a few agencies are investigating the Sykes kidnapping."

Liam nodded. "I like it."

"Assuming he's really our guy, either the texts or Bill's investigation could spur him into making a move. But we're also running a risk that he'll destroy any remaining evidence. We need more eyes on him."

"Already on it," Liam said. "He makes a move, we follow. Noah's going to pull Tony in for additional surveillance."

Dallas considered the ramifications, then nodded. "It's solid. Risky, but it may pan out."

"I damn sure hope so. And we'll also have the intel from the bugs you're going to plant, so let's talk about how that's going to go down."

"Should be easy enough. The point of the dinner is to show off the remodel of the house Colin bought in Brooklyn Heights."

"So you can wander freely and praise the woodwork and casually mention Bill's investigation."

"That's my plan," Dallas said. "I just wish Jane wasn't going to be there."

Liam frowned. "Why is she?"

"Adele invited her. So it's going to be one big happy family, and I'll have to plant the bugs without Colin or either of the women noticing."

"Easy enough for a crack spy like you."

Dallas rolled his eyes, and Liam sank down into one of the rolling desk chairs, then pushed backward a bit before kicking his feet out and studying Dallas. "So what's the real reason you don't want Jane there? Because it's Colin? Or because you still haven't told her everything she wants to know about Deliverance?"

"Both," Dallas said. "Neither. Shit, man—everything is such a clusterfuck right now."

Liam rolled his chair closer. "Tell me," he said. And despite everything Dallas had told himself earlier, he heard himself saying, "I hurt her. Goddammit, Liam, I had her slammed against the wall with my hand around her neck and I fucking hurt her."

To his credit, Liam didn't push himself up out of his chair and bash Dallas's brains in. Instead he said, very slowly and carefully, "I think you need to back up, buddy. Back up and tell me exactly what happened. And while you're at it, I think you need to tell me why."

It wasn't easy. Christ, it was one of the hardest things he'd ever done. To tell his best friend the way he'd been tormented as a teen by that fucking bitch. To explain his screwed up, violent, horrible fantasies. The kink he was into. Everything he craved with Jane.

He told Liam that Jane had said she could handle it, but he'd never fully believed her. Hell, he even told Liam about the play-room she'd had built in one of the old maids' rooms in her townhouse, part of a last-ditch effort to convince him that she meant what she said.

And then, worst of all, he actually confessed to his best friend that he hadn't penetrated a woman since he was fifteen.

"Wow," Liam said, blinking and looking a bit like he was in shock. "You really are badass. All those women saying you've fucked them."

"Yeah, I'm just like David Copperfield. Master of illusion."

"And seriously screwed up, too."

And despite the hell he'd just put himself through, Dallas broke down and laughed. "Thanks," he said. "Thanks a lot."

Liam waved it away. "I don't mean your angst or your cock. I mean that all this really is messing with your head if you're telling it to me."

"It is," Dallas admitted, running his fingers through his hair. "And I haven't even told you everything about last night." He did now, though. About the intense sexual violence of his dreams. About Jane taking advantage of his erection. About the way he'd taken her, not realizing it was her. And then had kept on going when his senses returned, wanting to claim her. Needing to know if she could go with him as far as she'd said.

"And that's why you don't want her at Colin's? You don't think you can be around her right now?"

"Honestly, I'm more concerned that she'll be okay seeing me. What I did to her . . . the way I just took her . . . Christ, I'm such an ass."

"An ass? Maybe. But you're also dense and blind."

"What the hell?"

"Are you even looking at her?" Liam demanded. "Are you

listening to her? Or are you believing whatever the hell you want to believe and seeing what you think you should see?"

Before Dallas could speak, his friend continued. "You're embarrassed and scared and yeah, maybe you have a right to be worried, but you're the one who ran, dude. Not Jane. Do you really believe she doesn't want to see you? That she doesn't believe you two can get past this? I mean, hell. She told you she could deal. Maybe you ought to do her the courtesy of believing her."

Dallas's stomach twisted, because Liam was right. He remembered her words from before they'd committed to being together. She'd said that he had her on a pedestal when she shouldn't be. She swore that his darkness didn't scare her. More important, she said it wouldn't break her.

He'd told himself he believed her, but he hadn't. Not really. She would always be on a pedestal to him. She would always be the one true thing in his life.

But maybe Liam was right. Maybe she could be both.

Hell, maybe she had to be. Because if she couldn't be right down there in the dark with the real Dallas—with all his screwups and faults and fucked up needs—how could she be his truth?

"Dallas, man? You gonna answer me this century?"

"Sorry." He drew in a breath. "I do want to get past this. Hell, I want everything with her. But the real bottom line is that I don't want to hurt her. I can't live with myself if I hurt her."

"No? What do you think walking away from her did?"

"I thought I was protecting her."

"Yeah? Well, that was—"

"Bullshit," Dallas finished. "Yeah. I get it. I screwed up."

"Big time. Doesn't do you a whole lot of good to bolt. I mean seriously, man, I thought you had bigger balls than that."

"She brings me to my knees, Liam."

Liam nodded. "I know she does. And I'm happy for you. Not

sure I could handle being so ripped up by a woman, but I get that you love her. And god knows I've spent enough time with you two to know you're meant to be together."

"So what should I do?"

"Talk to her. Figure it out together. And in the meantime, you litter her birth father's house with electronic listening devices."

Despite himself, Dallas chuckled. "And there's problem number 7,536 we have to get past."

Liam laughed. "You already told me that part will be a piece of cake." He stood. "And one last thing. I'm going to give you the same advice about Jane that I'll give you about me. Stop keeping shit from us."

"You're saying I should tell her about Colin?"

"Hell no. That shit you hide. At least until we're certain. One way or the other."

Dallas met Liam's eyes. "Let's hope for the other."

"No kidding, man."

They were walking out together when Dallas's phone pinged to signal an incoming text. "Jane," he said, glancing at the screen. "She says, 'Look.' "

Liam glanced at him. "What the fuck?"

Dallas frowned. "There's a picture attached. Hang on." He opened it, then froze.

"Holy shit," Liam said, obviously looking over his shoulder and seeing exactly what Dallas saw. Jane, and she was chained spread-eagled to a bed with a blindfold covering her eyes and clamps tight on her nipples.

Fear—cold and icy—cut through Dallas.

"Is there another message?" Liam asked. "A ransom demand? Someone sent this from her phone, but who the fuck would have—"

"*Wait.*" Dallas held up a hand, trying to think. Something about this was familiar. Something that eased his fear even though it didn't quell it. "Wait," he repeated. "This room. This room, it's—oh, fuck," he said, turning back to Liam. "This is the room she had built in her house."

"The playroom you just told me about?"

Dallas nodded.

"So someone's holding her in the townhouse?"

"I don't think so," Dallas said slowly. "I think she's baiting me."

Liam met his eyes. "You think she'd go that far?"

"Don't you?"

Liam hesitated, then nodded. "Yeah, I think she would. So what are you going to do?"

Dallas didn't even hesitate. "I'm taking the bait. I can't risk the possibility that we're wrong. And more than that, like you said, she and I need to talk."

"And right now," Liam said with a smirk, "at least she's a captive audience."

18

Fight Me, Fuck Me

I know that Brody is just upstairs, but it doesn't matter. I'm alone in here. In the dark.

The room isn't soundproofed, but it might as well be. I can hear nothing except my own breathing, which is growing more and more rapid the longer I lay here, tied down on this bed, unable to move, unable to do anything except remember—and hope beyond hope that Dallas is coming.

I'd thought this was a good idea. That by laying myself out like this he might finally, *hopefully,* understand that's what I truly am to him. An offering. I'm offering myself up to him. My hopes, my dreams, my body, my life. I'm his, and he's mine, and I just want him to finally get that. To embrace it. To love me so fully and completely that we go with each other as far as we can and need, no barriers, no qualms, no fears.

That's my dream—and I want it so badly it's palpable. But right now, that dream is shifting and moving. It's twisting. Knotting up inside me.

It's becoming a goddamn nightmare, and that is something that I didn't expect when I'd committed to this crazy plan.

Mentally, I know that I only have to scream and Brody will come release me. But emotionally I'm sliding back through the years. I'm in a dark room. I'm tied down.

I'm fifteen again, and I'm terrified.

Terrified that I will never get out of this place. That she will leave me here to starve. That she will never take me back to Dallas.

That Dallas will never find me here in the dark. That he is gone from me for good.

That he won't come for me.

That he won't forgive me for pushing him.

That I'll be bound here forever. Trapped here forever. Lost in this place between then and now.

This was a mistake, I think, as the tempo of my heart increases. I should never have let Brody tie me up. I should never have surrendered control. This was supposed to be about Dallas, but right now—like this—I don't know if I can take it anymore. The fears. The memories.

I feel like ants are crawling on me. Like the dark is turning red. And though I struggle against the bonds, I can't loosen them. On the contrary, everything is tightening. My wrists, my ankles. And I finally can't take any more of it and I open my mouth to shout for Brody—only it's Dallas's name that comes off my lips when I hear the door crash open. And it's Dallas's face that I see when the blindfold is ripped off my face.

Dallas, looking scared to death and pissed as hell.

Dallas froze in the doorway, tossed back seventeen years as he saw the terror reflected on her beautiful face. Then he rushed to her and ripped off that damn blindfold.

"Jane," he cried. "Jesus, Jane, who did this to you?"

"Dallas." Tears streamed down her face. "I—I got mixed up. It felt like I was back then, and I was afraid you wouldn't come to me. That they wouldn't let you come to me."

"I will always come for you, baby." He pulled off his T-shirt and covered her with it, certain she must be cold. "But you have to tell me what happened. Who did this to you?"

She was breathing better now. The wildness in her eyes fading. She turned her head to meet his eyes. "You did."

The words hit him like a slap. "What the hell are you talking about?"

"You pushed away from me, Dallas. I had to get you back."

He shoved back off the bed, her words like a blow. "Oh, Jesus, Jane. Christ. You were terrified when I came through that door. And now you're telling me there's no one else. This is all on you?"

She didn't say anything, but he saw the truth in her eyes. And damned if he wasn't sure if he was incredibly relieved or entirely pissed off.

Either way, he pulled out his phone, then dialed Liam. "You can stand down. We were right. There's no perp."

"Glad to hear it. Give her a hug for me."

"After I spank the shit out of her, I just might do that."

He heard Liam's chuckle before the line went dead, then he pocketed his phone and strode to the head of the bed and unfastened the ropes that held her wrists before repeating the process with her ankles.

She sat up, the cuffs still around her wrists, the ropes still dangling from them. The T-shirt was pooled in her lap, and her bare breasts combined with the restraints spread around her on the bed made a damned enticing picture. And despite the fact that he was pissed as hell, he felt his body tighten with desire. For Jane—always for Jane—but also for the idea of Jane here. In this room. This sensual playroom that she'd put together for him, but that they'd never once used.

He pushed it aside.

Enticing or not, he was too damn angry. "What the hell were you thinking?" he asked, pacing beside the bed.

She watched him, her head moving as she followed him. "What was *I* thinking? Maybe that I didn't know how to get through to you? That the only way to get you to actually listen and to hear me and not just run away because you think you've freaked me out, is to prove to you that it's okay."

"Okay?" he repeated, glancing around the room as he remembered the way he'd hurt her after he'd awakened inside her. "This is okay? You tied up? Me using you? Me taking you however the fuck I want? Me losing control because I'm too fucked up to hold back? Possibly hurting you? Probably scaring you? Is that what you're saying is okay?"

"Yes," she whispered, rising up on her knees and holding out her hands for him. "But say the rest of it. Say what it is you're afraid of."

He shoved his hands in his pockets. "I'm not having you play shrink, Jane. Not happening."

"Fine. Then I'll say it. It's more than just possibly hurting me—and guess what, I don't care. And it's more than just possibly scaring me, because you won't. But none of that really matters, because that's not what's really scaring you."

He swallowed, wanting to argue. To back away. But he didn't. Because, dammit, she was right.

"What you're really afraid of is that if you scare me—if you hurt me—that you're going to lose me." She rose up and got off the bed, trailing bondage ropes as she moved to stand in front of him, naked now that the T-shirt had fallen to the floor. "Well, you won't."

"You don't know that."

She didn't argue—he had to give her credit for that. Instead, she just reached out and slapped him hard across the face.

"What the fuck?"

"I don't know that?" she countered. "The hell I don't. And if you don't believe me, then fucking let me prove it to you. Take me, Dallas. Use me. That's why I'm here. That's why I brought you here."

"You don't even know what you're asking for."

"So you say," she taunted. She rose up onto her toes, all defiance and heat and so intense it made him want to lay her out and fuck her blind. "Show me."

And goddammit, he broke. He shouldn't. He should just walk away. But even as he told himself that, he was yanking her back to the bed. Positioning her on her knees. There was a hook extending from the ceiling at just the right height—the handiwork of her friend Brody, no doubt—and he lifted her wrists and slid the buckles of the cuffs over the hooks so that she was on her knees, her torso stretched tall. He considered spreading her legs and strapping her ankles to the sides of the bed, but decided against it. He wanted her somewhat mobile.

He reached down for the blindfold that he'd ripped away, then put it back over her eyes. He saw the way she bit her lower lip, but dammit, he wasn't showing her mercy. Not now. Not when she'd pushed him this far to take what he wanted.

And he was going to, dammit. He was going to take and keep taking, because if she ran the way he thought she would, he at least wanted this last memory to cling to.

"Dallas," she whispered, but he just pressed his finger to her lips. "No talking unless I say you can. Nod if you understand." She nodded, and he gave the chain that connected the nipple clamps a quick, sharp tug, making her cry out.

Good.

He slid off the bed and circled the room, glancing at the various items on display. He selected a small glass butt plug, some lube, and a leather flail. Then he returned to the bed and slid his hand between her legs. She was wet, and some of his fear and anger slipped away, pushed aside by his increasing desire and, yes, by hope.

He turned her around, then slid his finger from her cunt to her ass, teasing her and eliciting all sorts of soft sounds that made her moan. Then he lubed up the plug and, without telling her what he intended to do, spread her cheeks and slid it in, using one hand to manipulate the plug, and reaching around with the other to tug on the chain, tightening the pressure on her tits as he teased her ass.

She gasped, then moaned. And then, god help him, she squirmed in pleasure, and when he slipped his fingers inside her cunt and softly stroked her clit, she exploded around him, her muscles clenching around his fingers as a powerful orgasm rocked through her.

He kept his fingers inside her, but with his other hand he reached down to stroke his cock. He was rock hard, thrilled at how responsive she was. At how much she wanted it—everything he did to her. And he could do so much more. He looked around the room. The chains and hooks on the wall. The leather flails and crops and whips. All sorts of toys and devices, from relatively tame to incredibly intense.

He'd wanted that when he'd first released her—when he'd realized the way that she was pushing him. He'd wanted to push back. To lay marks across her back as he whipped her. To clamp her clit and watch as she writhed, working first through pain and then off into pleasure, totally at his mercy. Completely under his control.

He still wanted it—and so much more. But only when she was ready. And, yes, he believed that she would go there with him. But not as punishment. Not as a way to prove a point. But as an exploration. He'd take her down with him—damned if she hadn't convinced him.

Right now, though, he just wanted to give her pleasure. And, yes, he wanted to take his pleasure with her.

Slowly, he stripped. Then, naked, he got up on the bed and released her from the hook. Then he put her hands behind her and fastened the cuffs together before taking her by the hair and guiding her mouth to his cock. He wanted to be close to exploding when he fucked her—because, dammit, he was going to be inside her.

She took him deeply, eagerly, and he closed his eyes, his hand on her hair guiding her as his mind drifted back to another room like this one. Another woman's mouth on him. He'd fantasized about Jane then, and hated himself for it. Hated that the Woman was mixing Jane up in her vile game. But now that it was real—Christ, he wanted it. Wanted everything he could take from her. Everything she could give.

And as she gave, he felt the nightmarish memory slip away, losing power to the new reality. A reality he wanted. Craved. A reality that *he* controlled.

"Baby," he said as his body tightened. As he came just to the edge. But he couldn't go over. That much, he hadn't gotten back. For that matter, he didn't want it. He wanted to be inside her, and he roughly pushed her off him, then turned her over.

Her hands were still behind her, so that she was on her shoulders, her ass in the air as he thrust hard inside her, the pressure from the plug making her even tighter, and adding to her own pleasure when he pushed hard against her, his body pounding into her as he thrust deeper and deeper, wanting everything, wanting the explosion.

Harder and faster. And he hadn't lost it. He was inside her, fucking her, and damned if it wasn't incredible. Damned if he didn't feel like he could last forever.

Again and again they moved together, his erection never waning, his desire rising and rising. And although she was taking all of it—all of him—he still couldn't climax. He was right there on the edge, but he still couldn't fucking explode.

He pulled out of her, then rolled her over, his cock in one hand as he used the other to pull off her blindfold. He wanted to see her face. He wanted to look into her eyes as he jerked off. As he came on her belly, her cunt. He wanted to cherish the way she moaned. The light that cut through her as he shattered in front of her.

He wanted to drown in the pleasure that he could see was so goddamn genuine.

"How?" he asked when the tremors of his orgasm faded. "How can I need you so much?"

Her mouth curved. "The same way that I need you."

"Oh, baby." He was exhausted. Mentally. Physically. Slowly, he moved beside her, then unclipped her wrists. He pulled her close and kissed her forehead. "I'm sorry," he said.

She sat up, looking alarmed, and he laughed, then kissed her. "No, not for this. I'm not sorry for this at all. Although I am a little bit sorry that I held back. You could go with me a lot further."

"Yes," she said. "I can."

"One day," he promised, and was rewarded with her very genuine-sounding sigh of pleasure.

"So what are you sorry for?"

"For not believing you. Not trusting you to know your own limits."

She propped herself up on her elbow. "Just like secrets, Dallas. You have to trust I know what I can handle. What I want."

He nodded. What could he say? She was right.

She curled up against him and sighed. "You do know what I want, don't you?"

"Why don't you tell me?"

"You," she said simply.

He felt the smile touch his lips. "Baby, I'm already yours."

19

Happy Hour

I am deliciously sore—wonderfully fucked—and as a result I'm having one hell of a hard time paying attention to anything that Henry Darcy is saying.

"Don't you think?" he asks, and I curse myself and Dallas and my wandering mind.

"I'm sorry, Henry." I smile brightly. "I was trying to catch the waitress's eye and didn't hear what you said."

"Just that it's nice to get out of the office sometimes. Usually I lunch in. But when a beautiful young lady wants to interview me, how can I turn down such an invitation?"

"I'm really glad you didn't," I say as our waitress approaches. "You should try the yellow curry," I tell him. "It's basic, but delicious."

He takes my advice and we both order, and as soon as the waitress is gone, I start to chat him up about the kidnapping. I've done a lot of interviews—I've been writing articles about kidnappings for years, and I've researched two books—but I've never done research for a dual purpose the way that I am right now. Because with Darcy, I'm interested in how one goes about contacting a vigilante organization for my own research, and also in how Darcy heard the name Deliverance, so I can report back to Dallas and the team.

As for the first, when my phone rings, Darcy is telling me that he was initially clueless about how to contact a vigilante group, but—speak of the devil—it was my brother who helped him out in that regard. He nods to my phone, sitting buzzing on the table, Dallas's name larger than life on the screen.

I ignore it. "Dallas knows how to contact vigilante groups?"

"Oh, not exactly." He frowns at the phone. "Should you get that?"

I scowl, then pick up the phone. "Hey. What's up?"

"Are you on speaker?"

"No."

"Then it's okay for me to say how much I want to rip every stitch of clothing off you and bury my face between your legs?"

My entire body starts to burn and I clear my throat, hoping that Henry can't somehow sense the sudden spike in my temperature.

"Actually," I manage to say, "now's not the best time. I'm in the middle of a research lunch. With someone you know, actually."

"You're with Darcy."

"Exactly."

"I haven't had lunch yet. I could come join you. Listen to what he has to say. Slide my finger into your pussy under the table. He'd never even know."

I force myself not to squirm, then smile at Darcy as I tell Dallas, "I really don't think that's a good idea."

"On the contrary, I think it's an excellent one. Admit it, baby. Admit that the thought of me touching you in a crowded restaurant turns you on. That getting away with something so naughty excites you. Tell me," he prods. "Tell me you'd like that."

I clear my throat and squeeze my thighs together. "Actually, yeah, I'd like that," I say, as if he's offered to help clean my attic. "But I'm guessing that's not why you called." I turn my attention to Darcy. "Sorry. Sometimes my brother has trouble getting to the point."

He chuckles. "You like it when I don't get to the point right away. And the reason I called was to tell you I was thinking of you."

"Oh." I can't help but smile. "Well, me, too."

"You're working all day?"

"Yes. After lunch I'm going back to type up my notes."

"My schedule's pretty clear this afternoon. I should be done by six. Meet me at the Strand kiosk at six-fifteen," he says, referring to the permanent bookstore kiosk on Fifth Avenue.

"Need some new reading material?"

"Just be there," he says and hangs up.

I bite back a scowl, then smile at Darcy. "Sorry about that."

"Fascinating man, your brother."

"You could say that," I agree. "But getting back to the kidnapping. You were saying that it was actually Dallas who helped you find a private team to hire?"

Darcy nods, then sits back as the waiter brings our curry. "We had a business meeting scheduled not long after my girls were taken." His voice hitches as he speaks. "I remember I had canceled it, but Dallas showed up at my house anyway. Said he figured I needed an ear. He was right, of course."

"And he just happened to suggest you hire vigilantes?"

Darcy laughs. "I don't remember how it came up, but I do know that I couldn't get the thought of hiring someone out of my head. I just—I didn't have confidence in the authorities. And I told Dallas that, and he said he had a friend whose son was kidnapped and he'd hired a private team that successfully recovered the boy."

"So he told you how to get in touch with this Deliverance group?"

"Oh, no. Dallas didn't have a clue how to do that. But he put me in touch with his friend. Well, he set up a phone call. It was anonymous—his friend was nervous about his privacy. But we talked, and he gave me a contact number for reaching the group. I called and, well, even though it was clear he was using one of those voice alteration devices, I liked what the guy said. I hired them on the spot—it all happened fast. Had to if I wanted to get my girls back. Anonymous wire transfer to a numbered account. Could've ripped me off, but they didn't. I got my girls back. And I don't give a rat's ass that the slime-ball who took them got his throat slashed. I owe a lot to that group."

His mouth curves into a frown. "If it was up to me, I wouldn't be pushing for your husband's investigation," he adds, referring to WORR's efforts to track down Deliverance.

"Ex-husband," I say automatically.

"Right. Sorry. At any rate, that's my mother's mission. Me, I'd just let Deliverance keep doing its thing."

"How do you know that's what they call themselves?"

He tilts his head as if he's seriously considering the question. "The truth is, I don't think they meant to let me hear that. I got a call from one of the men on the team, and he was pissed. I'd fucked up."

"You? How?"

He shakes his head. "My girls—I knew from one of their friends who'd come back early from their Mexico trip that they'd bought some drugs from a guy they met at a club. But I—I didn't say anything because . . ."

"Because you didn't want to think of your girls that way," I say after he trails off.

He nods. "Anyway, Deliverance—the team—they learned about it, and one of them called me. Told me I'd wasted valuable time. That I'd withheld important details, and that they'd learned that the guy who sold my daughters drugs was part of their kidnapper's advance team. He said that I'd hired them to do a job, and that's what they were doing. But that Deliverance could only do the job if I gave them all the information."

His eyes are wet with tears. "He was right, of course. And even though he held it back, I could tell he was furious with me. I'd lost them time. Hell, I'd lost my girls time. And if they'd—"

A sob rips out of him, and I cover his hand with mine. "But they didn't. They survived."

"Yes. Yes." He sucks in air. "Anyway, I didn't realize what he'd said until after the fact, but then I made the connection. *Deliverance*. That's what they called themselves. And that's what they were. They delivered my girls back to me. They saved them. Hell, they saved me, because I would have shriveled up and died if my girls had been hurt."

I nod, understanding. I would have shriveled up and died if something had happened to Dallas, too.

We talk for another hour or so, and even though my primary purpose for this meeting was to get the information for Dallas and Liam about the leaked name, by the time I get back home, change into comfy clothes, and start working, my head is filled with details for my book and I dive in with gusto, ignoring the screenplay that I really should be working on.

I'm so deep into work that I actually jump when my cellphone buzzes, signaling a call from my mother.

I grab up the phone, realizing as I do that I've completely lost track of time. It's already five-thirty. I need to put on something other than sweatpants and get across the park in forty-five minutes.

"I can't talk for long," I say in lieu of a greeting. "I just realized I'm running late."

I save my file and then jog upstairs, figuring I'll change while I talk.

"That's okay, sweetie. I just called to see if you wanted to have dinner tomorrow. I'm going stir crazy in the Hamptons. I thought I'd drive in early and do some shopping."

"I'd love to," I admit. "But I'm having dinner in Brooklyn with Dallas and Colin. He's finally moved into that house he bought a year or so ago."

"Mmmm," she says, and I hear the disapproval in her tone.

"Mom. I know you worry about him, but I'm not just going to write Colin off. You know that." She does, too. Colin was there for me after the kidnapping in a way that my mom and dad couldn't be, and that was despite my mom and Eli having terminated Colin's parental rights years before. He could have washed his hands of me, but he didn't, and we've rebuilt what for a while was a very rocky relationship.

I understand why she's worried—apparently the IRS has been looking at Colin again, and she's afraid he's fallen back into the well of white-collar crime—but I just want to maintain a relationship.

"I know, sweetie. And of course I get it. So you're going with Dallas?" Her voice has a lilt to it, like someone forcing herself to make small talk.

"Yeah. Actually, Adele is going to be there, too. Apparently she invited me."

"Adele," she repeats. "That reminds me, why on earth is Dallas interested in a laundry list of the women Colin dated between me and Adele."

I balk. "I have no idea. What makes you think he does?"

"Well, because he asked me. Yesterday? No, the day before. I thought it was the oddest question."

"Can't argue with that." I've put the phone on the bed and have it on speaker as I pull on a skirt and sleeveless summer sweater.

"It doesn't matter. I just thought he might have explained himself to you now that you two are getting along so much better." There's a beat. "I saw the pictures from outside the Balcony."

I'm leaning over my vanity, and my hand stills as I apply mascara. "Yeah, that was a fun night," I say casually. "It was kind of a birthday present. We're, you know, trying to get along better."

"I'm glad." She clears her throat. "Jane, sweetheart . . ."

"Yeah?"

"Never mind."

I can see her soft smile in my mind as she shakes her head, dismissing her words. Normally, I'd press her. There's something on her mind. But I'm not in the mood to discuss my relationship with Dallas with my mom. Especially not now when I need to get out the door.

"Listen, I really am running late. I'm sorry I can't meet you tomorrow."

"No, no. That's fine. I'll let you go."

"Love you," I say.

"Love you, too," she responds. And then, right as I'm about to end the call, she says, *Jane.*

"Yeah?" I'm frowning, something in her voice making my insides tighten with dread.

"Your father—he saw the pictures outside the Balcony, too."

"Oh." I bite my lower lip, wondering what exactly Daddy saw in those pictures. Did he see more than the two of us getting in a limo? Did he see the truth?

Because Eli has known for years how Dallas and I feel about each other. Or, at least, how Dallas feels about me. He's never spoken to me about it. But he's made clear to Dallas that if anything happens, he'd disinherit us in a heartbeat. And years ago, the embers that burned between me and Dallas were one of the reasons that Eli sent Dallas off to boarding school in London.

I hold my breath, wondering if my mom is going to expand on her comment. We've never really talked about me and Dallas except to push the lie that he and I couldn't really be together after the kidnapping because it brought back too many dark memories.

So I don't know what she really thinks. What she really feels.

What she fears.

I don't even know if she sees what's really between her two kids.

She told me once that she sometimes regrets the spiderweb of adoptions that made Dallas and I brother and sister, but I don't know if that's because she understands that those machinations now keep him and me apart. I don't know, and I've never asked.

I'm not going to ask now, either.

"Well, anyway," she says brightly, "you need to run. I just thought I'd mention it. I love you," she says again, and then the line goes dead.

Weird, I think. And troubling. Because as much as I fantasize about not having to hide from the world or my parents, I know damn well that I'm really not ready for that fantasy to become a reality.

Dallas is already at the kiosk when I arrive. He's still in his work clothes, a charcoal suit paired with a crisp white shirt, all of which is perfectly tailored. He looks good enough to eat, and if the unapologetic stares from passing women are any indication, I'm not the only one who thinks so.

"You look amazing," he says as I approach, and I have to laugh.

"I was just thinking the same thing."

He starts to reach for my hand, apparently remembers that

we are standing on one of the busiest streets in the city, and pulls it away ruefully. "I thought we'd have a drink at The Pierre," he says, referring to the hotel that is just across Fifth Avenue from us.

"Sounds great." I follow him there—also forcibly keeping my hands at my sides—and we head through the opulent lobby to the Two E bar. The hostess clearly recognizes him and starts to seat us at a prominent table in the center of the room, but Dallas deftly steers her to something more private in one of the corners.

As we order, I remember what he said on the phone earlier today, and a little frisson of disappointment cuts through me when I realize that the tables don't have cloths. Apparently there will be no illicit touching happening. Which, sadly, is going to make happy hour a whole lot less happy.

As if he can read my mind, Dallas's mouth quirks up. "We can find another bar," he suggests, then leans closer so he's certain not to be overheard. "Or I can see if I can make you come without even touching you."

A trill of anticipation laced with desire runs down my spine, but I force myself to keep my cool. "Mr. Sykes," I say. "You couldn't possibly."

"A challenge?"

"A dare," I retort playfully, and when I see the heated look of a man recognizing a gauntlet being thrown, I wonder what exactly I've set myself up for.

"I won't say that I'm accepting your challenge," he says, "but if I were, I'd start by saying that I like your outfit. Your skirt that hits below your knees. Your sweater that doesn't show a hint of cleavage. It's very proper, Ms. Martin. But I know that you're hiding a secret."

I swallow. "Am I?"

"Mmm," he says, leaning back in his chair as the waitress brings our two martinis. She leaves, and Dallas takes a sip, his eyes never leaving mine. "A lacy bra," he continues. "And under that skirt, I bet you're wearing no panties at all."

I just lift a brow, trying to look unaffected. "I'll never tell," I say. "And you're not allowed to find out for yourself."

"Oh, but I will," he says. "I'll put my hand on your knee. On the soft cotton of that skirt, so simple it's sensual. I'll slide it up slowly, until I can brush the skin on your knee with the pad of my thumb, and you'll feel the shock of my touch all the way to your cunt."

"Dallas," I say, my voice hushed. I'm squirming a little, and I'm sure he can tell. "Someone might hear."

"They might," he says. "Does that turn you on?"

I look away, because he knows it does. And I don't like that it does, because I'm too damn scared of the reality. I draw a breath and turn back. "Dallas, we shouldn't—"

I don't finish, though, because my phone rings, the sharp tone startling in the quiet bar. I blush as the people at nearby tables turn to look at us while I rummage through my purse for my phone, then feel my chest tighten when I see who the caller is.

"Daddy," I say, my eyes meeting Dallas's as I answer.

He sits back in his seat, any sensuality still lingering between us vanishing like cotton candy doused with cold water.

"I saw that you and Dallas were at the Balcony."

"Um, you did?"

"Your mother said it was some sort of celebration for your birthday?"

"Yeah. Yeah, it was."

"So you two are getting along better?"

I look at Dallas. "Yeah. We're getting along." I frown. "Daddy, what's on your mind?"

He sighs, and for a moment I'm afraid he's going to tell me that he knows I'm fucking my brother and that I'm no longer a

Sykes and that tomorrow Dallas and I are going to be the feature story on Page Six.

It's not a pleasant feeling.

Then he says, "Bill came by. He knows about the kidnapping. He's going to pursue it."

Relief crashes over me. I'm not thrilled about Bill poking around the same places where Deliverance is poking, but this is a conversation I can have with my dad. The me-and-Dallas conversation? Not so much.

"I know," I say. "He told me. He's pretty much dead set on it."

"So he said. And I . . ."

"Yes?"

"I'm just afraid it's going to be hard on you. On Dallas. I wonder if now is the time for you . . ."

He trails off again, and I honestly have no idea where this conversation is going.

"Daddy?"

"Oh, hell. It's just that you and Dallas have kept your distance for so many years. And while I'm all for family reconciliations, I'm afraid that Bill's investigation is going to bring back a lot of memories. I'm afraid that it's going to hurt you. Hurt Dallas."

"Oh." I blink, holding back tears. The truth is that while my mom and I have a great relationship, my dad and I haven't ever talked that much. Especially not since the kidnapping. "Oh," I repeat. "We'll—we'll be okay, Daddy. I promise."

I hear him draw a breath as if he was starting to say something else, but changed his mind. For a moment, there's only silence. Finally, he says, "If you see Dallas, tell him what Bill is doing."

"He's right here with me. And he already knows."

"You're together?"

"Yeah."

"I see."

My gut twists again. "Dad?"

"Sweetheart, I have to go. I love you," he says, and then hangs up before I can even respond.

Dallas looks at me, his eyes searching. "What was that about?"

"He's concerned about Bill's investigation."

"No." He drags his fingers through his hair. "That's a front story. He's concerned about you and me."

I realize I'm hugging myself and force my hands back to the table. "What makes you say that?"

"Because he's always been concerned." He meets my eyes. "Because he's always had a reason to be."

I feel my cheeks warm. He's right about that.

"He's convinced it's all on me," Dallas says. "That I'm my father's son. That I'm just as much of a fuckup as Donovan was. And that I'm determined to corrupt my sweet, innocent sister."

"I'm not sweet," I say. "And you're sure as hell not Donovan."

Donovan is Dallas's birth father, Eli's brother, who drank and got high and fucked around and eventually drowned in the Pacific.

"No," Dallas says, "I'm not. And it would be nice if my father realized that."

"He does, Dallas." I start to reach for his hand, but he pulls his back with a shake of his head as he glances around the full bar. *Shit.*

I sit back, determined to change the subject. "We're heading down to Colin's together tomorrow?"

He's quiet for a second, obviously understanding what I'm doing. For a moment, I'm afraid that he's going to keep the subject on our dad. Then he nods. "I figure we'll just use a driver. Easier that way. We'll leave at six?"

"Perfect." I frown, remembering. "Mom said you were asking about all of Colin's ex-girlfriends. What's up with that?"

I see a flash of emotion in his eyes—surprise? confusion?—but it's gone before I can identify it. "Oh, nothing. A ridiculous idea I had for a housewarming present. I've abandoned it. I'm going with a plant. Bamboo. Gin swears that even Colin won't be able to kill it."

"I'm bringing candles," I say. "By the way, the conversation with Darcy went really well." I explain how Darcy heard the name Deliverance, and then relay my understanding of the role Dallas plays. How he pretends to know someone who's used the team before and puts the potential client in touch with them.

"I'm sorry about not running you through it beforehand," he says.

"No, this was good. It kept the interview real. But who's the friend you put him in touch with?"

"Me," Dallas says. "Sometimes the role is played by one of the other guys. We use computer software to alter our voices. Works out well, and keeps me out of the spotlight."

I nod, conceding that it's a solid ploy. I'm about to ask for more details when he checks his watch. "Are we on a timetable?"

"As a matter of fact, we are. There's somewhere we need to be."

I frown. "Now?"

He downs the last of his martini and tosses a hundred dollar bill on the table. Then he grins, wide and boyish. "Come on and I'll show you."

What he has to show me is a one-bedroom apartment in an exclusive building just three blocks from my townhouse.

"You're going to buy it?" I ask as the real estate agent wanders off onto the balcony, obviously giving us a chance to talk.

"I'm thinking about it."

"It's so close. You might as well move in with me."

"That's pretty much the idea."

Ohhh. "Camouflage," I say.

"Something like that. Plus, it's a short sale, so the price is right. I think it'll be a good investment. And . . ."

I frown. "And what?"

He shakes his head. "Nothing. I just want a place in the city."

I consider pushing, but I don't want to be that girl. It's one thing not to have big secrets between us. It's another to feel obligated to share every single thought and idea.

"It's only one bedroom," I point out.

"Do I need more? After all, as far as the world knows, the point of this place is so that I don't have to commute from the mansion. Go to work, come back to my Upper West Side apartment."

"You could afford something bigger. With an office."

"True. But I can pay cash for this place without tapping the trust."

"Really?"

He nods. "I want to do this on my own. And I have enough saved from work and what I make from Deliverance."

"Oh. I'd kind of assumed it was a charitable thing."

He chuckles. "We don't turn down cases if there's a need. But our services aren't given free. We invest back into the tech. And we compensate ourselves, too. Our time is valuable. For that matter, so is our service. So," he continues, "what's the verdict?"

"I think you should go for it," I say, then tug him into the bedroom long enough to give him a deliciously sensual kiss before we join the agent on the balcony to tell her the good news.

Afterward, we walk the short distance to the townhouse, and he steps back as I unlock the door. "You're not coming in?"

"No," he says. "I'm not."

I tilt my head, surprised. Then he moves in and stands very close to me as he reaches around to open the door, his arm brushing my shoulder. "Pretend I'm kissing you good night," he whispers, then backs away.

"Dallas." I hear the plea in my voice. I want him to come in.

But he just shakes his head and smiles. "Sweet dreams, sister mine. Until tomorrow."

"Tomorrow," I repeat. And when I go into the townhouse, I'm smiling, too.

20

Steak and Potatoes

Just a normal dinner party, Dallas thought. Just your average, every day evening around the table with the man who may well have masterminded your kidnapping, the sister you're in love with, and the older woman you used to sleep with.

No doubt about it—as a group, they made one hell of a Norman Rockwell painting.

"This is why I chose this house," Colin said, indicating both the dinner table and then, with another sweep of his hand, the patio upon which he had grilled their steaks and vegetables. "Entertaining. Family. And perfectly done steaks."

"Hear, hear," Jane said. "But don't forget the wine." As if to illustrate the point, she took a long, slow sip of an exceptionally smooth pinot, keeping her eyes on Dallas from over the rim of the glass. Damned if just the look in her eye didn't make him go hard.

"I could use a refill." Adele pressed her hand on his thigh while she leaned across him to grab the bottle. "Pardon my reach," she said as her sleeve brushed against his.

He knew she was trying to get a rise out of him, but he had no reaction at all. Not physical, anyway.

Emotionally, he wanted to tell her to calm the fuck down, because Jane was there. But Jane was sipping her wine and chatting with Colin, and so maybe Dallas was being hyper-aware and paranoid.

Maybe.

Hell, maybe he was being paranoid about Colin being their jailer. Because how on earth could the man just casually have them over for dinner—how could he have interacted as a friend for the last seventeen years—if he'd put both Dallas and Jane through that kind of torture?

The man would have to be so fucked up it was almost beyond belief. Dallas, however, knew better than most that some horror stories were real. And that some monsters looked like men.

For that matter, some monsters looked like women.

They moved to the patio for port and dessert, and the conversation flowed from the house to their jobs to the weather to travel. It was normal and pleasant and way too surreal.

And despite everything, he was actually enjoying himself. Which, frankly, added to the strange quality of the evening.

"You met him?" Colin was asking Jane when Dallas tuned back into the conversation. "Lyle Tarpin?"

Jane nodded, looking exceptionally pleased with herself.

"He's the sitcom actor, right?" Dallas asked.

"I've heard he's looking to do features," Adele said, then laughed when everyone turned in her direction. "Well, I do pay *some* attention to West Coast gossip."

"Yes to both of you," Jane said. "And the feature he's most interested in is *The Price of Ransom*."

"The movie based on your book?" Colin asked. "Sweetie, that's amazing." He pointed his finger at the group in general. "And that boy's a fine actor. I watched two seasons of his show when I dated the woman who played his mother."

"Did you?" Adele asked. "Dallas was just asking me who you dated between Lisa and me." She leaned toward him, then squeezed his leg as if to underscore the comment.

Dallas shifted, freeing himself from her touch, and saw that Jane was no longer looking at Colin, but was staring right at him.

"Mom said that, too." She peered at Dallas. "What was it you said it was for?"

Dallas frowned, wishing both women had kept quiet. "An ill-advised housewarming gift." He looked at Colin and forced a grin. "Trust me when I say you're glad I realized the stupidity of the idea."

"A montage of all the women in my life?"

"Something like that."

"Well, I can't say I regret any of them." He smiled at Adele, then turned his attention to Jane. "Not even your mother. Lord knows I put her through hell. Divorcing me was probably one of the two best things anyone has ever done for me."

"And the other?" Jane asked.

"It hurt, but terminating my rights to you. I'd gotten pulled in all the wrong directions. I needed a solid kick, and your mother and Eli provided it. I may not have realized it at the time, but I realize it now. And in the process, you got a good father." He looked from Jane to Dallas. "A good family."

Jane leaned over and kissed his cheek. "Thank you," she said, as Dallas's gut twisted. Christ, he didn't want it to be true. He didn't want to learn that Colin was as bad as they suspected. That all this warm fuzzy talk was just a load of bullshit.

And there was Jane, laughing and talking as if Colin was one of the best men she knew.

He should tell her the truth about his suspicions. But then her smile wouldn't be so bright, and for every moment from here on out, she'd look at Colin through different eyes.

How could he take that from her? Destroy that relationship? Twist it so radically?

He couldn't. Not yet anyway. Not until he was sure.

For the next hour, he tried to slide back into the groove of the conversation, but he couldn't get his mind off the job. He'd already planted a device in the kitchen and Colin's bedroom—thanks to Colin's offer to give them a tour of the house early on—but he still needed to hit the study. And he needed to tell Colin about Bill's determination to poke into the Sykes kidnapping. Once he'd done that, he and Jane could leave.

He wanted to get her home. He wanted her in his bed. He wanted to lose himself in her and block out all the memories and all of his fears about Colin. About everything.

But first things first.

He leaned back in his chair and then casually turned toward Colin. "By the way, you should probably expect a call from Bill."

Colin's brows rose, and he looked toward Jane. "Bill Martin? Why?"

Dallas kept his eyes on Colin, studying his face as he answered the question. "Because apparently he's learned about the kidnapping. And he's dead set on pursuing an investigation, working with the FBI, Interpol, I'm not really sure."

"Really." Colin's mouth curved into a frown. "Well, I'm sorry," he said, looking at both Dallas and Jane in turn.

"Sorry?" Jane asked.

"That he's going to force you to dig it all up again. Make it harder for you."

"For the whole family, I'm afraid," Dallas said. "I'm sure he'll want to interview everyone."

Colin nodded. "Well, I'll cooperate, of course. I want the bastard who did that to you caught and convicted, strung up by his goddamn balls. I just wish you didn't have to rehash it all in order to make that happen." He sighed. "If I could shield you both, believe me, I would."

"We know," Jane said, her expression soft. "And we appreciate it."

Adele had been quiet through the conversation, and now she picked up her wine and took a sip before slowly shaking her head. "It sounds like an epic waste to me. Not that I don't agree with the sentiment—whoever kidnapped you needs to be behind bars. But what on earth could they find now?"

Dallas kept his eyes on her, careful not to look at Colin. "I guess we'll know when Bill tells us." He pushed back from the table and stood. "I didn't mean to put a damper on the conversation. I'm going to the kitchen for some coffee and to clear my head. Back in a few." He started toward the door, but was halted by Adele's hand brushing over his hip, then tugging on his shirt to stop him.

He frowned down at her as she handed him her coffee cup. "Could you be a darling and bring me a refill when you come back?"

"Sure." He glanced at Jane and Colin. "Anyone else?"

With no other takers, he headed into the house, bypassed the bathroom, and headed straight for Colin's study.

The device was easy to plant, and he adhered it to one of the bookshelves and then quickly left the room. As he did, he almost walked straight into Adele.

"Get lost?" She took a step closer. "Or were you looking for someplace private because you're upset about Bill? Or maybe you're looking for a way to take your mind off of it?" she added, stepping close and sliding her palm down his arm.

He shrugged her off. "Stop it." They were done. They had been for a long time.

She lifted a shoulder. "You're so rigid. Always following the rules."

"You know better than that. But I'm not breaking any with you. Not now. Not anymore."

"Fair enough." Her eyes danced with mischief, the small lines at the corner the only indication of her age. "If you weren't looking for a tryst, then what were you doing in the office?"

"Trying to figure out how he set up that wireless sound system that he told us about. I want to do something like that for my home gym." He started back toward the kitchen.

"So now you're a handyman, too?" She patted his ass, and he twisted away from her touch. "Just pull out this nice, hefty wallet and pay someone to hook it up for you."

"I'll take it under advis—Jane." She was in the kitchen, her eyes more or less on his ass, but at the sound of her name, she lifted her gaze to his eyes.

"I was going to get more coffee, after all," she said, "but I think I'm going to call it a night." She looked between the two of them, then back to Dallas. "Are you ready to leave, too? Or can you find another way home?"

"I'm ready," he said. "Let's go."

Five minutes later they'd said their goodbyes and were heading to the corner where Dallas had told the driver to meet them.

"Jane, listen—"

"You son of a bitch."

"Excuse me?"

She stopped dead a few feet from the car and looked up at him. "Do you think I don't know what you've been keeping from me?"

His entire body turned to ice. *Colin.* How the hell had she figured out about Colin?

"Do you think I couldn't see exactly what you were hiding in there?" she continued, before he could respond.

He was frozen, but somehow he managed to thaw out his tongue enough to say her name. "Jane, please—"

But she just pressed on.

"You've slept with her," she blurted. And even as tears spilled down her cheeks, a wash of warm relief swept over him. "You've actually slept with Adele."

21

Mrs. Robinson

"Jane—"

"*No.*" I hold up my hand, my palm itching to slap him.

"Dammit, Jane, just listen to me."

"Honestly, Dallas, I'm really not in the mood." There's a cab moving slowly down the street, and I flag it. "You take the car. Enjoy the drive. Hell, maybe Adele needs a lift."

I almost regret saying the last when I see the hurt on his face. Then I remember that he hurt me first. I slam the cab door shut and tell the driver to take me to the Upper West Side.

On the way, my phone rings five times, each call from Dallas.

I send each one to voicemail. And then, for good measure, I delete the voicemails.

Jerk.

I mean, what the hell? He's more than willing to tell me he's slept with a zillion vapid women and yet he never thought to mention that he was fucking my stepmother?

Granted, she wasn't technically my stepmother, but that little fact didn't lessen the hurt.

I'm still pissed when I get home and my phone rings again. I'm about to just turn off the damn phone altogether when I realize the call isn't from Dallas but from the guy in LA who's producing the movie.

"Joel, I'm here."

"Janie, Janie, sweetheart, Tarpin's over the moon. Loves the material. Loves you. Everyone at the studio's excited about him. He's ready to sign on."

"Seriously? I was just talking about him and the movie tonight. That's so incredible."

"Just one little thing. He wants to meet you first."

"Me?"

"Since the screenplay's not done, he wants to chat a bit. Make sure he's confident in the direction of the story."

"And the book's not enough for him?"

Joel chuckles. "Baby, this is Hollywood. Just meet us at The Ivy at ten tomorrow for breakfast and all will be good."

I start to tell him that I'm in New York, but what the hell. It's not like I really want to be here at the moment anyway. And if I set up the flight right now, I can nap on the plane and still have time to go to my LA house, shower, then change before the meeting.

"Fine," I say. "I'll see you at ten."

I hang up and immediately call Brody. "Hey," I say when he answers. "I have to go to LA tonight so I can meet an actor for a breakfast meeting."

"Tonight? It's already past ten. You'll never get a flight."

"One of the perks of my family name," I remind him. "Nice, comfy private jet. Anyway, I just wanted you to know because I think I'm going to stay out there awhile and work on the screenplay and the new book."

There is a very loud pause from his side of the phone line. "You want to talk about it?"

I close my eyes and silently curse. The man really does know me too well. "You know, I really don't."

"Whatever he did, I'm betting he's not quite the asshole you think he is."

"Probably not," I admit, "but right now it doesn't feel that way."

"Well, do me a favor, and don't celebrate your birthday alone. Go out with your LA friends. Drink. Dance. Go to the beach. But don't sit in your house and work. More important, don't sit in your house and mope about Dallas."

"I won't," I promise, but even as I say the words, I remember the concert. Dallas and I were already planning on flying to LA tomorrow for the Dominion Gate concert and my birthday celebration. Now, it looks like I'm going all on my own.

And you know what? That's just fine by me.

At least, that's what I tell myself. And as I toss a few things into a suitcase, I try to convince myself that I actually believe it.

I don't have much to pack since I have a house out there already stocked with clothes and toiletries. And that's a good thing since I really can't focus and I feel like I'm moving through sludge. On the drive to the airport, I try to concentrate on the meeting tomorrow. About questions Tarpin might ask and how I can answer both honestly and in a way that will really entice him to sign on to the project.

I try, but I don't succeed. Instead, all that goes through my mind is Dallas.

No—actually, that's not all that goes through my mind. What *really* goes through my mind is the thought of Dallas and Adele. Talking. Touching. Laughing. Fucking.

Over and over again like one of those goddamn Nickelodeon movies that just go round and round and round on some endless loop. All through the drive and all through the flight, and even when I try to sleep, they infiltrate my dreams, so jarring that I'm yanked back to wakefulness by the thought of the man I love fucking my pseudo-stepmother.

Why?

And why the hell didn't he tell me?

And how the fuck long did it go on, and how long has it been over? Or is it over? Has he been with her since he and I got together?

Oh. Dear. God.

And now that the thought's in my head, I can't get it out, and all I can do is tell myself no. *No.* Dallas may have neglected to tell me that he and Adele romped between the sheets, but there is no way—no way in hell—that he would actually cheat on me with her.

Of that much, at least, I'm sure.

The brutal truth of that revelation calms me. It doesn't make me happy—he still fucked Adele, and what the *hell* is that about—but it calms me enough that I can sleep for the last hour of the flight. It's not enough, and I'm groggy when we land, but at least I won't be a total zombie at the meeting.

I've arranged for a car to meet me, and I sit in the back and watch the city go by as the driver whisks me to my house where I take a shower, eat a quick bite so I won't snarf food like a pig at The Ivy, and then jump in my car to battle traffic as I head over the hill to the meeting in Beverly Hills.

As predicted, traffic is snarled, but at least that gives me time to think about the meeting that I didn't think about on the plane, so that when I do arrive, I at least seem prepared. Joel is his enthusiastic, Hollywood self, and Tarpin is the real deal, an actor with both looks and genuine talent. And considering the scope and depth of his questions, he's not only intelligent, but he cares about the material. We get along great, and by the time the meeting ends, I'm not only confident that he'll sign on to the project, but also certain that I'll be disappointed if he backs out, because I can't imagine anyone better for the role.

And the best part? I realize as I tip the valet and slide into my car that I've spent two full hours without thinking about Dallas.

Frankly, that might be a personal best.

As I navigate my way to Coldwater Canyon and back up the hill to my house just off Mulholland Drive, I try to keep my mind from wandering in a Dallas sort of direction. Maybe I'll even go for a run when I get home. It's my least favorite physical activity, but I like the way it makes me feel after the fact. Like I've not only conquered something, but that I've made myself just a little bit stronger.

Alternatively, I can sit on my deck, look at the stunning view from my place just a block off Mulholland Drive, and conquer a bottle of wine. Which doesn't have quite the same psychological impact, but still sounds pretty damn appealing.

I'm still debating between good health and good wine when I pull into the driveway and see Dallas sitting on the front porch.

I freeze. My hand is on the gear shift and my foot is on the brake, and it would be so, so easy to just shift back into reverse and leave.

I don't. Because only part of me wants to run away. The other part wants to run into his arms.

In the end, I do neither.

Instead, I shut off the car, walk calmly toward my front door, and ask him what the hell he's doing here.

"Apologizing," he says, rising. "Groveling. Whatever it takes."

"How the hell did you find me so fast? I mean, what? You just assumed I'd run off to LA?" A horrible thought occurs to me. "Deliverance? Electronic surveillance? That is completely warped, Dallas. Intrusive. Invasive. Not to mention rude and just plain icky. How the hell can you justify—"

"Brody," he says.

"What?"

"I called Brody. He told me where you went."

"Oh." I make a note to sic a hundred telemarketers on Brody.

"Don't be too mad at him. I more or less suggested that I couldn't survive without you."

I grimace. "Brody has too soft a heart."

"I also told him that I still have the tickets to the Dominion Gate concert tomorrow night."

I cock my head. "What makes you think I still want to go with you?"

He reaches into his jacket pocket and holds out a small envelope. "They're your present. Your tickets—both of them. Go by yourself. Take a friend. Don't go at all." He meets my eyes. "It's completely up to you."

I keep my mouth closed, forcing myself to say nothing. Instead, I run my tongue over my teeth, then reach out and snag the envelope. I tuck it into my purse, then walk around him to get to my door. The porch is small, and he doesn't move, so I brush up against him as I pull out my keys. Immediately, I feel that shock of awareness, and it seems all the more powerful because I don't want to feel it. I don't want to want him. Not right now, when I'm feeling so raw.

"Jane." His voice is as gentle as the hand he places on my shoulder.

I shrug it off and open the door. I go inside, but I leave the door open. He can follow or not.

It's after noon, and I feel completely justified in having a glass of wine. I find one of my favorite Napa cabernets and pour a very full glass.

Dallas is standing on the other side of my kitchen pass-through. "A glass of that would be very welcome right about now."

I frown. "I'm trying to decide if I'm even letting you stay."

"Jane. Please. Let me—"

"What?" Fresh anger bubbles through me. "Change the past? Take it all back?"

"Explain. Just let me explain."

"Explain why you fucked her—yeah, I know you didn't actually. But for you, you did."

"Explain why I didn't tell you." He looks so lost. So sad. "And, yes, why I was with her. I just want—"

"What?"

He shakes his head, looking not at me but somewhere over my shoulder. "Never mind. I'll give you time."

He starts to head toward the door and suddenly the thought of him leaving seems to cut through me, slicing me to ribbons. "Wait!"

He stops, his back to me. I see the tension in his shoulders, the tightness in his back. And when he turns to face me, I see the hope on his face.

I look down at the ground. I want to hold on to my anger, but it's starting to diffuse. Still there, but now so hard to grasp.

I clear my throat. "If you go, I'll end up drinking the whole damn bottle by myself." I pour him a glass and set it on the pass-through. I nod at it. "You can stay for that long."

"All right, then." He takes a tiny sip. "I'll drink slow."

I almost laugh, but I manage to hold it in.

I stay in the kitchen and he stays on the other side of the bar. I like it that way because the longer he's here, the more I want him to hold me. I'm hurting—and even though it's Dallas who hurt me, he's still the one I crave to give me comfort. Whose arms I want around me while I close my eyes and draw strength.

I'm not sure what that says—am I that screwed up? Or am I just in love?

I take another sip of my wine and busy myself with wiping down my already clean counter. "So go ahead," I say. "You have an explanation. Tell me."

"It's fucked up," he says, and this time I have to laugh. Because honestly, where he and I are concerned, when isn't it?

"When I met her not long after she and Colin got married, I was feeling so empty. You were out of my life, forever I thought. I was raw. And I was attracted to her."

I wince, and he sees it.

"I screwed up by not telling you the truth before. I'm not going to pull my punches now."

"No," I say. "I don't want you to. I just—she was married."

"Nothing happened. But we both felt it."

"Well, something happened eventually."

He nods. "After they broke up. We—well, yeah. I slept with her."

I feel my insides twist. Because this isn't like Fiona or Christine or any of the others. With Adele, there was more. And I'm jealous. I'm so incredibly jealous.

"I thought you only did one- or two-night stands."

His smile is thin, and I know he can hear the jealousy in my voice.

"Adele was an odd exception, that's for sure. She—oh, hell, Jane. She knows about us."

My eyes grow wide. "You *told* her?"

He shakes his head. "No. But she's a therapist, remember? She heard the way I talked about you. And because of Colin she knew that we'd both been kidnapped. She figured it out. She knew I was still in love with you. And she—she was edgy."

"In bed," I say. "She—"

"Understood what I needed, probably even more than I did."

My mouth is dry, and I'm not sure if I feel sick or if I feel relieved that he had someone when he couldn't—wouldn't—have me.

"Did you love her?"

He looks at me as if I've completely missed the point. "Love her? Oh, god, Jane, no. She was the only one I could be honest with. The only one who knew my core truth. There was sex, yes. But sex with Adele was never about her."

His eyes lock on mine. "Don't you get it? Sex with Adele was always about you."

22

City of Angels

He watched her face, uncertain if he was doing the right thing by revealing so much. But he couldn't keep it from her. Now that he'd made the decision to tell her, he had to go all in.

"All about me?"

"I wanted you. I craved you. And I was so damn frustrated that I couldn't have you. She got that." He ran his fingers through his hair, knowing he had to tell her the rest. "She knew that I hadn't really been with a woman since you. And she's the reason that I thought it would be different with you."

She nodded, but didn't say anything.

"Jane? Jane, I really need to know if I'm making a huge mistake telling you all this."

She blinked, looking a little shell-shocked, but she shook her head. "No. No the mistake was not telling me before. Keep going."

He wasn't entirely sure he believed her, but he knew he had to get it all out. "After a while, Adele wanted to—I don't know. Role play, I guess. Pretend to be you. Have me—take you."

Her brows rose to her hairline. "Like what I suggested. About the Woman. Oh, god." She hugged herself, her brow furrowing. "She thought if you did that, you'd get over me?"

"No. No, it wasn't like that. Just the opposite. She thought it would get me off. That I'd be able to, well, fuck her if I pretended it was you."

"Oh." She dragged her teeth over her lower lip. "And did you?"

"Jane, come on. You know I didn't. I told you. You're the only woman I've—"

"No. I mean, did you try."

"Hell no." His words were harsh as he remembered his disgust with Adele. With himself. "That was when I ended it."

Her relief was so visible he would have laughed if he wasn't already so twisted up inside. "And that's it," he said. "That's the story on me and Adele. And I didn't tell you before for two reasons. It's done. Over. So I didn't see the point. But more than that, the thought of you was so wrapped up in my entire, screwed up relationship with her that I didn't—I don't—want you to feel like everything between the two of us ties back to sex."

She shook her head and came around the island with the bottle of wine. She moved to him and topped off his glass. A perfectly simple, perfectly normal thing to do, but it filled him with so much hope he could feel his heart expand.

"I don't think we're all about sex." She looked up, not smiling. But he thought he saw a spark in her eyes.

"Maybe not. But I was afraid you would start to if you knew how fucked up being around Adele made me. Like witchcraft."

"Bitchcraft is more like it." She smirked. "And yes, that's not fair. I mean, I liked her well enough before. And you're both consenting adults. Blah, blah, blah."

"Jane."

"No, let me finish." She polished off the rest of her wine. "I don't—I couldn't ever—think that what's between us is only sex. But it is a huge part of it. And I think that's why it hurts knowing you . . ."

"And that's the other reason I didn't tell you."

She crossed her arms over her chest. "What? You didn't want me to know? Figured it could just stay a big secret?"

"I was ashamed," he said, and felt ten times lighter after the admission.

She tilted her head, her expression softening. "Oh, Dallas. Oh, damn. No. *No.* What you did—why you did it—there's nothing to be ashamed of. But just because it's not shameful doesn't mean I like it. You know?"

"I do."

She poured herself a fresh glass and took a swallow. "It's just that it feels like a secret, after you promised not to keep secrets."

"It was history, baby. Not a secret. Just an empty place." That wasn't entirely true, but he damn sure wanted it to be. "I don't need an itemized list of who you slept with between Bill and me."

"But if I'd slept with Liam, you would."

He felt the kick in his gut. "Yeah," he agreed. "I would." He took a step toward her, wanting so badly to touch her, but he kept one hand on his wineglass and the other in his pocket. "So how many times do I have to say I'm sorry?"

She shook her head slowly. "I guess we'll find out." She set her wineglass down. "The couch pulls out into a sofa, so you can stay here tonight if you want. Or you can go grab a suite at the Beverly Wilshire or something."

"Room service and comfortable mattresses are highly overrated," he said. "I'll stay here."

"Okay, then." She licked her lips. "I have work and some errands to run, but I'll be back later. You can hang or call a taxi or—"

"I'll be fine," he said. He didn't believe that she had things to do outside of the house, but he did believe that she needed her space. Even so, he wasn't about to leave if she wasn't kicking him out.

"Cool." She bit her lower lip. "So, there's not much to eat in the house, but there's a basket of delivery menus by the microwave. And probably ice cream in the freezer."

"I'll be fine," he repeated.

"Right." She hesitated, and he had the distinct impression that she had to force herself not to move closer and kiss him goodbye. "I'll just get going, then."

She grabbed her purse and keys and moved toward the door.

He knew he should just stay silent, but once she'd opened the door and the reality of her leaving was slapping him in the face, he couldn't keep quiet. "Jane," he said, then waited for her to turn. "Are we going to be okay?"

She hesitated, and in those few moments, he felt as though he were dying. "I don't know," she finally said. "But I didn't kick you out of the house. That must count for something."

23

Boy Toy

I bounce from shop to shop, spending the day at the Beverly Center and Rodeo Drive and then hitting up all my favorite boutiques around Melrose Place. That doesn't eat up nearly enough time, however, and so I add a massage and a facial into the mix, then follow that with dinner and a ten o'clock movie. Afterward, I sit in my car and consider calling my film agent to see if she wants to meet for drinks at the Chateau Marmont, but considering it's already past midnight, I nix that plan.

I consider going by myself, but the thought sobers me. I don't want to be alone anymore.

The truth is, I want Dallas. I've wanted him all day. But I've been avoiding him because it feels like that's what I should be doing.

I *should* be staying away.

I *should* be keeping some distance. Evaluating. Figuring things out.

The trouble is, I figured out me and Dallas years ago. And it's not a question of *should*, but of *how*.

I know we should be together—I've always known that. What is still tormenting us is the question of how. And that's a much trickier one.

But I'm pretty damn sure that the answer doesn't lie in a bar or a mall or a movie theater. And it sure as hell doesn't lie in running away.

And the truth is, as much as I hate the thought that he slept with Adele, of all people, I do understand why he didn't tell me. I wish that he had, but I understand.

No, if I dig really deep I have to admit that my biggest problem isn't that he kept a secret, but that I'm jealous. All those other women are anonymous. Even Fiona and Christine are anonymous at the core. Fungible women that aren't really part of his life.

Adele is, though. Like it or not, she's right there in both our lives. Maybe not at the center, but she's sure as hell sitting comfortably on the periphery. Which means I'm going to continue to see her. To be around her. And each and every time I'm going to think about how Dallas touched her. About how she knows the truth about us. About how she played those mind games with him, and put the thought of me right there in bed with the two of them.

And honestly, I really don't want to be thinking any of that.

With a sigh, I grab hold of the steering wheel then close my eyes and rest my forehead on my hands. I want to erase Adele from my thoughts, but that's not possible. There's no turning back time. There's no changing the past. If there was, god knows I would have done it a long time ago.

So I just have to go forward—and it's Dallas that I want to go forward with.

Which means it's time to go home.

It's time to cry in the arms of the man that I love, then let him dry my tears as we move forward, leaving Adele and all the shit behind.

It's almost one in the morning when I get home. I expect Dallas will still be up, but I'm surprised to find him asleep on the sofa bed, an empty bottle of scotch on the table next to him, along with a mostly empty glass. The television is still tuned to ESPN, the volume low, and the flickering light illuminates his sleeping face.

His clothes are on the floor, and I see his briefs and realize that I'm wet simply from the knowledge that he's naked under the sheet. I stand for a moment, debating whether I should wake him up to talk, but then he rolls onto his back. I see the way the sheet tents over his erection, and my whole body tightens with desire. I want him, plain and simple. But more than that, I want him to know that I forgive him. That I'm sorry, too.

I also think about the last time that I took advantage of his erection while he was sleeping. My throat still hurts, and he'd been so incredibly freaked out that he'd bolted. If I try again, how will he react? Will he get lost in the nightmare? And if he does, will he wake in time, or will he hurt me? Because god knows he could have gone a lot further the last time.

But I also need him to understand that I still trust him, and what better way is there?

I strip off my clothes, tug down the sheet, and carefully straddle him. Slowly—so wonderfully slowly—I lower myself, relishing the way he fills me and hoping that this time we can take this all the way. I want to see the passion and power when he explodes inside me. And we've already gotten so close—so damn close.

My thoughts are as wild as my breath, and I ride him hard—harder than I have before when we've done this, and I realize it's because part of me wants him to wake up. I want to see his face and know that he's in the now. Right here. With me.

I want to make this work. Dammit, somehow we have to make this work. Sex and life and everything.

I have one hand on his chest and the other on my clit, and

I'm stroking myself and his cock, rock hard now and deep inside me. He is filling me completely, and my eyes are so focused on his face that I don't realize that his hands have moved. They're no longer at his sides, but now cup my ass, his fingers squeezing me as he works with me, pushing me down onto him harder and harder so that this ride is growing wilder and wilder, and I don't know if he's dreaming or awake. I just know that I love the way he's filling me. Taking me.

And then he opens his eyes and I gasp—*He's awake.* Awake and aroused and with me. He's right there with me, his eyes on mine. His breath coming in time with mine. We're in perfect sync, his cock inside me, and that knowledge is even more of a turn on than the way his body feels locked with mine.

I see a wicked, triumphant grin spread across his face, but I'm unprepared when he moves suddenly to roll us over so that I'm on my back and he's on top of me.

He's still hard, and I shudder with pleasure as he thrusts inside me, again and again, our bodies slapping together in a wild fury that I so want to lead to an explosion. And we're close—we're both so deliciously close. I can see it on his face. I can feel it in the tension of his body. Just a little bit longer and—

But it's no good, and with a raw curse, he pulls out of me, soft now, and rolls onto his side, pulling me along with him, his arm around my waist, my eyes looking into his.

"Dallas." I don't know what to say. I want to soothe. I want to celebrate. I'm afraid that he's disappointed, but he quiets me with a kiss so deep and passionate that it erases all my worries and sends me floating off to a place where there's only desire and pleasure as Dallas marks a trail of kisses down my neck, between my breasts, and then all the way down my abdomen to my pelvis.

His tongue teases me, and the instant he closes his mouth over my sensitive clit, I explode against him, all of the built-up passion and energy radiating out of me in one vibrant, massive, overwhelming orgasm that he draws out by teasing my clit with his tongue, playing me like a finely tuned instrument from which he is determined to coax a concerto.

Finally, when he has drained me fully, he slides up my body and cups my face with his hands. "I'm sorry," he murmurs, then kisses my temple and teases my earlobe. "I'm so sorry."

I brush a kiss over his lips. "Thank you," I say sincerely. "I'm sorry, too." I reach for his hand and twine our fingers together as he pulls me even closer and I rest my head in the curve of his shoulder. "We're stronger together than apart, you know."

"Because we're meant to be together, Jane. We've known it our whole lives."

I nod, acknowledging the truth of his words. "But it only works if we *are* together. Don't you get that, Dallas? I can't be with you, if you don't let me in."

I see his throat move as he swallows. "I know," he says. "I should have told you about Adele. About Deliverance. About what the Woman did to me after they released you. All of it." He shifts, so that he is looking at me more directly. "But, Jane, you have to know that whatever I've kept from you, I did it because I thought it was right. I had a reason. I would never deliberately hurt you. All I ever want to do is keep you safe."

"I know." I brush a kiss over his lips. "I really do know that."

He reaches over to grab his phone and check the time. "It's tomorrow," he says, then grins. "Happy birthday. What do you want to do today?"

I snuggle closer. "I'm already doing it."

My ear is pressed against his chest now, and I both feel and hear his chuckle. "You know, yesterday you were pretty mad at me."

"Yeah, well, you're my brother." I prop myself up on an elbow. "I've spent my life being mad at you and getting over it." I see his face and roll my eyes. "Don't look like that. It's our reality. We can't exactly hide from it."

I push up and then straddle his waist, forcing him all the way onto his back. "So this is what we're going to do on my birthday. I'm going to work on scene revisions. You're going to lounge on my deck looking like my gorgeous boy toy. Then we're going to go to a concert. And when we come back, you're going to fuck me hard."

"Am I?"

"Oh, yes. Tie me up. Spank me. Fuck me however and wherever you want." I slide my hand over his now-hard cock. "I have a few interesting toys in my bedside drawer, so feel free to help yourself. But that's what I want. To be used by you. Very, very thoroughly."

His eyes are alight with a very wicked shade of green. "Sounds more like a present for me."

"Believe me, I want it."

He slides his finger between my legs, and I'm so sensitive that even that gentle touch on my clit makes me shudder as electricity tingles over every inch of my skin.

"Yeah," he says. "I guess you do."

We snuggle close again and sleep until almost lunchtime. And then we spend the day exactly how I said we would. It's LA, so the weather is gorgeous, and my deck has such a wonderful view of the hills and city beyond that it's easy to pass the time out there, me working and Dallas reading, with only small breaks for food and conversation. It's nice and comfortable. It feels like home.

Hell, it feels awesome.

As the afternoon draws late, I shut down my laptop and head to the railing, then look out over the green hills below and wisps of white clouds above. After a moment, Dallas joins me, his arms encircling me at the waist. I lean back against him and sigh deeply. "This is nice," I say. "If I didn't have two tickets for a concert tonight, I might have to stay here and do naughty things with you."

He tightens his grip and kisses my ear, then whispers, "I promise we'll be naughty tonight," with such heat that I'm tempted to forgo showering and changing clothes in favor of pulling him down on a chaise lounge and having my way with him.

Soon enough for that, though.

"I need to get ready," I say, then start to push back from the rail so I can head inside to my bedroom.

He tugs me to a stop. "If you don't mind, I thought we could go with some friends tonight. They can swing by and pick us up."

"Oh." I'm a little surprised; I hadn't expected that we'd be going with other people.

"But only if you're cool with having company tonight," he hurries to say. "I'm more than willing to have you all to myself."

"Who?"

"Damien and his wife, Nikki," he says.

"Damien Stark?" I ask, referring to the professional tennis player turned entrepreneur turned multi-billionaire.

"Westerfield's is his club, and he's the one who scored the tickets for me."

I nod, the pieces falling into place. "You invested in that island resort one of his companies launched recently, right?" I try to remember what I read about the high-end retreat just off the coast. "The Resort at Cortez?"

"I did. And the architect and project manager would be joining us, too. Jackson Steele and his wife, Sylvia. But only if you're okay with company. It's your birthday, and that means your wish is my command."

I slide my arms around him and press close. "I like the sound of that," I admit. "But I'll issue my commands after the concert. I'm happy to go with your friends. Honestly, I'd like to hear more about the resort. It sounds amazing."

"We can go tomorrow, if you want. I've got a little bungalow there, actually. An investor perk. What do you say? Concert in public tonight, with both of us on our best behavior? Island getaway tomorrow, alone and being very, very naughty?"

I laugh, remembering the last time we were alone together on an island; frankly, *naughty* is an understatement. "Actually," I say, "I think that sounds like an absolutely perfect plan."

24

Tsunami

We arrive at Westerfield's in a Stark International limo and get the full VIP treatment. I walk up the red carpet with Nikki and Sylvia, with whom I've been chatting and drinking during the drive from my house down to West Hollywood. The guys are behind us, talking about the resort and plans for a retail complex that the three of them are considering working on together.

Honestly, it's far too much business talk during my birthday celebration, and when we get to the door, I step back from the girls and tell the men that it's time to be festive. I almost put my arm through Dallas's, but he steps back at the last second, and I shoot him a grateful glance. I've been so comfortable with these four all evening that it's far too easy to let my guard down.

And while I don't get the impression that any of them—Jackson or Damien, Sylvia or Nikki—would judge us harshly, that's not a theory that I'm willing to put to the test.

"My birthday," I point out. "My rules. Fun and dance and drinking from here on out."

"And right next to the stage," Damien says. "Best seats in the house. Except for the fact that it's standing room only. But if you want to sit we can go up to my office and watch through the window."

"Not on your life. I want to dance."

Beside me, Sylvia laughs. "Sounds like your brother got you the perfect present."

I flash Dallas a smile. "He knows me well. I love this band."

"You're lucky," she says. "I adore my brother, but as far as birthday presents go, he has no imagination whatsoever. He usually gets me a Starbucks gift card. Or wine."

"Both good choices," I say as we follow Damien through the crowd toward the stage. "How about you?" I ask Nikki. "Good sibling presents or crappy sibling presents?"

"My sister died when I was a teenager," she says, and I freeze, because it's really hard to walk after putting your foot so firmly in your mouth.

"It's okay," she says, squeezing my hand. "You couldn't know, and the truth is she always gave great presents, but never something I thought I wanted. The best was my camera. It's what got me started with my hobby. I love it."

"And now you have a sister-in-law," Sylvia says, indicating herself. "And I have absolutely no idea what to get you for a present ever." She meets my eyes. "You probably already know this, growing up in the family you did, but it's really hard to buy a gift for people who can afford to buy themselves whatever they want."

"That's Damien," Nikki says, laughing. "I'm still getting used to having money in the bank."

They're both talking so casually and openly that I forget about my faux pas and relax again, taking the time to look around the space. We've passed into a roped off area that is apparently only for holders of VIP tickets. According to Damien, there will be more room to move in this area which is good news as that means there will be room to dance. I can already tell that the general admission area is going to be so jammed that the crowd will be doing well simply to sway.

I suggest to Dallas that we go get a drink, but that's handled for us as well. Damien taps something into his phone, and seconds later a jean-clad waitress brings us all a drink. Honestly, it's all pretty awesome, and I break protocol long enough to grab Dallas's hand, then rise up onto my tiptoes so that I can whisper to him. "Thanks," I say. "Even before the band comes on, I can honestly say this is the best birthday ever."

I see Jackson pushing in through the crowd and only then realize that he'd stepped away. I glance at Sylvia, and must look confused, because she leans in to tell me that he'd gone to a quieter area to call their nanny and check on their kids, a four-year-old daughter and a three-month-old son.

"Everything's good," he says, kissing her temple. "I caught them right before Ronnie went down, and she said to tell you she loves you."

Sylvia smiles wide, and I feel a tightening in my gut. *I want that*. I want a family. I want kids.

I want Dallas.

And I don't want to hide.

I turn toward him—though I don't know what I intend to say. It's not as if I'm going to jump up on stage and announce our love. I guess I just want to look at him, this man with whom I share such a vexing love.

I'm about to pull him aside on some pretense when the opening band comes on, so I forcefully push my melancholy aside—tonight is about being festive, after all—and let myself get swept away in the music.

The VIP section fills up quickly, but there's still room to dance, and I'm doing so much of that I'm slick with sweat, even though I've dressed simply in a cotton halter and low-rise jeans. I'm drinking vodka like it's water to cool down, and I'm already a little bit buzzed, which is perfectly fine by me. I didn't catch the band's name, but they're awesome, and when they finish and we all applaud, I make a mental note to ask Damien later. Meanwhile, my eyes are glued to the stage as the host introduces the main act.

Dallas is standing right behind me, and though his hands aren't touching me, he sways forward and I sway back, so that our bodies brush just slightly. And I know that while we both hope that it looks like an innocent brush of two people moving on a dance floor, in our minds, we're both fucking right here in the crowd.

And damned if I don't want to reach back, hold his hips still, and grind my ass against his erection. The urge is so powerful, in fact, that I clasp my hands in front of my belly button, afraid that if I let go I will give in to desire. Because I'm wired on music and drink and my inhibitions are very, very low.

Then Dominion Gate comes on, and everyone around us goes completely crazy, and when they lead into their first song, I start to dance and Nikki and Sylvia soon join me, and I can feel Dallas behind us, swaying to the music, his eyes hard and hot on me. And, yes, I add a few extra shimmies knowing that he is watching me.

Soon enough, though, I just get lost in the music. I don't even realize that a tall, blond guy has moved in close to dance with me, and when I do, I start to move away. But then I think, fuck it. We're supposed to be playing the role of siblings, right?

And, yeah, maybe some part of me wants Dallas to see. To have the tiniest inkling of what it was like for me every time I saw one of those women at his side. And it's not like I'm going to fuck the guy. But I am touching him, our hips brushing as we move to the music. Our bodies finding the music as I wish that he was Dallas and that I was grinding hard against him. And it's only when Dallas moves in and roughly shoves the guy out of the way that I realize just how much I've gotten to him.

"What the hell do you think you're doing?" He's leaning in close because he has to practically shout to be heard over the band.

I hold on to his shoulder for balance as I answer. "Dancing."

"Dammit, Jane. You—"

"No. *No.* You're the one I want to dance with. Hell, you're the one I want to press against," I add. "To kiss." And then, because I've drunk too damn much, I move in closer, then grind against him before boldly lowering my hand to brush his erection.

"Christ, Jane." He pushes me away, then roughly pulls me back.

And even though I know it's a mistake, I rise up onto my toes and close my mouth over his.

I'm not sure what I intended. Maybe just a quick, chaste brush of lips. A tease.

Dallas doesn't take it that way. He's had as much to drink as I have, maybe more, and between us we're a walking billboard for impaired reasoning. Because god knows he shouldn't be sliding his arm around my waist. Shouldn't be pulling me close. Shouldn't be slanting his mouth over mine and sliding his tongue inside, kissing me deep and hard and making me so goddamn wet right here on the dance floor.

He shouldn't, but he is. And only when the bright flash of cameras breaks through my haze and reality finally crashes through my addled brain do I realize the consequences and push him away from me.

But it's too late. We've been recognized, and camera phones are still snapping and people nearby are pointing and yelling, and though I can't hear what they're saying over the band, I don't stay to find out. Instead, I turn away, ignoring both Nikki and Sylvia who reach for me, and race out of the VIP section.

I shove through the crowd, or at least I try to. But it's only when bouncers open a path that I am finally able to move, and I realize belatedly that Damien and Dallas are ahead of me, and that Damien's had security clear us a path.

Dallas and Jackson are on either side of me as Damien holds the door open and says something to the bouncer, who signals for the limo to pull up.

The driver steps out to open the door, and we start to hustle that way. "Just take it," I hear Damien say. "I can get another one easily enough."

"Thanks, man," Dallas says. "I can't—"

But Damien just shakes his head. "I don't need an explanation." He turns and smiles at me. "It was great meeting you, Jane. You're going to be just fine."

I somehow manage to respond, and Dallas and I head across the parking lot to the limo. But we don't make it.

Someone inside must have made a call, because now the small crowd of reporters and paparazzi that had been hanging around outside the club hoping for pictures of Damien Stark or the band or Dallas has turned feral, and I can feel my panic rising. I can't believe that I've done this. That I started this avalanche. Me, who only wants to be in control. Who fantasized about being open in my relationship with Dallas, but never, ever wanted this. The media. The attention. All the trappings and bullshit.

But that's what we have, and now the press is surrounding us like a pack of dogs, and although Damien and his security guys tell them to back off, they continue to shout questions and flash pictures.

Finally, Dallas simply stops. "Come on, folks," he says. "There's not a damn thing to see here. You people know my reputation. Bad boy billionaire, right?"

"Are you fucking your sister now, Dallas?" one bold reporter asks. "Doesn't get much more bad boy than that."

Dallas points a finger at him, and I watch as his face changes to the personable media whore that he plays so well. "You have to admit she's gorgeous, even as sisters go. But what you guys witnessed was a dare—nothing more. Somebody dared me to kiss my sister like I kiss all my women." He lifts a shoulder. "I'm sure she'll give me shit for it later, but I never turn down a dare. Especially when money's on the table."

"How much money?"

"Who dared you?"

"So is your brother a good kisser, Jane?"

As they shout questions, Dallas takes my elbow and leads me toward the waiting limo. I can tell from his expression that he knows the story that he made up on the fly is completely absurd. And, frankly, I'm in a little bit of shock, because even though I know it won't last, in this moment, they actually seem to believe his bullshit story.

And suddenly, surprisingly, that pisses me off. I know Dallas was trying to protect me. That he manufactured this story of a dare to try and keep the press away from me. To keep me safe. And while I love that he tried, at the core, I'm annoyed with myself. I've spent a gazillion dollars and at least as many hours in self-defense classes and strength training, and I'm still a damn victim, too scared to stand up and fight for what I want—and what I want is Dallas. A real life out in the open, the judgment of the world be damned.

And yes, I hate the thought of the media attention that will inevitably follow. And yes, it makes me twitchy knowing that I'm tossing away privacy in exchange for a life as tabloid fodder.

But it would be a life in the light. A life with Dallas.

And with him at my side, I know I can get through it.

"Jane." Dallas's voice cuts through the dialogue in my head, and I realize I've zoned out, lost in my fantasy of freedom. Even freedom at a price. "Go on. Get in."

We're at the door of the limo, and I start to comply. But then I shake my head and turn around to look out at the crowd that has gathered around us.

And then, before I can talk myself out of it, I blurt, "It wasn't a dare."

"*Jane.*"

I take his hand, but otherwise ignore him. I have to say this fast before I lose my nerve.

"It wasn't a dare," I repeat. "It was a kiss. And it was real." I turn so that I'm looking straight at Dallas. "And it was right."

For a moment, I think that he's going to argue. Then he inclines his head. For a moment, our eyes lock. Then he takes my hand and urges me into the limo.

He follows, then shuts the door, firmly cutting off the shouted questions and camera flashes from the crowd we're leaving behind.

"Oh, god," I say as he pulls me close.

"You're amazing. Absolutely amazing." He bends to kiss me, but is interrupted by the sharp ring of his phone.

I meet his eyes—we both recognize the ring tone. The caller, I know, is our mother.

Dallas answers on speaker. "Mom," he says.

But it's not Mom, and I cringe when Daddy's very formal, very cold voice comes across the line.

"Imagine my surprise when my business manager calls and tells me that I need to tune in to TMZ, of all things."

"Daddy—" I begin, but he doesn't let me get a word in.

"So here is what's going to happen. You're going to instruct your driver to take you to the NBC affiliate. I've already got my team making arrangements. You'll go on air. Jane, you'll explain that you were irritated at being jumped by the press on your birthday. You'll say you decided to bait them. That you don't know what came over you, but of course there is nothing between you and your brother. A stupid dare. Foolish and silly but not real. Then you will end the statement and you will come immediately home to New York. I'll arrange for a longer appearance on a few talk shows. We'll have to spin this, but it will be spun. And this family will not be destroyed in the media because of the stupid, ill-conceived actions of my children. Do you understand?"

"I understand," I say, looking hard at Dallas. "And I'm sorry, Daddy, but I don't think we're going to be doing that."

"Dammit, Jane, you—"

"She already answered you, Dad."

"I will not be—"

"Goodbye, Daddy," I say. And then, with my heart pounding painfully in my chest, I take the phone from Dallas and press the button to end the call.

25

Sanctuary

Dallas watched—astounded, amazed, pretty damn impressed—as Jane hung up on their father.

The second she did, he pulled her to him. "Baby," he said. "Jane, baby, are you sure?"

She nodded.

"It's going to get crazy, you know that, right? The press isn't going to leave us alone. But our parents are. We're going to be cut off. Mom won't be calling you, sweetheart. You know damn well that Dad won't let her. At least not right away. Not until he cools down."

He could tell from her expression that she hadn't thought of that, but he also saw the determination in her eyes and loved her all the more for it.

"It's all good," she said. "I'm good." She drew in a deep breath, like a drowning victim coming up for air. "It's better this way. And look—I pulled back the curtain and it didn't kill me."

He chuckled. "No, it definitely didn't."

"I know it won't be easy," she said seriously. "But even the kind of hard we're going to be facing is better than living a lie. At least, I think so." She took his hand, and he saw the uncertainty color her face. "I sort of took over for both of us. I'm sorry. I shouldn't have made that decision for you. I just—"

"*No.*" His voice was harsh. Firm. "Don't you dare apologize. You were brilliant."

"Yeah?"

"Beyond brilliant," he said, then pulled her close. He wanted to hold her and never let her go. "Brilliant and ballsy."

She smiled up at him, her hand going to cup his crotch. "Is that good?"

"Very good," he said, then slanted his mouth over hers and lost himself in the feel of her for the rest of the drive to her house.

"I want more wine," she said once they arrived. Thankfully, no reporters were waiting in the streets. They hurried to her door, and she fumbled for her keys. "And then I think we need to get naked, get in bed, and properly celebrate our emancipation."

He took the key from her and deftly inserted it, then opened the door. "I like the way you think."

As they entered, he heard the beep of her cellphone. "Voicemail," she said. "Someone must have called while we were in the dead zone coming up the canyon." She pressed the button to play the message, and he heard their mother's voice saying, "Sweetie, your father—well, he asked me to call and tell you to check your email. I—well, you'll see. There's a letter. Baby, I'm so sorry. I love you both so much, and—yes, Eli. I'm getting off right now—Goodbye, sweetheart. I have to go."

Even before the line went dead, Dallas had his phone out and was checking his mail, and Jane was only seconds behind him.

"Got it," she said. "Come on, open. Open."

He was cursing his own slow connection, too, but when the

attached letter finally opened he both wished that he hadn't bothered and knew that he'd been expecting it all along.

He read it once carefully, then again more quickly. Then he looked at Jane and waited for her to finish. He watched her eyes skim the page once, then twice. Then a third time.

He saw when her hand began to shake.

And he was there to catch the phone when she dropped it.

"Dallas," she whispered. "I shouldn't have done it. I should have thought. I guess I never really believed he'd go this far."

"I did," Dallas said.

"But completely disinherited? He's really taking our houses away? Cutting us off from our trusts? He's firing you from Sykes Retail? What the hell? He's our father. How can he do that? I mean, I knew he'd threatened, but I guess I never really believed he'd go through with it. And I should never have taken the risk. What was I thinking putting you in that position?"

"You're in it, too."

She shook her head. "Not as deep. He can't touch my book or film money. But you work for him." She pressed her fingertips to her temples. "God, I'm such a selfish idiot."

He took her by the shoulders and forced her to look at him. "If you are, then I am, too. Because there's nothing I want more than to be with you—nothing."

"But Deliverance—your lifestyle. It's all driven by Sykes money. You need your reputation and—"

"No." He shook his head. "No, the money isn't a problem. Deliverance is self-sustaining now. I haven't funded it out of my trust in years. You're right about the parties and the reputation. The reputation I'll abandon." He squeezed her shoulders as he spoke. "But don't write me out of the parties, yet. Considering the nature of gossip, I probably have a good six months of the kind of notoriety designed to garner all sorts of party invitations. But you are right that this is going to inconvenience us. Hang on."

He pulled out his phone and dialed Archie's cellphone. "We have a code nine."

"I assumed you would be calling. I've been watching the news. I take it you've spoken to your father since Miss Jane's announcement."

"Looks like I'll be finding a new place to call home. Eli says we can both store our stuff in our houses until we come to our senses. But we both feel remarkably sane, so I think it's best to have our personal belongings packed up and sent to storage."

"I'll take care of everything. I'll contact Ellen and have her begin working on Miss Jane's belongings at the townhouse. Where will you be staying?"

It was a good question. He turned his attention to Jane. "Your LA house, is it part of the family trust?"

She shook her head. "No, I bought it when I sold my film rights."

"We'll be staying in LA for a few days," he said to Archie, "then coming back to New York and moving into that apartment I was considering. Would you call my agent and tell her I want to move in mid-week? If we can't close the sale that quickly, then I'll rent the place until closing."

"I'd be happy to arrange that for you."

"Wait a second. Tell her that title will be held by both me and Jane."

"What?" Jane said.

"Of course," Archie said. "Good luck, Dallas. I'll speak to you both soon."

They ended the call, and Jane lifted her brow.

He shrugged. "Don't you want to buy an apartment with me? Short sale, remember? It's definitely a good investment."

"Is that why you want to buy it together? Because you're concerned about my investment portfolio?"

"I want to buy it with you because I want us to have something tangible. Something that is ours. A symbol that we're stepping out and moving on." What he didn't say was that he couldn't drop to one knee and offer her a ring the way he wanted to. Maybe he'd never be able to do that. But he'd damn well give her this. And as much and as often as he could, he'd make sure that in the eyes of the world, they were a couple.

"So," he pressed. "Are you in?"

Her smile bloomed so wide it made his heart swell. "Yeah," she said simply. "I'm in."

"In that case, I think we need some of that wine." He moved to the kitchen and got a bottle from her wine fridge, then deftly uncorked it. He took the bottle and two glasses back out to the living room and set them both on her coffee table. Then he sat, and when she moved to join him, he shook his head. "No. You stand."

"Really? Why?"

"Because I'm going to watch you. And then I'm going to fuck you."

She licked her lips, and he saw the color rise in her cheeks. "What if I say no?"

He just shook his head. "That word has no meaning tonight." He let his eyes graze over her, noting the way she shifted her weight. The way her nipples hardened beneath that skimpy little halter. The enticing way she sucked on her lower lip.

Christ, he was hard.

"Take off your jeans," he demanded.

She complied immediately, first kicking off her heels, then unbuttoning the fly, then easing the jeans down over her hips until she finally stepped out and tossed them aside. She was clad only in tiny pink panties and her triangle-style halter.

"Shirt next," he ordered, and felt his cock twitch when she obeyed without even the slightest hesitation.

She reached up to the middle of her back and pulled at the string to untie the bow. Then she lifted both hands to her neck, undid that bow as well, and the skimpy top slid off her to the ground.

She stood there in only her panties, her hands still behind her head, her hip cocked to one side and a sexy little smile on her face. Her nipples were hard, her areolae tight and puckered, and all he wanted to do was stand up and take one of those perfect tits in his mouth and suck until she felt it so damn intensely that she came in his arms.

Soon, he thought. But not yet.

"Slide your hand down inside your panties," he ordered, then watched her mouth open as she gasped in pleasure when her finger skimmed over her clit. He watched her touch herself, stroking his cock as she did, and getting harder and harder as he imagined the feel of her. The heat of her.

"That's it, baby. Play with your clit. Tell me when you're close."

Her posture tightened as she touched herself, her breathing coming faster and faster. She was close—and damned if he wasn't, too. He wanted to watch her explode. Wanted to see the way her face lit as she went over the edge.

But that wasn't the game. Not yet. And the moment she whispered, "Now," he ordered her to stop and pull her hand away.

She whimpered, but she complied, and her easy obedience made him all the more hard.

He stood, still fully dressed, his cock straining painfully against his jeans. "Why did I make you stop?"

With a little sigh, she licked her lips. "To tease me."

"Oh, no, baby," he said, stepping right in front of her and running his fingertip lightly over her breasts, making her sigh, then roughly flicking her left nipple and changing her sigh to a startled little cry. "Not to tease, but to punish."

He watched as she closed her eyes, her throat moving as she

swallowed, then he took her arms and lifted them above her head, until she was the way he wanted, hands clasped, body stretched up, her back slightly arched. *Beautiful*. And his.

"Why am I punishing you?"

"I—I don't know."

Her eyes were still closed and so she wasn't expecting it when he spanked her tit, eliciting a surprised cry. He kept his eyes on her, watching her reaction. He'd never done that before, and he'd stop if she wanted him to. But goddamn it, he hoped she didn't want to. She'd promised him she'd welcome whatever he needed, and right now—tonight—he needed this. He needed her.

He needed her to be his. Completely. Fully. No holds barred.

He moved closer, cupping both her breasts and squeezing, then lowering his mouth to suck on the nipple of the tit he'd just spanked. He released his hand from her other breast and slid it down until his fingers dipped beneath the band of her panties and he found her soaked, her clit swollen and so sensitive that she shuddered at the softest of touches.

He bit back a smile; apparently she liked it just fine.

"Why am I punishing you?" he repeated after he drew his mouth off her breast, scraping her nipple with his teeth as he did so.

She continued to hold her arms above her head, and he couldn't help but smile at how well she was obeying. "Because I was bad."

"How were you bad?"

"Because of what I did. Hanging up on Dad, and—"

"*No*." He cupped the back of her head. "Open your eyes. Look at me. *No*," he repeated when she complied, then watched as the relief flooded through her when she realized that he meant it. "Why?" he repeated, this time more gently.

Her teeth dragged over her lower lip as she considered the

question. And then he saw the moment she knew the answer. "Because you didn't like me dancing with another man."

"I damn sure didn't," he said, fisting her hair and tugging her head back, leaving her neck exposed to his mouth. He shoved her thong to the side and thrust two fingers inside her, so that he was holding her in place by the pressure on her hair and her pussy. He knew it was awkward. He knew she felt unbalanced; hell, she was. With her hands still above her head and her weight shifted, if he let go she'd tumble to the ground.

Which was exactly what he wanted—for her to be completely in his control. "You're mine," he whispered, then trailed kisses along her exposed throat, alternating soft busses that made her moan with sharp bites. "Mine," he repeated. "Hell, I just paid a few billion dollars for you." He didn't mention that by the same argument, she'd paid a few billion for him. They both knew that he belonged to her as fully and completely as she did to him. But right now, he was the one in charge.

"Tell me I'm right," he demanded. "Tell me I own you."

"You're right. You own me. I'm yours."

The words rolled through him, filling him. Hell yes, she was. "What does that mean?"

"Only you. Whenever. However. Anytime. Anywhere."

"Does that frighten you?"

She shook her head as much as she could, fighting against his tight grip.

"Does it excite you?"

"Yes."

"Tell me what you want."

"You." The word was ragged. Raw. "God, Dallas, I want you."

"You have me, baby."

He released her hair, then steadied her before cocking his head to indicate the couch. "Bend over it," he said. "Hands on the cushions. Chest on the back. I want your ass in the air."

She met his eyes, and he saw desire as thick as his own. "Yes, sir."

Her easy compliance just about did him in, and he felt his cock throbbing with need. Dammit, he was going to fuck her. He *had* to fuck her. To claim her. To prove to both of them that they were together. Completely. Wholly.

He moved behind her, then held on to her hair with one hand, his other on her hip. She still wore the tiny thong panties, and he considered just ripping them off her, but there was something so enticing about taking her with them on. About urging her legs apart, shoving the damn panties to the side, and thrusting his cock inside her just like he wanted to do. Just like he was doing now.

And he was.

He was hard and he was inside her, and her back was arched as she moaned with the pleasure of being filled by him. Oh, fuck. Oh, yes.

He grabbed her hips, certain that this wouldn't last, but damn sure hoping he was wrong. He held her, then pounded roughly into her, faster, deeper, wilder.

She moaned, crying out his name. Begging him to fuck her harder. And damned if he didn't do just that. She was his—*his*—and he was inside her. Owning her. Taking what he wanted. What he needed.

He reached forward with one hand, holding her around the throat, making her submission complete. With his other, he reached beneath her, finding her clit and teasing it as he thrust harder and harder, then felt his balls tighten with the familiar sensation that led to an explosion.

And oh, holy shit, he was actually going to come inside her. For the first time in seventeen fucking years, he was going to come inside the woman he loved.

"*Jane*," he cried as his body shattered. He fell over her, his chest to her back, as his fingers continued to stroke her.

"Oh, god, Dallas," she cried as he still trembled against her. "Dallas," she repeated as he pulled out, then turned her around so that he could draw her to him, embracing her, holding her, loving her.

Tears ran down her cheeks, and she started to say his name again, but he cut her off, silencing her with a kiss, his mouth taking her as wildly and eagerly as his cock had.

He'd claimed her.

He had no idea if he'd be able to manage every time. If he was cured, or whatever the fuck you wanted to call it. But as he lifted her into his arms and headed for the bedroom, he realized he didn't care.

Right now, this was enough. Right now, they had everything, because they had each other.

Yes, they still had to face the judgment of the world. And, yes, there were still lingering secrets between them. Dallas knew damn well he was playing with fire by not telling her his worries about Colin. But despite all of that, he felt closer to her now than he ever had. They were together. They were whole.

And they were resolved to get through whatever the world threw at them. It wouldn't be easy. But, dammit, it would be real.

Gently, he laid her on the bed, then just about melted at the tender way she smiled up at him. "Are you okay?" he asked, knowing he'd fucked her too damn hard. Hell, he could already see a bruise rising on her throat, and he brushed the pad of his thumb gently over it, hating the thought that he might have hurt her, but also loving the fact that he'd marked her. With his hands. With his cock.

"Okay?" she repeated as laughter bubbled out of her. "Dallas, my god. Are *you* okay?"

"Baby, I couldn't be better."

"Can you—I mean, are you—oh, *fuck*. Are you going to be able to do it again?" Her cheeks bloomed pink.

He grinned as he got on the bed and straddled her, already rock hard again. "Sweetheart," he said, meeting her eyes as she spread her legs and he stroked the tip of his cock against her core. "I have no idea. But I can think of at least one way to find out."

26

Enemy Mine

Stacks of boxes surrounded Dallas as he stood in the middle of his office at the Sykes building. Or, rather, in the middle of the room that was once his office and now belonged to no one.

He glanced at his watch. Just thirty minutes ago, he'd been inside the apartment that he now owned with Jane.

More accurately, he'd been inside Jane inside the apartment.

He smiled, remembering all the ways he'd fucked her over the last week, both in LA and now back here in New York. He wasn't one hundred percent—not yet—but he damn sure wasn't complaining. "Practice makes perfect," Jane had teased when she'd pulled him to the bare hardwood floor only minutes before he'd rushed off to be here.

The floor had been newly polished and damned uncomfortable, but he wished he was there right now, his back against the wood as she rode him. Or Jane on hands and knees as he thrust hard into her.

He pressed his hand against his stiffening cock. *Soon.*

Right now, he had to take care of business.

He'd hired movers to come by after working hours to get the boxes and the desk—it had been a birthday present and he was damn well keeping it—but apparently they were running late. Which meant he was stuck in this room with nothing to do, playing the role of the disgraced leader. The immoral son of Eli Sykes, the king of the universe. The goddamn Father of the Year.

Fuck.

He dropped down into the chair—*not* a present, so it would be staying behind—and wished he hadn't packed away his laptop and personal Wi-Fi router. At least he could have spent the time going over some Deliverance files. As it was, he had no choice but to answer emails on his phone. And considering his and Jane's current notoriety, half his emails were from celebrity chasers who'd managed to track his account address.

He was just about to start deleting the bullshit when Gin popped her head in, her eyes still red from her crying jag earlier when she'd told him in a hushed whisper that Eli had it all wrong and that she couldn't be happier for Dallas and Jane.

It had warmed him, but it hadn't changed anything.

"It's late, Gin. Why haven't you left for the night?"

She sniffed. "I'll go when you do."

He nodded, moved by her loyalty. "Fair enough."

"I came in to tell you that Mr. Foster is here," she said. "He says it's important."

"Liam? Send him in."

She didn't have to because Liam was already striding past her. He tossed a blue envelope onto Dallas's desk as Gin left, closing the door behind her.

Dallas reached for the envelope, careful to pick it up by the corners even though he knew it made no difference. "Where'd you get this?" he asked as he opened it.

"In the pile of mail on Gin's desk. I recognized it, grabbed it. And it's not why I'm here."

"No," Dallas said. "I didn't think so." He let the paper slide to the desk then growled low in his throat when he saw the words written there:

> She's a slut.
> She's a whore.
> I'll make you see you deserve so much better.

Without thinking, he grabbed the note and balled it up, then sent it flying across the room where it smashed ineffectually against the window. Liam strode over casually, flattened the paper, and slipped it in his jacket pocket. "Just in case."

"You're supposed to be in London," Dallas said, forcing his mind away from the letter-writing bitch. Away from Jane. Away from all the shit that was going down around them and messing with his head. "It must be bad."

"It is."

"Colin." At Liam's nod, anger and regret coiled inside Dallas. "Tell me. What have you found?"

"I'll send everything over to you digitally so that you can review it yourself. But right now, if I had to call it, I'd tell you to put a bullet in the back of the fucker's head." Liam ran his palm over his head. "But we need to make sure."

"You want to interrogate him."

"Actually, I want Quince to interrogate him."

Dallas nodded, thinking of his former roommate turned MI6 agent and his exceptional skill at extracting confessions.

"If we grab him and he's innocent—"

"I know," Liam said. "I don't think he'd invite you around for lunch anymore. It's your call, man," he said. "We can keep poking around, but I don't think we're ever going to be sure until we look the man in the eyes."

Dallas nodded slowly. "Grab him."

Liam nodded. "The team's already in position. We'll have

him within the hour." Liam started to turn toward the door, then paused. "Do you want in? Not on the snatch, but the interrogation?"

Dallas shook his head. "No. If he really is the one—if I see the truth of that in his eyes—I swear to god I'll kill him on the spot. And I don't want him dead that fast. I want answers. I want to know why he did it. Why he put Jane and me through hell. And I damn sure want to know who the Woman is. So you have Quince interrogate, and you call me in after."

"And then?" Liam asked.

"And then I kill him."

27

Goodbye to You

Compared to the Southampton mansion and my townhouse, the West Seventy-Fifth Street apartment is tiny at only eighteen hundred square feet. But I don't care. It's ours—mine and Dallas's—and despite the shitstorm that has engulfed our personal and public lives, that fact alone makes me positively giddy.

We haven't said anything more to the press, but they've been buzzing around us constantly. And pictures of us holding hands as we came and went from my LA house to the airport and then again in New York are all over social media.

It feels as if the whole world is commenting on our relationship. Some people say we should just be left alone to do what we want. Others say we're disgusting. Sinful. That even without a blood relationship, the fact of our adoption makes our relationship both illegal and vile. Some say we got what we deserved when Eli disinherited us. Others say our parents are horrible.

As for the two of us, we've said nothing.

Reporters have been begging for a statement, an interview, anything. And Dallas and I agree that we should give it to them.

We'll do that, but later. There's nothing they can print that is more than the truth, and we're hoping that by letting them run loose with speculation, that by the time we officially speak, our relationship will have been so gossiped about it really won't even be news.

Probably won't happen, but we can hope.

And besides, even with all the chatter and gossip, we're both too happy in our new bubble to think about bringing the press into our world just yet.

Now, I turn in a circle, taking in the obstacle course of boxes and furniture. It's a huge mess—and I have absolutely no idea how we're going to make everything fit—but I'm looking forward to the challenge. Craving it, really. My life may have literally exploded, but I'm surprised by how much of a relief it is to have shed the secret that Dallas and I have been carrying. So much of a relief that even doing normal, mundane stuff is making me a little giddy.

And, yeah, I feel a bit guilty about that. I know my mom is in a huge funk—not because she thinks Dallas and me being together is bad, but because my dad is being so damned unreasonable. And, yes, because she hasn't got the balls to stand up to him and support her kids.

I know that Dallas and I are going to have to deal with that. With him. And with the press. And with sideways looks from strangers.

I know that Dallas is going to have to figure out how to regroup on the Deliverance side of things. He can no longer be the King of Fuck—at least not to anyone but me. Which means that Dallas may have to shift his role within Deliverance, and one of the other guys—I think briefly of Quince with his sexy British accent—will have to dive into the playboy role.

These are all real problems, and we're going to have to find real answers. But for this week at least, I officially don't care. For the next seven days, I'm all about this apartment and the man I share it with. The real world is out there—I know it. He knows it. And we also know it's not going away. But for this bubble in time, we're going to focus on us.

Right now, in fact, I'm searching the room for the box into which I'd packed all the bar supplies. Because Dallas is going to return from clearing out his office soon, and when he does I intend to greet him at the door with a martini—and absolutely nothing else.

I'm interrupted in my rummaging by the buzz of the intercom. I hurry to the door and punch the button on the speaker. "Yes?"

"Sorry to disturb you, Ms. Martin," the doorman says. "But I have a man here who wants to see you, and I don't think he's a reporter."

"Who is it?"

"He says he's your ex-husband."

I frown, not entirely sure how Bill got this address—probably my father—but absolutely certain I don't want to talk to him. I'm positive that the press about Dallas and me has both confused and hurt him, but I'm not in the mood to talk about it. Soon, but not yet. "I'm sorry. Tell him it's not a good time."

"He says it's important. That it's about Colin."

Colin?

I start to ask what he means, but instead I tell the doorman to just send him up.

"What's going on?" I ask, the moment I open the door for him.

"You're not going to like it," he says. "Not any of it."

I cross my arms over my chest, feeling suddenly vulnerable. "Just say it."

"You know how we've been investigating your brother's kidnapping?" He stumbles slightly over the word "brother."

My throat is so dry I can barely speak. Somehow, I manage to say, "Yes."

"Well, first of all, we weren't the only ones investigating."

I look at him sharply. "What do you mean?"

"Someone else was trying to find Dallas's kidnapper, too."

"Who?" I walk to the couch, because my knees are so weak now I'm afraid I'll fall if I don't sit. It's Deliverance of course. It's Dallas and Liam and Quince and the rest of the team. I know that.

What I'm wondering is if Bill knows it as well. But he, thank goodness, is shaking his head. "No idea. I wish we did because— well, I'll get to that. The point is, we suspected someone else was poking around. We're certain now."

I don't want to ask. I'm positive the answer will be bad. But I have to know. "Why? Why are you sure now?"

He meets my eyes. "Because when we made the move to bring Colin in for questioning earlier today, someone else had gotten to him first."

Questioning?

I try to move, but I'm frozen. I try to speak, but my hand is glued to my mouth. *Seriously?* They think Colin had something to do with the kidnapping?

Oh, god.

The room starts to turn gray, and I realize that I'm not breathing and that Bill is by my side, his hand on my back telling me to just inhale. To take it slow and breathe deep.

"Colin?" I say. "You're really telling me that Colin was behind the kidnapping? Are you sure?"

"It's looking bad for him. I'm sorry," he says. "God, Jane, I'm so sorry."

I swallow, trying to make sense of what he's saying.

"And he's gone?"

Bill nods.

"And—and someone took him."

"They did."

I stand. I have to move. I have to—*oh, god. Oh, god.*

"How long have you suspected him?"

He looks away. "A while."

"And you didn't tell me?"

He turns back to face me. "Come on, Jane. It was an official investigation—"

"That's bullshit."

"—and I didn't want to hurt you unnecessarily. What if we'd been wrong?"

"You shouldn't have kept it from me," I insist.

His expression turns ice cold. "Seems like you've kept a lot of things from me."

I start to lash back at him, but I bite my tongue. Instead, I look straight into his eyes and very calmly ask, "So why are you telling me now?"

He shoves his hands into his pockets. "Christ, Jane. I still love you, you know that. Even with . . . everything else, do you really think I'd let you hear about this through a news leak? From someone in the FBI coming to investigate? From anyone other than me?"

I cringe, thinking of the way he heard about me and Dallas. Not from me, that's for sure.

"It's classified," he continues, "but no way in hell am I keeping this from you."

I open my mouth to answer and taste the salt of my tears. "Thank you. Really. But I—I need you to go now. I need to be alone."

"Jane—please. We need to talk. About this. And—and the rest of it, too."

I shake my head violently. "No, no, please. I'm sorry about—well, everything. But not now. I can't—I—" I draw a breath and try again. "Thank you for coming. I mean that. But right now, I need to be alone."

Right now, I'm falling apart, even more than he realizes.

Because I know something Bill doesn't. I know who has Colin.

Deliverance.

Deliverance has been investigating my birth father. *Dallas* has.

And he never once told me.

He lied to me. He shut me out.

And right now, I think that he's broken my heart.

I've reamed Dallas out in my head at least a dozen times before he even walks through the door. Finally he comes home, and I'm so well-practiced that it's almost anti-climactic when I cross the room in five strides, lash out, and slap his handsome face.

"What the hell?"

"No," I shout. "That's *my* line. What the hell, Dallas? What the *fucking* hell?"

He shuts the door behind him—probably a good idea since we haven't even met our neighbors yet—and eases around me into the apartment. He's moving warily, like someone who's found himself trapped in a cage with a tiger, and he raises his hands in an effort to either soothe or protect. I'm honestly not sure.

"You want to tell me what's going on?"

"Oh, that's rich," I say. "But sure. Yeah. Why not? I'll tell you what's going on." I cross to him and shove him hard in the chest with the heel of my hand. "What's going on is that you lied to me. What's going on is that my boyfriend and my best friend and their friends have been investigating my birth father. What's going on," I conclude, my voice so hard it's painful, "is that you think Colin kidnapped us and you didn't fucking tell me."

I step back, breathing hard. Dallas has gone completely white, but he moves toward me, his green eyes glowing. "Jane—"

"You grabbed him." I have to force the words out. "Did you kill him?" I force the question out on a sob. "Oh, god, Dallas. Did you kill Colin?"

"*No.*" He tilts his head back and draws a long breath, and I watch as he visibly steels himself. As his color returns. "I didn't want to tell you until we were certain. But today—well, dammit, it doesn't look good. Liam's sending me everything we've gathered, and I'll show it all to you, I swear. But right now, we need to interrogate him. He's locked up. And Quince is going to talk to him."

"Talk? Is that what they call it?"

"What the hell, Jane? I'm pretty damn certain that the man fucking kidnapped us." He's in my face now, and I'm glad. I want him fighting back. I want a battle. "You damn well better believe I'm interrogating the fucker."

"You promised me no more secrets. Damn you, Dallas, how the hell could you keep this from me?"

He seems to deflate with my words. "Oh, baby. Baby, I swear I didn't mean to hurt you. I didn't want you to think—I mean, if it turned out our suspicions were wrong. I just—oh, fuck. I was going to tell you. I swear I was going to tell you as soon as we were absolutely certain."

"You were certain enough to take him in."

"Today," he says. "It all came together today, Jane, and Liam's sending me all the evidence. I'll share every bit with you. And you're right, I didn't tell you before, but I would have told you soon." He meets my eyes. "I truly am sorry. Hell, I'm sorry for both of us. He's my friend, too."

I nod, feeling numb. But the truth is, I haven't even started to process all my feelings—rage, confusion, anger, hurt—about the possibility that Colin could have done that. To me. To Dallas.

My hurt is still focused on the deception. On Dallas. "I trusted you. You're my heart. My lover. My brother. Jesus, Dallas, you're everything to me and you just—you just—"

I turn away as a sob rips through me. "Everything is public now because of you. And we promised each other we'd be okay. And even in all of that—that *mess*—you didn't say anything?" I look back at him. "I can't believe you did this to me."

"I'm sorry—I am. I was trying to protect you, not hurt you."

"No? Well, guess what? You did. All those times we talked about secrets. About finding out who did this to us. Hell, I point blank asked you if Deliverance had any leads, and you didn't have the balls to tell me the truth."

"I screwed up, I know that. But it's because I wanted to keep you safe."

I wince. Him. Bill. Everyone is trying to coddle me. "You can't keep me safe, Dallas. Not by lying to me. How can you not see that?"

"Jane, please."

But I just shake my head. I don't want to hear any of this. What was it I'd told myself in LA? That I knew that Dallas and I should be together, I just didn't know how?

Well, maybe there is no how. And maybe a lie this big completely erases *should*.

"Jane—" His voice is soothingly gentle, but I'm not ready to be soothed.

"No—*no*." My breath is coming fast and shallow, and I force it to slow. "I need you to go. Will you please just go?"

I sound so calm and commanding, that I'm almost baffled when he says, "No."

"No," I repeat. "No? Okay. Right. Fine." The calm in my voice is cracking around the edges. "Fine. If you won't go, then I will." I grab my purse and head for the door, fueled by a mix of anger and the need for action. Any action. He reaches for my elbow, but I yank my arm away so that his fingers only graze over me, the touch so damn familiar. And right then, so unwelcome.

I skip the elevator and hurry toward the stairs, both relieved and disappointed when he doesn't follow. I want to go—or I want him to go—but I also want a fight. I want to release all the shit that's building up in me. I want to explode, and I really don't know how.

It's not until I reach the street that I realize I don't know where I'm going. Obviously not to the townhouse since it's no longer mine. Honestly, though, it doesn't matter. Right now I'm so fired up all I want to do is walk, and so that's what I do.

Maybe when I'm tired I'll catch a cab to Brody's. Or maybe I'll go splurge on a hotel. Hell, maybe I'll go sleep on a park bench. I don't know. All I know is that I can't think. I can't focus.

I have to move.

I'm not walking with any particular destination, so I'm meandering through a pattern of long and short blocks. Now I'm on a dark residential street, the canopy of trees making odd shadows on the asphalt.

I hear footsteps behind me and move to the side, expecting a resident or dog walker to pass me by. But the footsteps slow, and even through my haze of anger and hurt, my skin begins to tingle with awareness and my heartbeat quickens.

Mentally, I curse myself, because I am never this unaware when I'm outside. I always watch my surroundings. I always pay attention. And yet here I am, wandering blind in an emotional haze.

I'd left with only my small cross-body purse and my keys, and now I slide my hand into my pocket and curl my fingers around the keys, letting the metal slip between my fingers so that I can not only punch, but do some damage in the process.

I continue walking forward, listening, and when I hear the footsteps again, I turn.

Mistake.

The word screams in my head as voltage rips through me, stealing thoughts. Stealing the world. Stealing reason.

I don't remember falling, but suddenly I'm on the ground, terrified and lost as my body writhes in the wake of the Taser assault.

I feel my lips move as I form his name. *Dallas.*

And above me I see a woman. Tall. Lean.

She's wearing a red dress and a mask, and is carrying something long and black, like a thin telescope. I'm confused at first, and then realize it's an extendable billy club.

"You," I croak.

"He's mine," she whispers.

Then she leans over, lets the club fly, and lands it square against my temple as the world fades to black and my heart screams for Dallas.

28

Lady in Red

Dallas paced the living room, or tried to. The place was so full of boxes it's a wonder he could even move.

He'd fucked up and it was his own damn fault. He'd known he was taking a risk not telling her about Colin, and now that choice was biting him in the ass.

Frustrated, he glanced toward the door, wondering now if he'd made the wrong choice again by not following her. He was trying to give her space, but already the gap between them was too wide. He needed her beside him. And, dammit, he was certain she needed him.

As if in evidence to the thought, his cellphone pinged, the tone signaling a text from Jane. He snatched it up, praying she wanted him to meet her somewhere.

But when he opened the text, it was as if he'd been punched in the gut.

His knees gave out, and he fell to the ground, the phone tumbling from his hands.

It didn't matter. The picture was burned in his mind.

Jane, her face bruised and battered.

And on the sidewalk next to her was an all-too-familiar carnival mask.

The Woman.

And now she had Jane.

•

The S.I.N. series continues with the concluding book in
Dallas and Jane's story,

SWEETEST TABOO

From the *New York Times* bestselling author of
"red-hot and angsty" fiction that "keeps readers guessing"
(*Publishers Weekly,* on *Under My Skin*).

Read on for a sneak peek!

Available soon from Bantam

He couldn't think. He couldn't breathe.

Him. Dallas Sykes. The man who always kept it together.

But not now. Not with this.

Fear curled in his gut like acid, and he fought the urge to put his fist through a goddamn wall.

He'd hid the truth from her, thinking he was making it better. That he was sparing her more pain. But those buried secrets had burst free, wild and vicious and dangerous. They'd sunk their teeth in her. They'd scared her. And now he feared they had destroyed her.

She was gone. Missing.

He didn't even know if she was alive or dead—except she couldn't be dead; the thought was too big, too horrible to even fit in his head.

But captive? Oh, dear Christ, what if she'd been thrust back into the horror of their childhood, and all because of him?

Blindly, he groped behind him, searching for something to grab, needing to steady himself.

He would find her—he had to find her.

She was his best friend. His sister. His lover.

Jane.

She couldn't be gone. He couldn't lose her.

Because if he lost her, he would damn sure lose himself as well

1

Gone Girl

"She's not here. Goddammit, she's not here."

Dallas Sykes's blood burned with dread as he stalked down the dark, residential block of West 82nd Street, his eyes scanning every nook and cranny, searching for a woman he knew wasn't there.

"I'm showing a signal." Liam's voice—firm, controlled—filtered through the speaker.

"She's not here," Dallas repeated, his voice rising. "And neither is her damn phone."

"Stay with me, Dallas. You can't help her if you lose your shit."

"Fuck." A fresh wave of fear crested inside him, and Dallas had to tighten his grip on his own phone in order to fight the almost irresistible urge to hurl the damn thing to the ground. But he couldn't. As impotent as his smart phone was at the moment, it was his lifeline to Jane.

Jane.

His lover. His sister.

His heart. His soul.

The one person in all the world he loved, needed, *craved* more than any other.

And Liam was right—he couldn't help her if he lost control. If he let himself get pulled back under into fear and memories.

So he wouldn't. He'd stay on the street. He'd search. He'd follow every lead. But in the end, he would find her because no other option was even conceivable. He'd find her, he'd rescue her, and then he'd kill the fucking bitch who'd taken her.

Slowly, he drew in a breath, then exhaled with just as much precision. "You're sure this is the location?"

"I'm sure. I'm logged into her account. I can see the phone's location on the map. And we're looking at a circumference of about eight meters."

Dallas nodded, trusting his friend because he knew damn well that he couldn't rely on himself. He wasn't thinking straight at all. The last thing he remembered with any clarity was standing in the new apartment that he shared with Jane, a little shell-shocked after she'd laid into him about the secrets he'd been keeping. She'd stormed out, and he'd forced himself to hold back, knowing that she needed to get her anger out of her system. He'd expected her to take a walk, maybe visit her friend Brody.

He hadn't expected that she would be attacked. Taken.

He hadn't expected a repeat of their goddamn childhood.

And he sure as hell hadn't anticipated that his phone would ping with a text message showing Jane splayed out on the street, her eyes closed and her face battered.

That image had been horrible enough. But what really gave him chills was the carnival style mask on the ground next to her prone form. A mask just like the one the Woman had worn when she'd entered their cell. Like she'd worn when she took him away from Jane. When she'd tortured him.

His stomach twisted as his mind filled with images of what she'd done to him. Only this time, it wasn't Dallas who was the victim of the Woman's cruel abuse, but Jane.

No. Please, God, no.

"No mask, no Jane. Christ, Liam, this isn't even the same stoop that was in the picture. Hang on." He pulled up his text messages and studied the screen. The image was tight on Jane, but part of the stairs was visible, lit by the white light of the camera flash. "Different colored concrete. Texture, too."

"She sent the picture from one location," Liam said, "then ditched the phone somewhere else. Could have even been a different block."

"Maybe. Probably." Dallas turned in a circle as he examined the area. At almost midnight, the residential street was quiet, the front steps and awnings that lined the way down the street each illuminated by the glow of stoop lights. It could take hours to try to match reality up to the picture, but it was a lead. Because Jane had to be somewhere, and maybe the Woman had dragged her into one of these brownstones. Maybe Jane was only meters away, maybe she was watching from a window, her hands tied, her mouth gagged, hope fading as she saw him fumbling in the dark.

Fuck that.

He took another hard look at the area he'd already scoured. No phone.

He stepped off the sidewalk and into the street. Same as it had been two minutes ago. Except . . .

"The drain," he said to Liam even as he dropped to his hands and knees, then thrust his arm in up to the shoulder. Absurd, really. If the phone was down there, it would be at least a meter away, sitting on the damp concrete, ready to be washed away in the next storm. He couldn't reach it, not without—

"I have it." The words, though his, surprised him, and he laughed. "Holy shit, I think I found it."

"Where?" There was no laughter in Liam's voice, and the simple word sobered Dallas.

"Drain," he said, as he pulled the phone free, then exhaled in relief that it really was hers. "There's a small concrete lip just inside that it was balancing on. The plastic case must have kept it from sliding off."

"Open her photos," Liam ordered. "There wasn't any location information buried in the picture you received or the text, but the photo on her phone might have GPS information embedded."

"Already on it," Dallas said, as he tapped and swiped the screen to get the photo to open. Sure enough, he found the time and place attached to the image, and exhaled with what he prayed wasn't premature relief.

Maybe his luck was starting to change.

"These things are never that accurate, but we should be able to get within a door or two," he said as he hurried down the street to the next block and the address the phone had assigned to the photo. "Give me an update," he demanded as he jogged. "Colin awake?"

"Still out," Liam said. "We loaded him up with tranqs."

"Tony and Noah?"

"I just dispatched them to you," Liam said.

"Good," Dallas said, unsurprised that his friend had anticipated Dallas's next request. "How about Quince? What's his ETA?"

"He just checked in. He should be landing at JFK within the hour. Soon as he gets here we'll start the interrogation."

Dallas nodded. The five of them—Dallas, Liam, Quince, Tony, and Noah—made up Deliverance, an ultra-secret, elite vigilante team that did whatever it took to locate and rescue kidnap victims. Dallas had formed it with the hope of locating his and Jane's kidnappers—their *past* kidnappers. He scowled at the irony, because now that search was being conducted in the present. And the stakes were a hell of a lot higher.

Ironic or not, Dallas was grateful that Deliverance existed. It may have been his brainchild, but Dallas was only a small part of the reason the organization was so damned effective. He'd populated it with men he knew and trusted. And, more important, who were exceptionally good at their jobs.

As far as Dallas was concerned, Quince couldn't get to the States fast enough. The London native had been his roommate at St. Anthony's, the prestigious boarding school just outside of London where Dallas's father had sent him back when he'd been fucking up royally as a teen. Now Quince was an elite MI6 operative who had acquired certain unique skills over the years that tended to make the interrogation process go a lot faster. A nice perk for the team needing the information. Not so nice for the asshole in the chair.

Right now, that asshole was Jane's birth father, Colin West, and just thinking about that single, horrible, inescapable fact made Dallas want to slam his fist through the windshield of one of the parked cars.

Dallas had known Colin since he was five years old. He'd grown up around the man. He'd comforted Jane when Colin's boneheaded decisions had put her in danger. He'd held her when Lisa, their mom, had filed suit to terminate Colin's parental rights so that Eli—Dallas's uncle and adoptive father—could adopt Jane, making Dallas and Jane full-blown brother and sister.

Dallas never had doubts that Colin could be a dickwad. After all, the guy had served jail time for insider trading. He'd been investigated for tax fraud. He'd made bad decisions and he'd pulled with the wrong crowd.

But Dallas had also seen the way Colin had comforted Jane after the kidnapping. When she was vulnerable and confused and needed to get away from her family. What had hurt the most was that it was Dallas she'd been trying to escape. Their connection—their passion—had sustained them in captivity. But it had been the one thing they absolutely could not take with them beyond those concrete walls.

So she'd left. Put up walls. And turned to Colin for support.

Dallas had hated the distance, but he'd been grateful for Colin, who had seemingly put aside his hurt at having his rights terminated in order to be there for his daughter. So grateful, in fact, that Dallas and Colin had rekindled their own friendship as he'd moved into adulthood. And over time, Colin and his new wife, Adele, had become part of Dallas's circle of friends.

Never once had Dallas suspected that Colin might have been the force behind the kidnapping of Jane and Dallas. Never once had it even crossed his mind that the man he'd grown up around—the man who Jane still loved like a father—had been the Jailer. The man who'd locked them in a room. The man who'd whispered to Dallas that he deserved every bit of agony he suffered in captivity.

The man who allowed the Woman to play her sadistic, sexual games on a fifteen-year-old boy.

Now, he suspected it. Hell, now he believed it.

It made him sick, but he believed it.

And it took all of his strength not to head to Deliverance's East Harlem safe house and curl his fingers around the fucker's throat until he confessed to everything. Until he revealed where Jane had been taken.

"He knows," he said now into his phone as he reached the address tagged in Jane's photograph. "Colin knows where she is."

"Maybe," Liam said. "Probably. But we have to work the evidence. We can't risk taking a wrong turn. Not when Jane's safety is at stake."

"You saw the image. The carnival mask. I know damn well who took her."

"The Woman. The one who did all that fucked-up shit to you back then," Liam said. His voice sounded hard. Raw. Dallas had only recently told him the full truth about what had happened during the kidnapping, and he could tell from his friend's voice that he was still processing the horror of it.

"Damn right."

"Maybe—hell, probably. But it could be the bitch who's been sending you those letters. And I know Jane thinks the Woman is your mysterious correspondent, but we don't know that for sure."

"The carnival mask is one hell of a clue," Dallas protested.

"Except it's not the most original disguise," Liam pointed out. "And if I was going to snatch someone tonight in that neighborhood, it's a disguise I'd probably use."

Dallas tilted his head. "What are you talking about?"

"I've been poking around online," Liam began, "and there was a benefit at the museum tonight. A masquerade."

"*Fuck.*" Dallas ran his fingers through his hair, not wanting to acknowledge that Liam had a point. The Museum of Natural History was only a block and a half away, and now that Liam had mentioned it, Dallas remembered the benefit. Hell, he'd even been invited, and more than five hundred people were expected to attend. A carnival mask really would be the perfect camouflage for anybody up to no good in the area tonight.

"Our perp might be the Woman. Or she might be your letter writer, assuming they're different. But it could also be a man. Or it could be some nutjob who read about you two and has made it his mission to erase the scourge of sin between brother and sister. We don't know, Dallas. We just don't know."

"*I* know," Dallas said. Because even though everything

Liam said was entirely true, Dallas trusted his instincts. The Woman had attacked Jane. The Woman had taken Jane.

And Colin was the only one who might know where they were now.

The squeal of brakes pulled him from his thoughts, and he whirled around in time to see a gray Mercedes slam to a stop in the street beside him. The driver's door flew open even as the engine died and the hazards lights started flashing, and Anthony Sanchez sprang out while Noah Carter emerged from the passenger side, his usually cheerful face twisted with worry.

"We're going door to door," Dallas said to his men. His friends. "Find out if anyone saw anything. See if you get any sort of vibe that she's being held inside one of these buildings. The entire block," he stressed. "And then the surrounding ones."

"Figured that would be your first step," Tony said, pulling out a fake NYPD badge. "We came prepared."

"You're not on this one, man," Noah added, his eyes fixed on Dallas.

"He knows," Liam said, his voice tinny over the phone speaker. "His face is too recognizable to pull off a fake badge. Besides, he has somewhere else to be."

"Damn straight," Dallas said. "I need to have a chat with Colin."

"The hell you do," Liam countered. "You already told me that if you saw him right now, you'd kill him. Quince is on his way. Let the man do his damn job. Besides," he added, before Dallas could retort, "there's someone else you need to talk to."

"Who?"

"Dallas." Liam's voice was uncharacteristically gentle. "Jane's not just your girlfriend, she's your sister. You have to tell your parents she's been taken."

J. Kenner (aka Julie Kenner) is the *New York Times, USA Today, Publishers Weekly, Wall Street Journal,* and #1 international bestselling author of over seventy novels, novellas, and short stories in a variety of genres.

Though known primarily for her award-winning and international bestselling erotic romances (including the Stark, Stark International, Dirtiest, and Most Wanted series) that have reached as high as #2 on the *New York Times* bestseller list, Kenner has been writing full-time for over a decade in a variety of genres, including paranormal and contemporary romance, "chicklit" suspense, urban fantasy, and paranormal mommy lit.

Kenner has been praised by *Publishers Weekly* as an author with a "flair for dialogue and eccentric characterizations" and by *RT Book Reviews* for having "cornered the market on sinfully attractive, dominant antiheroes and the women who swoon for them." A four-time finalist for Romance Writers of America's prestigious RITA award, Kenner took home the first RITA trophy awarded in the category of erotic romance in 2014 for her novel, *Claim Me* (book 2 of her Stark Trilogy).

Her books have sold well over a million copies and are published in over twenty countries.

jkenner.com

Facebook.com/jkennerbooks

@juliekenner